THE
TROUBLESEEKER

"Alan Lessik's *The Troubleseeker* is an extraordinary novel and a deeply moving expression of love. Gathering its beautifully numinous mythic and cultural materials, the book deftly tells the story of our hero's journey, a gay Cuban man in the midst of life and historical tumult. With a soulful daring to take risks, Lessik pulls us to witness the full heat of life and love inside the human heart."
—Tim Miller, Performer and author of *Body Blows* and *1001 Beds*

"In this remarkable debut novel, author Alan Lessik weaves the modern day struggle of a gay Cuban man's sprawling journey with mythological import. Our hero receives intervention from gods and demi-gods both loving and capricious, proving our very human fragility."
—Jim Provenzano, Lambda Literary Award-winning author

"Alan Lessik combines several unlikely fictional elements and an unexpected point of view in this auspicious debut novel. But it pays off: *The Troubleseeker* is an engrossing read about one gay man's life-voyage that manages to be fantastic and yet quite real, with a wonderful overlay flavoring of the Caribbean that you can almost taste."
—Felice Picano, author of *True Stories* and *Nights at Rizzoli*

"A book you won't want to stop reading, *The Troubleseeker* offers the best that literature can give: a moving human chronicle that both entertains and lingers in our hearts."
—Elías Miguel Muñoz, author of the novels *The Greatest Performance*, *Brand New Memory*, and *Diary of Fire*

THE
TROUBLESEEKER

A NOVEL BY

ALAN LESSIK

CHELSEA STATION EDITIONS

NEW YORK

The Troubleseeker
by Alan Lessik

Cover and book design by Peachboy Distillery & Designs

Published by Chelsea Station Editions
362 West 36th Street, Suite 2R
New York, NY 10018
www.chelseastationeditions.com
info@chelseastationeditions.com

Paperback ISBN: 978-1-937627-27-0
Ebook ISBN: 978-1-937627-65-2
Library of Congress Control Number: 2016940537

First Edition

A mi Bebito,
René J. Valdés López.
May your story never end.

Estoy pensando en usted. Yo sin cesar pienso en usted. Usted se duele en la cólera de su amor, del sacrificio de mi vida; y ¿por qué nací de usted con una vida que ama el sacrificio?

I am thinking about you. I never stop thinking about you. You who ache in the wrath of your love and the sacrifice of my life. And why was I born with a life that loves sacrifice?
—José Martí to his mother, Lenor Pérez Cabrena

Odysseus, not one of us who sees you has any idea that you are a charlatan or a swindler...there is a style about your language which assures me of your good disposition. Moreover you have told the story of your own misfortunes as though you were a practiced bard... The evenings are still at their longest, and it is not yet bed time—go on, therefore, with your divine story, for I could stay here listening till to-morrow morning, so long as you will continue to tell us of your adventures.
—Book XI, The Odyssey

A GUIDE TO THE CHARACTERS

The Gods
Aganju—Santería *orisha* of the mountains
Apollo—Greek god of the arts, of light and healing
Athena—Greek goddess of wisdom, courage, law, and justice
Babalú Ayé—Santería *orisha* of disease and healing
Changó—Santería *orisha* of wind, hurricanes, and thunder
Elegguá—Santería *orisha* of highways and crossroads
Hera—Greek goddess of women and marriage
Hermes—Greek god of travelers, thieves, and merchants
Obatála—Santería *orisha*, creator of the earth
Ochún—Santería *orisha* of love and beauty
Oko—Santería *orisha* of food
Olokun—Santería *orisha* of the ocean bottoms
Oyá—Santería *orisha* of change
Ozain—Santería *orisha* of forests
Yemayá—Santería *orisha* of earth and sea, mother of all *orishas*

The Demigods
Hadriano—Hadrian, Roman Emperor
117–138 AD, deified after his death
Antinous—lover of Hadrian
111–130 AD, deified after his death

The Hero
Antinio—lover of men, the Troubleseeker
His Chorus
Reason
The Lamenters
The Shriekers
The Siren

The Humans
Akos—asylum seeker in Cuba, judge of the dead in the Underworld
Alethia—block leader in Cuba, from the Greek word meaning *truth*
Anticlea—mother of Antinio, twin sister of Erastos, from
the Greek tale *The Odyssey*, meaning without fame
Apolion—a bully in Cuba, from the Greek word meaning *destroyer*

Archon—an immigration official in Minnesota,
from one of nine ancient Greek magistrates
Atropos—third lover of Antinio, from the third
Greek Fate, who cuts the thread of life
Avis—Antinio's aunt in Cuba, from the German
word meaning *refuge from war*
Boreas—a lawyer in Minnesota, from the
Greek word meaning *the north wind*
Brontes/"Ciclope"—a mill superintendent in Cuba,
from the giant, one-eyed tribe in *The Odyssey*
Calypso—a proctectress in Cuba, from the Greek nymph in *The Odyssey*
Circe—Antinio's wife, from the Greek sorceress in *The Odyssey*
Cloto—Antinio's first lover, from the first Greek
Fate, who spins the thread of life
Diotima—Antinio's friend at the hospital,
from the name of the Greek oracle
Dr. Paean—Antinio's doctor, from the Greek physician of the gods
Erastos—Antinio's uncle, from the Greek word meaning *an early disciple*
Erato—Antinio's best friend, from the Greek
muse of love and erotic poetry
Euterpa—a cello player, from the Greek muse of music
Fineo—Antinio's friend, from Phineus, Greek
blind seer who revealed the path to Jason
Icario—Antinio's twin son, from Icarus, a
boy who flew too close to the sun
Laquesio—Antinio's second lover, from Lachesis, second
Greek Fate, who measures the length of life
Minos—A hospital doctor, from the judge of the dead in the Underworld
Oydis—Antinio's coworker, from the Greek goddess of good luck
Philippides—guard at the Pergamon in Berlin, from
the courier who ran the original marathon
Polideuces—Antinio's twin son, from Pollux,
Roman twin, meaning *very sweet*
Pothos—Antinio's lover, from the Greek god of sexual longing
Theron—a gay journalist in Minnesota, from
the Greek name meaning *hunter*
Tiresias—prophet of Apollo, a man born to anger the gods
Tityus, Tantalus, Sisyphus—hospital patients, from
the tortured mortals in the Underworld
Trajan—Roman Emperor
Tyro—asylum seeker in Cuba, from a heroine in the Underworld
Volodya—a Russian soldier in Cuba

THE

TROUBLESEEKER

PROLOGUE

Three voices remained now having taken residence in every cell of his body, a collective of sounds not unlike the chorus of an ancient drama.

The first and loudest were the Shriekers with their high-pitched yells and screams. While over the years they changed in time and timbre, they had always accompanied him, embedding themselves deeper and deeper into his being, refusing to let him be on his journey alone. They had evolved from specific screams of threats to wails of despair and terror. Their sound filled him from toe to head, rising higher in his body until it streamed out of the soft spot on his skull that had never healed from birth. Their effect was to stretch thin every nerve in his body to the snapping point, which produced a pain like a blackboard being scratched—shuddering, unstoppable, and impossible not to look at. The worst part was that he could not prevent himself from searching for the source of the pain, which was everywhere at once and nowhere to be located.

The second were the Lamenters, their deep voices aching with loss and agony. As the basses in the chorus, they resonated in waves that erupted from his belly and merged with his heartbeat. Like military ordnance exploding in regular patterns—*doom, doom, doom*—day and night the bombing continued—*doom, doom, doom*—building up imperceptibly at first, but soon the full throes of a new hit every three seconds, then every two, then every second, until finally each explosion built on the last and he had the impression that every organ in his body was being blown up.

The third was only a single voice—the Siren. In a voice full of desire, love missed and to be realized, it came from his loins and snaked around his body. The Siren's voice was simultaneously Antinio's own and a mixture of the sounds of voices of all he had loved and each he had forsaken. *I am truly you, there is no other*, the Siren sang. *Follow me, follow me now and forever to safety.*

There was once a fourth voice, Reason, which he had not heard for a while. In the last weeks, Reason, once so notably present in his brain, was getting quieter and quieter. Or maybe it was just that the other voices were getting louder and louder. Whatever the case, Reason—the cool, unimpassioned voice of logic, the voice that had guided him through the hardest times, that had helped him to sort out the competing chorus members in his mind, and that made sure that the emotions and grievances and terrors were kept in place—had abandoned him. The rest of the chorus now had free reign over him.

Antinio never slept that night. All night long, he felt himself pushed and pulled and tormented. Pain was everywhere and all-encompassing. Nothing existed but pain. The wailing of the Shriekers stripped his very soul to pieces. He saw—not imagined, but saw—rats gnawing away at his soul, defecating and eating their own shit and then repeating the cycle until every last bit of his identity was gone.

Meanwhile, his heart beat out a litany of every failure, every loss, starting with his mother; every insult, every mistake, every unfulfilled desire. Each beat dredged up a long-stored feeling to be smashed and pounded under the weight of a doomed history—a history of being born to fail and to suffer, a history where love only brought pain around him, a history that only achieved greatness and success to be knocked down lower and harder from the memory of that success, a history that would be forgotten; and, therefore, a history that from its beginning never existed.

Early in the morning, at the dawning of the sun for a new day, the major players of his Greek chorus—the Shriekers and Lamenters—subsided. He often had these moments of peace, perhaps a false peace, but a peace where he could remind himself, where Reason would step in and repeat his mantra, *I am awake, it is a new day, and the world is before me.* If he worked it right, this peace could stay with him for a while as he washed, shaved, and dressed, made some breakfast, took his pills, talked with his partner, read the newspaper, made his protein shake for the gym, checked his emails, put together the grocery list, and walked out the door. As long as he had his lists and routines, he had order in his life.

But this morning it was the Siren who called: *You can have peace, Antinio. Surrender. I can keep the pain and despair and torments away. Only I can make you feel good. You are a beautiful boy,* mijito, *you have always been the most beautiful boy on earth. You were born never to suffer, never to be harmed, and now I come to protect you, my son, my beloved son. You have lit candles to me every day; you have never forgotten the mother who brought you into this world,* mijito, *come to me. I remember your perfection, I held you when others only desired to use you, you were never safer than you were with me. Come home, come home, your journey has been long and difficult, you have faced horrors that no son should ever face, come with me, I will bathe you with my tears of despair and loneliness so that you will be clean again and renewed, so that your desire and pain will disappear and be replaced by love, love that will be felt in every pore of your skin, every atom in every molecule of your body, come, come to me, follow me, follow me, put this chain around your neck, it is made of gold for my golden boy, my Antinio, who has been revered by the greatest, who will have coins of the realm made in his likeness, who will be remembered for his beauty, his strength, his singing, his wisdom, his command of languages, his smile, his sexual desire, his ever-ready dick that satisfied all and left all wanting more, come, Antinio, step on this chair, it is strong, it will hold you,* mijito, *you are so strong and handsome, you just have to take the step into my arms, I am here to hold you, I have lived and died for this moment to hold you,* mijito, *my son, my son, leap into my arms, the golden chain will hold you high, you have no fear any longer, no pain, no torment, you have only love, you have only love, you have only love, you have only love, yes, you at last only have love.*

I

Sprawled across the cool terrazzo floor of his family's home in Havana on a sweltering, humid day, Antinio flipped through the pages of his favorite book, *The Golden Ages*. It was a book his mother, Anticlea, a teacher of the classics and ancient history in a high school just down the street from his house, had given him for his fourteenth birthday a few weeks before. The Cuban government still allowed ancient history and mythology to be taught relatively unfettered. El Comandante wanted Cubans to make the connection between the ancient heroes and the New Cuban Revolutionaries, equally brave and wise.

Antinio had not made it past the first four chapters. Methodical in approaching any new project, he paced his reading, as he absorbed each word and pored over every detail until he committed it to memory. He was fascinated by the stories of men and gods and tried to keep all of their names— Zeus, Apollo, Poseidon, Athena, Aphrodite, Hermes—and their responsibilities straight. These were unruly deities who frequently fought with each other and seemed to enjoy making life difficult for humans even when some of those humans were their own progeny. Although his family did not believe in the Afro-Cuban religion Santería, originally brought over by slaves from Yorubaland, Antinio saw the similarity between the gods he was studying and the Santería *orishas*, Elegguá, Yemayá, Obatála, Babalú Ayé, and Changó.

In a small notebook he was not using for school, he carefully printed his name (he had the best printing skills in his class, each letter carefully but distinctively written out), wrote the date, *el 15 de septiembre 1962*, and the names of each of the gods as he encountered them, with notations of their origins—Greek or Roman—their powers, and, if available, the meanings of their names. For, above all, Antinio loved languages and logic. The voice of Reason guided his studies and shaped his approach to the world around him. In addition to his native Spanish, he was already fluent in German, taught to him by his *tante* Avis who had accidentally found herself as a young woman on the island through the vicissitudes of war and, even more unexpectedly, met and fell in love with his uncle. To Antinio, language was as fascinating as the gods. Every word in each language that he knew or was to learn not only had its own meaning, but had its own particular feeling and sensation. His mind instantly cross-referenced the new word and its sensation with every other word that already was stored in the logical maze of his brain. He was oblivious of this gift and never would understand the challenge others faced learning languages.

He loved to roll his tongue around the Greek and Latin names of gods, people, places, and objects, and in doing so was transported back in time. He was intrigued that his Spanish had emerged from these ancient languages. At this particular moment, on the hard floor of his living room and aware of an excitement growing in his groin, he was fascinated that the Spanish word *pinga*, which in his case was getting erect, a word derived from *pingar*, to hang, could be traced to the Latin word *pendicare*. Even at this young age, Antinio tried to imagine the pathways that a word took through the centuries, traveling through countries and changing sounds, inflections, and meaning. When he discovered that the word for the part of the body he most loved to observe, *culo*, was nearly identical to the Latin word for buttocks, *culus*, he felt the electric charge of a two thousand–year divine connection.

Living with his mother and father, aunts and uncles, cousins and grandparents all in the same house, there was little privacy, so he struggled to remain still despite the growing pleasure his body was experiencing. As he flipped through *The Golden Ages*, Antinio's eye lingered on the pictures of gods and emperors, gladiators and centurions: muscular men teeming with life and vitality in their bodies, but cool and calm with vacant, distant gazes in the demeanor of their faces. Naked men, men with robes, men without arms or heads, but always men with *pingas*, men that had no doubt that they were men.

*   *   *

Before we proceed further with this tale, let me introduce myself. I am Caesar Publius Aelius Traianus Hadrianus Buccellanus Augustus, generally known in your less formal time as Hadriano in Spanish and Hadrian in English. I was born to Roman parents in the year 76 in the region of the world that would become known as Spain. My schooling covered all of the important subjects—philosophy, rhetoric, mathematics, theology, and archery, but my passion for Greek culture and language was so great that they nicknamed me "the Greekling." To this day, I love to see how my beloved Greek and more workaday Latin have survived, sometimes openly and other times hidden in the roots of English and Spanish words. Their survival is part of the legacy of my reign. My father's cousin was the Roman Emperor Trajan, and when I came of age I served under him in the army. Right before his death, he adopted me as his son and I became heir to the throne of the Roman Empire. Historians note that I was one of the most powerful emperors, uniting my far-flung territories in what is now referred to as Europe. I won't dispute this. During the almost nineteen hundred years since my death, my curiosity about the world keeps me alert to its concerns and changes.

Although Antinio's mother had previously told him the story of my life and how a mighty Roman emperor had as a beloved *compañero* Antinous—"Yes, your namesake," she said—until now, he had never seen a picture of any of the thousands of statues I had ordered to be created of my beloved after he drowned in the Nile at the age of eighteen.

While Antinio was only four years younger than the age at which Antinous had been recast in sculpture, they looked nothing alike. Antinio was skinny, with straight black hair and a body browned by the sun. In contrast, from what he saw in the book, Antinous was white as snow—but the boy saw in Antinous what I had seen in him: beauty, courage, desire. Each muscle of Antinous was defined and hard, especially those of his sturdy legs. His *culo* (Antinio sighed at the sound of the roundness and the fullness of the word—*cooolooo*) was magnificent, and Antinio fantasized caressing that *culo*, as he correctly imagined I had done many times. The *pingas* he saw in the statues excited him as well. Already, at fourteen, Antinio had a quite large one that had gained the notice of his friends and, occasionally, men on the street. But he knew that to appear more like his namesake, he would need to build up his musculature.

Not being a boy who waited after he made decisions—a trait that often got him into trouble—Antinio went downstairs to the garage to take action.

"*Tio*," he called out to his uncle Erastus in his workshop, "can you help me?"

"What can I do, *mijito*?"

"I want to make a set of barbells so I can be strong and have muscles."

Erastus was always willing to aid the firstborn child in this extended family, especially since he knew his brother-in-law had little time for the boy.

"Okay, let's see what we have here. Bring me those two coffee cans while I find that bag of cement I was using to make repairs around the house."

After mixing the cement, they poured it into the two cans and placed a stick in-between them before the cement solidified. The next morning, Antinio had a passable barbell. Over the years that followed, the little gym in the garage grew with homemade pulleys and bars. Once in a while, when a real barbell could be found in one of the state stores and there was some money to spend, it was added to the gym.

A few days later, Erastus found a well-used bodybuilding book in the market and brought it home. Eagerly, Antinio perused the pictures and illustrations and began a regular routine that he decided he would follow to some extent every day of his life. Each workout was recorded in the same notebook that contained the names of the gods.

I had made sure that to all mankind Antinous was frozen in time and would be forever young and virile, with ringlets of hair circling his white, full, beautiful face. Only I remembered him differently, having seen him after he was pulled out of the Nile bloated and scarred. With tears rolling down my face, I did not tarry in deifying him, and by that act restored his beauty. This living and breathing Antinio, however, realized, as young as he was, his fate was to get old and die like his *abuelo* or *tio*. He dedicated himself to staving off this inevitability, to be the one that outlived death.

He was only one month into this new regimen, secretly checking himself out in the mirror to see if his muscles were growing (much to the amusement of the rest of the family, for whom there were no secrets), when the crisis started. El Comandante announced that the *yanquis* were going to invade and destroy the missiles that their friends the Russians had recently given the Cubans to protect themselves. Everyone needed to be on alert and ready to defend their home against *yanqui* bombers and soldiers.

At school, there was a lot of talk among the boys about joining the Army. Their young age was no barrier to becoming a *Revolucionario* and protecting the homeland. Antinio's teachers explained the special role of the Army in Cuban society and stressed the importance for every boy to be ready to fight to protect the Revolution. But Antinio was repulsed by guns and fighting. He turned a deaf ear to all this talk about war and invasion and continued to concentrate on his studies and exercises. While other boys would resolve problems with fists, he used his charm and laughter to divert his interlocutors.

One Tuesday afternoon, the boys were called into the school auditorium. The pompous and chronically disheveled principal announced that in two days, buses would take the eligible boys to an army camp in the distant countryside. Upon dismissal, the boys ran out in a cacophony of excited screams. Antinio tried to ignore their enthusiasm, although he felt an already familiar longing in his body when thinking of all the boys together, sleeping, working out, showering, and being alone at night.

I watched this scene with a mixture of bemusement and sadness. Although I was condemned for it at the time by the Roman Senate, I retreated from Mesopotamia because I knew those lands were indefensible. I fought the battles that were winnable and used diplomacy to gain peace and, ultimately, greater power in the region. Armies must be trained, and trained well. Each man must be fit, prepared, and willing to obey orders. Sending untrained boys into danger was reprehensible and not something I would have ever considered.

Later that evening, after Antinio told his family about what he had heard in school, a loud argument broke out that lasted half the night.

Anticlea was horrified. "I cannot believe that the school would endorse sending such young boys—they are children, not soldiers. If they come to recruit, I will chase them away."

"Now, be careful, Anticlea," her twin brother, Erastus, warned. "You could get in trouble by doing that."

"I have spent my life teaching boys how to become civilized young men, and despite how good the Revolution has been for Cuba, I won't let these boys become cannon fodder." The other women voiced agreement with her point of view.

Erastus chimed in, "The Army is rough and dangerous. And I agree with the women. Given Antinio's kind and loving soul, if we are allowed to use that word anymore, he is exactly the type of boy that should not go into the Army."

Antinio's father countered angrily, "This is what men do. It's time for Antinio to grow up." He had been casting a wary eye on his son for years. He added, "This might be the only way to toughen up a mama's boy."

Anticlea's response came quick and with a frozen look at her husband that ended the conversation. "If you believe that, then you can sleep on the porch," she said. "Maybe that will toughen you up."

Antinio, for his part, was dead set against going. He tried to forget about the Revolution, burying himself in his book. Though the pictures of Roman soldiers aroused him, the story of the foolishness of the Trojan War, with its wanton waste of life, disgusted him. When he went to school two days later, he tried to keep away from the rising commotion. When his classmates asked if he was going, he would shake his head no. After school, the boys were to go home for their belongings and come back in an hour.

On the way home, a girl from his class walked with Antinio. She asked, "Do you realize what the other boys are saying?" He cast his eyes downward. "They say you are weak, a sissy, and will never be a *Revolucionario* like El Comandante. How can you let them think that?" she asked. "I notice how you look at the boys. I wish you would look at me like that. What will you do when there are all girls in the class except for you and that blind boy? How will you live with that?"

Antinio continued his silence because he did not have an answer. When he got to the house, it was empty except for his grandmother dressed in black, perennially mourning her long departed husband, asleep in her rocking chair on the porch. He looked in the stained bathroom mirror and no longer saw the muscles he had been dreaming about, but a skinny, sad boy who was afraid. He did not have an answer to the girl's question. He was not strong enough to go, but he was not strong enough to stay. He became aware of his heart beating, and he heard for the first time the low-pitched Lamenters in his head. *If you stay you will die a coward, if you leave you will die a hero.* With each beat—*a coward, a hero, a coward, a hero*—the voices took over his body and drowned out Reason, who spoke to him every day. In a trance, he found the small, battered valise that he used for trips to the countryside to his uncle's tobacco farm and quickly put in his only underwear without holes, two pairs of shorts, a pair of rough pants, all three pairs of socks that he owned, two shirts that still might look good if they got dirty, and a pair of sandals. He found his toothbrush, took his father's shaver (because surely once he was in the Army his beard would start like all of the *barbudos*, the bearded ones who commanded the country) and the pocketknife that Tio Erastus had given him, and rushed out of the house. He was halfway down the block when he ran back to his room and slipped *The Golden Ages* into his suitcase. He would need its strength and wisdom if he was to survive.

II

The Army was Antinio's introduction to an entirely male world. For the first time in his life, there were no mothers, aunts, grandmothers, and neighbor ladies to fuss over him, to lovingly comb his hair, to talk to him softly, and to cook up his favorite dishes. Technically, one had to be sixteen to be in the Army, but in emergencies like this one, age did not matter to El Comandante. Antinio was one of the youngest of the hundreds of boys and men who temporarily populated this dry piece of rocky terrain far away from his home.

I loved the military life and, unlike most Roman emperors, spent the majority of my time away from Rome, leading my command as I traveled to its far reaches. I was always more comfortable sleeping among my men than I was in my bed in Rome with my wife. In most regions of the Empire, it was common to start military training around puberty. My own service began when I was fourteen, just like Antinio. But I was not ready for the rigors of the military life and soon was sent to Rome for more schooling. My real military career began at eighteen when I was stationed in Germania.

Antinio adapted to army routine relatively easily, and it was here he discovered the traits that would carry him through life: geniality, intellect, and good looks. In this new male playground, he was easygoing and curious. If he had a fault, it was that he constantly asked questions of his comrades and superiors—*Where are you from? What are you doing? Isn't there a better way to do this? Are you sure that is right?* He was curious not only about how the rocket launchers functioned, but about what life in a small village was like for the boys who came from the *campo*.

Aside from some army manuals, his cherished book *The Golden Ages* was the only reading material available. He finished reading and making notes on the remaining chapters and then restarted the book from the beginning. Since many of his young companions from the countryside were illiterate, they pestered Antinio to look at the pictures in his book and wanted to understand what the words meant. He thus began nightly readings in their tent-bunkroom lit by lanterns and, like the bards of old, recounted the stories of Troy, Athens, the Peloponnesian Wars, and the tales of Odysseus and the Argonauts. At particular points, Antinio would sing in his tenor voice a familiar song relating to the test that the hero was facing, and all of the boys would join in.

The only story he did not tell to others was that of my love for Antinous. He reserved it for himself, for quiet moments when the other boys had drifted away in sleep. Though he could not put a word to it, he knew I had had a profound connection to Antinous. When Antinio slept, I would creep into his dreams—hold him in his bed, cradle him in my arms, and feed him figs as I used to do so often with beauteous Antinous. Other nights, struggling to understand deep alliance with another being, Antinio would remember his family and feel my everlasting grief, the heaving of my chest and the burning of my tears at the memory of that moment when I was informed that Antinous had sacrificially drowned himself in the Nile. *Sacrificus* originally meant performing priestly duties, but Antinous was not a priest. He gave up his own life so I would achieve the glory foretold by the oracle to manifest only when I lost that which I loved the most. Antinio knew nothing of my own afterlife, my state of being in the heavens watching over the world searching for what I had lost.

Antinio's good looks and his curious, open nature were remarked upon in the camp. He was drafted into the laundry brigade, washing and pressing the uniforms for the *barbudos* in the Army command, most of whom had served with El

Comandante in the mountains. He used that position to keep himself clean and made sure that the few pieces of clothing he had brought plus the army shirt he was given (there were not enough uniforms for anyone to have a complete set) were clean and ironed.

Even in the most rustic of circumstances, uniforms must be starched and pressed; such are priorities of military life, I remember well from my times. Whether on horseback or foot, my own uniformed men struck fear and awe in all that beheld them. A uniform separates the military man from the civilian, the powerful from the powerless, and those in command from the ones that must follow. Throughout history, all militaries have placed as much emphasis on the impression a uniform makes as they have on its protective qualities necessary for combat. While the *barbudos* lacked for fine uniforms, they had their trademark beards and cigars to set themselves off in the popular imagination.

Antinio's intellect soon caught the attention of the officers. With so few boys who could read or write, they considered him a godsend (well, perhaps not a godsend since they lived in a country that had officially banished the church). More importantly, his ear for languages helped with their most difficult task, working with the Russian soldiers and technicians who supported the Revolution and provided armaments against the *yanquis*. The officers observed young Antinio picking up phrases from their foreign counterparts who, for the most part, did not understand Spanish. One day a captain found Antinio in the laundry area intently studying a handwritten page, which he tried to hide from the officer.

"What is that you have there? Give it to me." The captain grabbed the page and encountered a strange list in Cyrillic and Spanish. "Explain this gibberish to me."

"I am learning the numbers and letters in Russian. It's not really so difficult, although their alphabet is different from ours. But once you learn it, the letters are the same as we have. What I really find interesting is that in addition to verbs changing forms from past to present, the nouns change in this language depending on how they are used in a sentence. For examp—"

"Stop with your chatter, boy. Come with me."

The man led the young boy to the Russians' barracks and managed to make them understand that Antinio would now work with them and become their translator. This was how, in a misbegotten camp in the Cuban hinterlands, Antinio was for the first time transported to another world and culture. The Russians had created their own outpost against these backward Cold-War allies, and they had brought with them not only guns, missile launchers, and bombs, but their own food, vodka, books of poetry, and musical instruments.

Volodya, a handsome nineteen-year-old, had a sprinkling of Spanish-language proficiency and was charged with working with Antinio. The Russian had a cherubic, ruddy face, blond hair, and soft, blue-grey eyes that showed both joy and intense sadness at the same time. He began to formally teach Antinio Russian, laboring intently with the boy, holding his writing hand as Antinio practiced forming the Cyrillic letters and leaning in to listen and correct his pronunciation. After their lessons, Volodya would open a can of Russian marmalade and offer it to Antinio with tea, a treat so exotic and yet so simple.

Antinio was especially curious about anything musical. He already held a sizeable repertory of songs in his head: popular Cuban melodies old and new, Mexican *rancheras*, Brazilian love songs, and from his aunt, German *lieder*. He could imitate Nat King Cole's enunciations in English and Spanish to a T, but since the regime banned all rock and roll and American pop music, hit songs from the '60s were not in his vocabulary.

Volodya taught Antinio songs of his homeland and accompanied him on the guitar. Antinio soon learned a treasure trove of Russian laments and love songs, songs so poignant in their longing for faraway homes, missing mothers, and misplaced lives—*nostalghia* was the Russian term he learned—they immediately spoke to his heart even though the words as yet were incomprehensible to him. I was pleased to see these two form a bond so quickly. A young boy always needs an elder to mentor and guide him.

Three long months had passed since the day Antinio left home. His mother and family were initially shocked to find him missing, even more so when none of his remaining friends had a clue to his whereabouts. Erastus eventually tracked down one of the schoolteachers who had loaded the boys onto the buses and confirmed that Antinio had been among the group sent off to the hinterlands.

Antinio's father bragged to his friends, "My one and only son is finally becoming a man in the military." While they played along, most of the men felt sorry for Antinio and thought less of his father for not preventing the boy's departure.

His mother had stopped speaking to her husband since the boy left home and put all of her pent-up feelings into her weekly letters, some of which Antinio received. Other members of the family tended to Anticlea, making sure she ate and took care of herself, all the while *tsk-tsk*ing Antinio's father, who sat smoking a cigar and reading the paper in his chair on the porch. Even his own mother, in her perpetual mourning reverie, would occasionally open her eyes, glare at him, and let loose a torrent of invectives indicating her displeasure with his cavalier attitude.

Finally the family gained permission to visit Antinio. They packed themselves into Erastus's 1956 Chevrolet, filling the trunk with food and clothes and anything else his mother thought her son might need. Once beyond the city limits, they drove seventy miles into the countryside, passing sugar cane and tobacco fields and small villages with no names. It was hot away from the sea breezes, the air thick with smoke and dust from the fields. Although there were six of them, the car was quiet except for Erastus, who tried to bring some levity to cheer up his twin sister, Anticlea. But tensions within the family would not be broken until they saw Antinio. To each of them, he was lost on a lonely and perilous voyage without a destination.

Antinio's family reached the camp and were let through the gate. They saw the large guns to be used to shoot down *yanqui* missiles, young boys walking around with machine guns and machetes, Russian soldiers and technicians talking in their mumbled language so unlike Spanish, and the *barbudos* leading the command. All of this they expected. What shocked them were the two hundred young boys running around this battle camp as if it were a school playground.

"It looks like break period in my schoolyard," Anticlea exclaimed, "if our boys had not washed or eaten in months."

Antinio had been alerted by a letter a week before that his family would be arriving. He was sitting on the side of the drill area talking to Volodya. The Russian soldier had his guitar and was teaching Antinio the words and chords to the song "Moscow Nights," *Podmoskovnye Verchera.* He sang soulfully, *"Chto zh ty, milaya, smotrish' iskosa, Nizko golovu naklonyaya? Trudno vyskazat' i ne vyskazat' Vsyo, chto na serdtse u menya."*

"I understand the words 'my heart' in the last line, but not much else."

"Ah, my Antinio, you are coming along well in your studies, and the rest will come quickly. The last stanza is, *Why do you, dear, look askance with your head lowered so? It is hard to express and hard to hold back everything that my heart holds.* As he sang those words with a sly smile on his face, he peered deeply into Antinio's eyes. For a brief moment, the camp receded from Antinio's mind, and he felt carried away to Volodya's homeland.

The two were so immersed in their song that neither noticed Antinio's mother standing across the way crying at the sight of her son. Antinio finally looked up and rushed over to hug his mother, who covered him with kisses while casting a wary look at the Russian soldier.

Since the family had to be back in the city that evening, they wasted no time in unpacking the food and gifts. They were quickly surrounded by boys who had no families or missed their own mothers or were just hungry. Antinio's mother tried to discreetly hand her son some new clothes and socks. The passing months had physically changed him; he was taller, and she could detect the outlines of muscles in his thin arms and legs. His hair was shorn, and he was clean, especially compared to the other boys. Antinio appeared to be happy, although Anticlea could detect a glimmer of fear behind his eyes. She always knew what he was feeling even without words. My own mother, Domitia, died when I was ten, yet I still remember how she would look at me with a tenderness that only Antinous could later match.

As quickly as the family had arrived, they had to leave. Each aunt and uncle and cousin kissed Antinio good-bye, his mother last. She whispered in his ear, "Are you okay, *mijito*? Are they treating you well? Remember I love you and will always love you no matter how far you are from me. Do not forget this, son. Never forget this."

"*Gracias, mamá.*" Although Antinio acted stoically, he did not want to leave his mother's embrace. He felt her tears burn into his skin as her whispers burnt in his ears.

As soon as the car pulled out of the gate, Antinio ran to find Volodya. Seeing the tears in his eyes, Volodya led him away from the boys to a nearby field behind a large rock outcropping.

"What's the matter, Antinio?"

"My mother—this was the longest time I had ever been away from her. Seeing her made me realize that I already had forgotten some of the details of her face, the softness of her skin, how her eyes crinkled, and how warm her kisses felt. How can this be? I think about her every day. When I get her letters, I lift them up to my face to detect the faintest whiff of her perfume. I run my hands over the written words hoping to feel the vibrations of the pen in her hand."

Volodya smiled and caressed the boy's head. "I miss my mother, too. She is home in Sverdlovsk and doesn't know where I am."

"She is the only one who knows me," Antinio said, "and now that is fading. Without her, I am so alone and afraid."

It was getting dark. Antinio's sobs turned to wails, mimicking for the first time the voices that swirled in his thoughts. He felt immobilized. It became difficult to breathe or move his legs, and he felt the world had shrunk and he was all alone. The Lamenter in his head softly repeated, *Your mother suffers for you. She knows you will bring her pain, and for this suffers over you.*

Volodya sat down beside Antinio. "Don't worry, *moi dorogi malchik*. I am here with you. You are not alone."

He rubbed Antinio's head and chest until his crying stopped and his breathing returned to normal. As Antinio returned to consciousness and recognized his friend, he cast a weak smile. Volodya continued rubbing Antinio's chest and slowly made larger circles around his chest and leg, lightly brushing over his *pinga*, watching the reaction in Antinio's eyes. Seeing pleasure, Volodya concentrated his strokes on the boy's crotch, which produced a strong erection. The Russian undid Antinio's pants and lowered his lips, taking Antinio's hard cock into his mouth, stroking it with his tongue, coaxing it until Antinio felt the explosion throughout his body. Only then did the soldier kiss him on the mouth, wet with Antinio's fluid, a taste both salty and sweet.

This was not the first time this had happened to Antinio. Other boys at the camp had noticed right away that he was different, that he met their gaze directly and would often bump up close when they were lining up. During their twice-monthly group showers, ten boys at a time under a small tap, Antinio always had a group that wanted to shower with him, all bumping and soaping each other, touching each other's *pingas* and *culos*, watching to make sure that no one else entered the room while the bravest put their mouths on Antinio's cock. While he enjoyed this play, when a boy tried to put his *pinga* on Antinio's ass, he pushed him away. According to the code of Cuban manhood, he could only participate in this sort of play if he were the one in control.

It was common in Rome and Greece for an older man to have a relationship with a teenage boy that included sex.

Our word was *paiderastia*, from *pais*, which means boy, and *erastos*, which means lover—a beautiful word that in modern times has taken on a repulsive meaning. That is how my love for men began while I was being schooled and how I, in turn, brought Antinous into my life thirty years later.

Volodya helped Antinio off the ground and pulled up his pants for him. The Russian was distracted momentarily—he thought he noticed movement nearby. In the near darkness, he could not detect anything and returned his attention to Antinio.

"How do you feel now?" the Russian softly asked.

Antinio smiled, "Wonderful. I never thought you would do that."

"Why not?"

"You treated me like you cared about me. That was so different than what happens in the shower."

"Sex can be tender and loving. While both ways might end in release, the feelings are different. Men can care for each other. And they may kiss each other."

"When you kissed me, I felt closer to you than ever before, than I have ever felt to another boy."

"That is a good memory to keep of me. You are a sweet and wonderful boy. Let me kiss you again."

Assured that Antinio was fine, Volodya gave him another lingering kiss and left. Antinio brushed himself off and began to walk slowly back to the main camp, his mind filled with feelings of missing his mother mixed with a glow and other sensations he could not quite yet understand. One of the big, rough country boys jumped in front of him. Antinio avoided these boys who had neither the education nor sensibilities of the capital city. This one, Apolion, nicknamed Destroyer, was one of the worst.

Apolion opened up his pants and took out his dirty *pinga*. He stroked it until it was hard. "Suck on it. I saw what that Russian soldier did to you. Now you do that to me."

"No. Take that dirty thing away from me. Go and wash up and then come back. Maybe then I will do it, but I doubt it."

As he tried to brush past Apolion, two other boys jumped out of the darkness, pulled him to the ground, and tore at his pants. Antinio struggled, but they were stronger and held him facedown. He heard Apolion spit as he jumped on top of Antinio's legs and pressed hard against his body. He felt a pain between his butt cheeks like none he had ever felt before. Apolion grunted and plunged while the other boys covered Antinio's mouth to muffle his screams.

After a long battering, Apolion let out a deep groan and pulled away. The other boys released Antinio and smirked as he sniffled. Apolion turned to him and said with a sneer, "Now you're my girl. I will fuck you every day. If you say anything, El Capitan will call you into his tent and fuck you even harder. And since you're my little girl and can't defend yourself, I'll watch over you, don't worry."

The boys laughed and slapped each other's backs and ran off. Antinio wandered back to the camp dazed and in pain. This time not one but many different voices were in his head, all accusing him: *You deserved what you got. You are being punished for being a sick little boy, or really a little girl, like he said. You will never be a man and will spend the rest of your life being fucked by men whenever they want to. You are so obsessed about* culo, *well you will never have any control over your own ass ever again. Your fate is set, and your mother cannot protect you, and in the end, when she realizes who you are, she will reject you.*

He tried to run to get away from the Shriekers, as he named them now, but they followed right beside him. Reason, always calm and logical, spoke up and plainly stated, *You must get out of the Army. They hold hearings every week, and those who are crazy are sent home. You have talked to others who have practiced how to be crazy and what to say. You can do that.* This provided him a temporary peace, and he returned to his bunk. I whispered in his ear comforting, calming thoughts until he fell into a deep slumber.

The next morning, Antinio began a routine of acting crazy, saying strange things to people and appearing disoriented.

When, a few days later, his turn came before the medical board, he spoke in a mixture of Spanish and Russian, seemingly unable to differentiate between the two. The doctors laughed and told him to practice some more. He wasn't crazy enough to be released.

As he left the doctors' tent, Antinio saw Apolion and his friends waiting near the bunkroom. The Shriekers returned, warning and admonishing, *You cannot escape, your mother cannot protect you, you deserve this fate, you are meant to be someone's* puto. *You will never be a real man.*

He ran to his bunkroom and picked up a heavy handgun, the only protection his platoon had against the *yanqui* invaders. While Antinio had been trained in shooting guns, he had never thought of turning one on a human being. He could aim at targets or bottles or fences, but people, never. When Apolion entered the room, the Shriekers were deafening to the point that he thought his head was going to burst. He could barely control his hand as he lifted the gun. Apolion stopped in his tracks, but Antinio did not notice. He took aim, and his last thought as the bullet left the antique gun was that he would get out of the Army if he survived this.

Antinio turned the gun and shot himself. Time moved slowly as the heat of the bullet passed through his belly. I could not allow this to happen, I had already lost one young boy in my life. I was determined to make amends and not allow another boy to die. With the forces entrusted to me, I deflected the bullet so that it missed Antinio's spine and organs. As he dropped to the floor, I protected his head so that he would not be further harmed. I whispered to the frightened boy, "Trust me, my love. You are safe in my arms once again." Blood had pooled across the floor by the time the doctors made their way into the bunkroom. When they bent over him, they saw he was smiling.

III

That the bullet emerged at all from the barrel of the old, rusty gun was remarkable. The doctors found that no vital organs were injured, but so much blood had been lost that an emergency field transfusion was arranged. Volodya volunteered, and after determining that their blood types matched, the Russian's blood was mixing with that of the young boy on the stretcher. The doctors, however, could not remove the bullet, as it was lodged behind Antinio's stomach and would be too dangerous to take out. Antinio would have this reminder stay in his body.

He was let go from the Army, leaving in his wake a spate of copycat shootings as his companions saw this as an easier way out once the doctors stopped releasing the boys pretending to be crazy. After two months, the casualty list added up to include seven shot-off toes, four arms broken from bullets piercing the bones, three ears blown off, and one shot buttock (no one could figure out how the boy managed that). All were released, and the firearms were taken away. The camp closed soon thereafter since the *yanqui* invaders never showed up. Then the Russians themselves left, taking their missiles with them.

I was taken aback by this incident. Demigods like myself do not have the ability to see the future, so I had no idea that Antinio might turn the weapon on himself. But even more surprising was my reflexive intervention. Never before in my years of roaming the heavens and earth had I saved anyone's life. This was not my intention; I did it unconsciously. Afterwards, an oddly exciting and familiar feeling coursed through what remained of my soul. I also felt a bit tired, something that I had not experienced since becoming deified in the days after my physical death.

Antinio never spoke about the bullet wound, leaving his family, their friends, and the world at large to fill in the gaps. His father began spinning the story right away.

"My brave son, Antinio, was wounded in a *yanqui* night attack. There were two of them crawling through the fields, and he fired at them first. His actions saved the platoon leader's life. I always knew he had it in him."

Erastus was the first to respond. "Wait a minute. There were no reports of *yanquis* landing in Cuba. And if they did, how did they manage to go undetected seventy miles from the coast to that camp in the middle of nowhere? You must have gotten that wrong. And this is the first time I have ever heard you say anything good about your son."

"You misunderstood me. He is a fine boy—maybe he was a little weak before, but the Army fixed that. What I meant was that there was a *yanqui*-influenced traitor in the ranks. Antinio discovered him and threw himself in front of his leader to protect his life." His father's friends liked that story better, and after a few drinks it even seemed to make sense.

But Erastus and Anticlea were worried. "What do you think happened there?" he asked her.

"I don't know. He won't talk about it with me," Anticlea said. "Didn't you find out anything from the army personnel when they brought him back?"

"They wouldn't say much, I think for fear of getting in trouble. They did say there was another boy in the barracks when this happened, and he was very upset by what he saw. They interrogated the boy. He had a reputation of bullying some of the younger ones like Antinio. But he denied doing anything."

"I was always worried that something awful would happen to Antinio from the moment he disappeared," she said. "Why would he ever shoot himself? I could have lost my baby forever. It is miraculous that he lived. Another inch and that bullet would have killed him. He must have someone looking over him."

"I'm afraid that something bad happened," Erastus answered. "He's too quiet and seems preoccupied most of the time. I've tried a few times, but he won't open up to me. He's always been different than the other children—in some ways more mature and worldly, and in other ways so naive."

"And so sociable," Anticlea continued. "He used to talk constantly about the new things he was reading or discovered. Now he stays alone and appears to be hiding some secret. Let's hope that time will heal his wounds."

Antinio recuperated for several weeks at home, tended to hand and foot by the women and Erastus. Eventually he became well and regained an eagerness to return to school. Meanwhile, enough time had passed for the story of his bravery to expand. It was now accepted that several *yanqui* traitors had been involved and Antinio had single-handedly routed an attempt to kill El Comandante's brother who was due to visit the camp. His stature grew, and boys and girls (and even his teachers) wanted to see the scar from the bullet, which he freely showed off. Since he did not talk about the incident, school administrators determined that it must be a classified military secret. They duly noted in his school records, "Antinio is an upright young Communist and continues to show the virtues of leadership and confidentiality that he exhibited so bravely defending the homeland." As stories spread about his prowess, both boys and girls began openly flirting with him.

Alone, Antinio often touched the scar, bringing back a vision of my rescue of his life. He was not sure what to make of this memory. Reason was quite adamant that it was the emotional shock and trauma that concocted my presence. Yet he could remember the physical touch of my hands holding his head, the smell of my skin, and the sound of my ethereal voice. All of these were as real as anything he had experienced.

Sometimes he felt this foreign object in his body burning, aching, and pulsating with his heart; and he remembered me comforting him, easing his pain, loving him back to life. He also knew that Volodya, who had returned to the Soviet Union, had given him a new life force, one steeped in thousands of years of *nostalghia*, pain, and longing. Love and desire were now so intertwined that Antinio could not tell the difference between them.

The months passed, and then years. Excelling at school, Antinio graduated ahead of time and prepared to enter the university. In those days, Reason was his constant companion and guided him through logic, mathematics, and languages. Both his mother and I steered him toward the Greek mathematicians Pythagoras, Euclid, Ptolemy, and Archimedes. Reason rejoiced at the precision of lines and angles and the formulas that spoke to him as he studied how they applied to the world at large.

I understood this fascination well, as I had singlehandedly commissioned and designed temples and buildings in all of my lands, the highlights being the Temple of Zeus in Athens and my villa outside Rome in Tiburtina. I spent years planning my villa and all of its surrounding outbuildings, baths, and temples. Many an architect was fired for not following the designs I sketched out. Over the years, hundreds of the finest craftsmen plied their trades in building my vision. Guided by my inspiration, Antinio decided to become an architect.

Cuba in the late sixties was undergoing a transformation as a revolutionary country. The blockade from the United States combined with misguided economic policies focused on unattainable sugar cane harvests led to shortages of food and supplies and almost anything anyone would need in life. There was only one life necessity that the government did not try to regulate; only one sphere of life free from the mind control, meddling, and constructive education efforts; only one thing that everyone freely shared day and night, on the streets, in back alleys, on rooftops, in parks, in fields, at the beach, in the ocean's waves, on the Malecón, in backseats and front seats of cars, in buses, up against trees, under bushes, in open hospital beds, everywhere except perhaps in bedrooms since those were inevitably shared with several other people, sometimes these days with people not even related.

That was sex.

Havana, more so than other Cuban cities, had sex in the air all the time. It was languid, thick, hot, and moist. Clothes, especially during the hard times, were reduced to a minimum of light, gauzy-thin cotton—anything heavier would cause the sweat to accumulate and mark deep patches under breasts or armpits or crotches. The odor of human sweat mixed with the sea air. The tartness of the unwashed human body mingled with the smells of ripe bananas and pineapples sold on the street. The smell alone was enough to keep everyone stimulated waiting for the chance encounter that would release the pent-up desires surrounding them.

The vegetation in the city, lush and full, matched this headiness. Flowers bursting with fragrant smells, their pistils enlarged, long and pointed to attract bees and insects, all but said, *Look at me! I am a sex organ. Come enjoy what I have to offer.* The banyan trees with their huge entwining trunks that wove around each other appeared to be in a constant state of erotic motion with branches hanging low, dripping with moss and vines. Nothing that grew was exempt from excess. Despite the hunger gnawing in everyone's bellies, trees would drop their overly ripe fruit on the ground, where ants and other insects would roll around picking up pieces until they were sated.

With the scarcity of housing, few people had private spaces in their homes. So, at night the parks and any available spaces were filled with men and women taking advantage of the temporary respite from the heat of the day and the lack of adequate lighting to have sex and banish away the miseries of the new, regimented order.

Havana brought back memories of my first journey to Asia. Unlike the stately order and uprighteousness of Rome or the dazzling purity of Athens, the sweltering cities of Bithynia were as chaotic as they were erotic. Upon entering new, unknown parts of my realm, I often roamed the streets and plazas in disguise to learn what I could from my own senses rather than rely on the incomplete written reports of my lieutenants. The bazaars with their winding narrow paths were filled with sultry men, lithe and dark-skinned, lurking in the shadows. I still remember the smells, masculine, spicy, and musky. In small, enclosed stalls men lounged on rugs and cushions drinking tea. I noticed the fullness of their lips as they sipped their drinks and the ease they had with each other, their countenance that of anticipation. When I walked in as a traveling stranger, they opened their arms and their masculine hospitality to find out what I had to offer.

It was in such a place that I first spotted Antinous, who had come to town with his father, a merchant. As they walked into the stall where I was lounging, I immediately noticed him, lithe of step with an intelligence that went beyond his young age. He looked at me and made me believe that he saw through my disguise. I quickly decided to send him to Rome for a proper education and upbringing. I spoke to his father quietly, telling him I was an emissary of the great and mighty Hadriano. "Bring the boy to the *agora* in two hours," I said, "and he will be granted an audience."

When they arrived at the *agora*, I was dressed in my military uniform and crown. I bade the father and son to come forward and asked the boy his name.

"Antinous, my Emperor," he answered in a clear and confident voice.

"Antinous, would you like to travel to Rome to join my service? If so, you must say good-bye to your father now."

"Father, what choice do I have but to accept our Emperor's offer? Do not fear for me as I have always dreamed of a life in Rome, the imperial center."

As he looked away from his father, our eyes connected. I said, "Tomorrow you will go to Rome for an education in all that a young man needs to learn to take his rightful place at the side of the Emperor. Come sit by me right here to watch and listen to the entreaties of your fellow countrymen, and mark well my beneficence and justice."

In his late teens, Antinio's body had ripened and matured and could challenge even Antinous in beauty and form. He was lean and muscular with a beautiful, sensitive face. A full, black moustache perched on his lips, and his smile lit up the world. His dark eyes were piercing yet could twinkle with delight, inviting flirtations from across the street. He wanted to understand the form and function of each gender, although men attracted him most.

He kept a list, not merely to remember his conquests, but because statistics and data were important to him. In neatly ruled columns, he carefully scribed each name, the date, location, the particular sex acts, and a final column with comments—*beautiful ass, sweet nipples, wow, 3x*. He frequently examined the listings and looked for patterns, monthly differences, and annual cycles. He cross-referenced correspondences with cycles of the moon, the weather, the economy, and the price of pork. All these were variables to be examined, and the only constant was sex itself. He tried to figure out the formula that would equate with happiness and add up to love.

The University opened a new world for Antinio. There were ideas to be discovered in architecture despite the oppressive nature of the regime. As had been true in the time of the Greeks, the line still existed as itself; it did not need to bend to Marxism and become a different thing altogether. Buildings were still constructed on foundations, walls still needed to bear weight, and roofs were still needed for protection from the elements. While cement, glass, steel, and wood might be in short supply at any given time, even El Comandante could not reimagine a revolutionary way to construct a building.

Antinio met Cloto on the first day of his second semester. During roll call, he was immediately intrigued by the unusual name of a new classmate. Over the class break, he introduced himself and asked him about it.

"My father was a Greek seaman and married a Cuban woman," the young man told Antinio. "They were always planning to go back to Greece, but waited too long to leave after the government was overthrown. So here I am."

Antinio peppered him with more questions about his family, where he lived, what school he had attended. "Have you been to the part of the Malecón where fishermen congregate? Why did you choose architecture? What songs can you sing?"

Not giving him time to answer, he then asked, "Would you rather have a short, glorious life or a long life that was common and without adventure?" Although in the end Cloto would go for the long life, quiet and thoughtful, in this moment with this strange yet attractive man, he nodded his head without an answer.

Antinio replied to his own question, "I'd opt for the exciting, the experience, and the pleasure, even if that meant a shortened life span. Cuba is such a small world," he added. "Anything would be better."

Cloto smiled at this and mysteriously murmured, "I will do the best I can." It was Antinio's turn to nod quietly, wondering what that might mean.

Antinio scanned Cloto's body, noting the arched butt on such a long, skinny frame, the crooked smile that made the left side of his face crinkle up, the clear brown eyes that met his glance, his curly brown hair, and lean arms covered with a soft fur.

When class was finished for the day, they walked out together already friends. Waiting in line for a snack, Antinio stood close behind Cloto, feeling the waves of heat from his body.

"*Mira,* look over there." Antinio pointed to a building across the street in order to graze his arm across that of Cloto. Cloto did not back off from the touch, but met Antinio halfway, turning to him with a smile. Thus was born Antinio's first love.

The two young men wasted no time discovering each other's bodies. In the early evening darkness, they ambled along the Malecón, jumped over the wall, and fell among the large boulders to a place big enough yet tight enough to cram together two bodies waiting for their chance. As the sea crashed a few feet away and a full moon lazily rose in the sky, they kissed for the first time—not a timid kiss, but a kiss of expectation, a kiss of two people who each had been waiting to find the other, a kiss that would have been enough to satisfy most mortals. But in this moment they were beyond life itself, plunging the depths and rising to the heights of the sacred, the gods, the angels. Cloto rubbed his face against Antinio's furry chest, grazing his brown nipples and eventually discovering the deep scar the bullet had left. Cloto's lips caressed the scar, his tongue neatly fitting in the crevasse hidden by hair. He lingered there for hours; at least that is how they both remembered it.

The scar was a sacred entry point previously undiscovered by the men who had concentrated solely on Antinio's glorious *pinga*. Antinio himself had often absentmindedly rubbed that spot, discovering that doing so gave him an erection that was not simply sexual, but much deeper, a feeling of fullness, fertility, bringing all life to fruition. When I deified my beloved after he drowned, I accorded him the powers of fecundity and fertility and associated him with the Egyptian god Osiris, who brought the annual overflowing of the Nile. Antinio, too, had this overwhelming charge that would satiate the desires of each and every man or woman he engaged. His own search would be for the few that could bring him this same depth of satisfaction.

For his part, Cloto experienced a jolt of understanding, compassion, and expansive love that overcame his body as his tongue gently explored this unknown aspect of his new friend. With each tender movement, Cloto traveled the shape and depth of this entry point, finding himself drifting out to sea and lifted upwards, floating above the city with a single thread trailing behind him to Antinio. An eagle, Aquila, carried the young man up to the constellation shimmering with stars that outlined Antinio's body. Cloto's body opened itself up to take in the fullness of Antinio without pain, without physical sensation, and with complete acceptance as natural as the tide. In this embrace Antinio was born anew.

The two young men awoke with the early morning sun, wet with dew and sweat and semen. They never spoke of this first night, awed by its power and dumbed by its inexplicability. But from this point on the two men were inseparable. Both lived in overcrowded homes with three generations of relatives in close quarters. While Antinio still had a private room, that did not guarantee any level of privacy. They would meet at the bus stop and stand together in the crush of humanity pushing and shoving for a space in the infrequent buses. On the bus, they stood front to back, Antinio always pressing against Cloto, leaning into each other, unnoticed by others in the crowded aisle.

Five blocks from the University they would depart the bus and linger in the shadows of the memorial in the Parque de los Martires Universitarios, stealing a kiss and a long embrace. They wrote odes of love that they would hide in each other's pocket to be found later in the day. Over the months, they created their own pathways throughout the city, seeking out deserted alleys, walking through the backs of yards, and resting in abandoned buildings where they could celebrate a few minutes of time together, alone and unobserved, or so they thought.

Perhaps it was inevitable that such a love could not be kept hidden. As Antinio had noted, Cuba was a small world. Secrets were common currency, especially when the real currency was worthless. Enshrined in the Revolution and any dictatorial regime, the secret police are aptly named: seeking out clues that could harm and constrain its citizens, keeping confidential what could damage the regime.

And there were those who kept secrets to protect their own secrets, a category that contained most homosexuals. Except for the times when one wanted to retaliate against a spurned lover or harass a lover to return, these men maintained a code of silence. Those at the highest ranks of government and academia held themselves to an even higher code of silence; that is, until they were trapped, intimidated, or blackmailed themselves.

The School of Architecture was one such place where a secretive love could flourish. Almost all of the faculty and students were men. It was not unusual for them to gather, sing, read poetry, trade banned Beatles records, and have long, complicated, obscure architectural discussions that were subterfuges for that about which they could never publicly talk. In their desire for time together, Antinio and Cloto would not engage in these conversations and rarely attended parties, which were never announced but whispered from friend to friend. Perhaps this aloofness is what condemned them. Maybe it was jealousy.

Whatever it was, eight months, fourteen days, and five hours from the date that the two men met, Antinio walked into class to find a rector from the University sitting in the front and all of the students gathered in a circle. He was pushed to a chair in the middle, and the rector dropped a piece of paper in Antinio's handwriting on his lap.

"Who was this poem addressed to?" Antinio did not answer. "It's your lover. What is his name? Why don't you tell us? Does he fuck you? Should we examine your asshole to see if it is red and bleeding?"

Each student in the room was required to add to the verbal assault. This was the way delinquents, those who would destroy the Revolution, were treated when discovered. The questioning went on for hours, and Antinio said nothing. Even when he was offered clemency. Even when it was offered that his family would never learn a thing if he would only give up a name. By the end, his interrogators were pleading, "Any name. Just give us a name."

Antinio's refusal scared the group. The usual chain of events was to get a name, and then a mob would find that person and repeat the process. Antinio's only consolation was that Cloto was not present to be made to participate in this "self-criticism session." But Antinio had to warn him, to tell Cloto to go visit his sick aunt in the countryside for a few weeks and to burn all of his papers before it was too late.

46

The University, being a cultured institution, did not beat people up, pummel them senseless, or bash their teeth in. In the end, Antinio was kicked out of the room, expelled, and told to never return. It took him three desperate tries before he found a working phone on the street to call and warn Cloto. Despite a connection riddled with static, Cloto heard the deadness in his lover's voice and instinctively knew what had happened. Fear always had lurked under the surface of their time together, a fear that never disappeared even in the most private of places and in the most intimate of acts. Telephones were no place for private conversations. Static was assumed to be from government listeners. Without any further words between them, each man disconnected.

Antinio walked the long way home, raging with anger born out of fear and shame. When his mania subsided, the Lamenters, his doubting chorus, took over. *They are right, I am not a real man. I don't deserve to live. I am lower than a worm. I can't tell anyone what happened. I can't let my family find out what happened today. I am so embarrassed. What will my mother say, the one who believes in me? Even she will reject me. All my friends will be afraid to be seen with me. My uncles and cousins will shun me like a leper.* His heart beat louder and louder, taking over his body, making it shudder. As he made it closer and closer to home, the beating became like hard bricks smashing against his body and his soul. He walked up his front stairs. In front of his uncle, he tripped and fell and vomited.

For three days Antinio lay unconscious with feverish dreams of an impossible voyage across the sea. He battled seasickness, monsters, and a gale that blew his ship half apart. He was surrounded by people half-dead, rotting and stinking, that would be pulled into the ocean by giant sharks with black, deadly teeth leaving a trail of blood. He was tossed on strange islands inhabited by cannibals, another by a one-eyed being, and a third swarming with animals that were at one moment men and the next wild boars. In each place he was tempted and tested. He lost track of time and direction, heading off in one vessel to wind up in another back at the place he began.

At the end he was abandoned in a strange land with strange customs, where nothing was soft and a disease afflicted people, causing them to shrivel up, to be covered with open wounds, and to suffer endlessly without cure. Yet even in this harshest of harsh places, he heard me singing to him, a song that held him up and filled him with warmth again. As he listened, I massaged the bullet entry on his belly and blew into it, giving life back to his weakened body.

He woke up in his own bed on a sunny day to a new world. As before, he never spoke about what had happened. His family had gathered around, watching him toss and turn, whimper and scream. They caught the name Cloto and heard Antinio warn him away, to watch out for Paris's arrow, and they wondered where Antinio's delusions were carrying him. After his fever broke, they ended their watch. When he did not speak of what had befallen him, no one dared to ask. In Cuban families, secrets were respected.

As secrets go, the biggest secret happened a day later when the sub-administrator in the School of Architecture who had admired the men from afar was given the proceedings from Antinio's inquisition to file in the official records to document his disgrace. This sub-administrator who shall remain forever nameless simply wrote a note in the file—*withdrawn due to illness*. He ripped up the official report and later, on his way home, scattered it on the Malecón, coincidentally at the very spot where Antinio and Cloto had consecrated their love. Their secret was maintained.

IV

By the early seventies, Havana was slowly melting away. As the oldest city in the tropics, it had only survived due to constant care and rebuilding. The salt air, the hurricanes, the hot sun relentlessly bearing down day after day, the rapid growth of trees and plants with their roots pushing through any crack they could find were enough to crumble concrete, rot wood, rust metal, and burn away color and paint. For hundreds of years, the battle had been fought against decay—wood was varnished and painted and protected until it needed to be replaced and the process started over again. Limestone and imported marble used to construct the walks and buildings of the University or the Capitolio were cleaned and polished daily. And the rampant growth of the vegetation was chopped and trimmed back to a manageable length by machetes.

Maintenance and care of the city were not the priorities of the new regime. The thousands of workers whose pride it had been to care for Havana were sent to the countryside to cut sugar or teach the illiterate *campesinos*. It only took a short time for the deconstruction of the city to begin. Simply enough, one day a hole would appear in Calle C, and soon all of the alphabet streets would be pockmarked. Bird poop containing undigested seeds would land in one of the holes, and within weeks plants were sprouting up. With the shortage of gasoline, cars were a rarity, and the bicycles and people walking by would skirt around these holes, allowing the plants to grow unimpeded.

The need to fight the process of decay was familiar to me. I restored the Pantheon in Rome and redesigned its dome after my predecessors had let it decline. I rebuilt aqueducts originally created by the Greeks, paved roads, and left a trail of new and reconstructed public works wherever I traveled. Storms, salt water, earthquakes, all under the control of Poseidon will destroy what man has designed and built. Only by constant diligence could I counteract his destruction. This was my responsibility to my people. After I died, I watched much of it collapse again.

The worst was not being able to prevent the decline of Antinopolis. After he drowned himself, I deified Antinous and built a new city in his honor on the banks of the Nile. It had the finest statues, temples, and public buildings, all created in the Greek style. Yet, after my death it was slowly buried by the desert sands, its marble looted and hauled away for other projects.

It was in this environment of decay in Havana that Antinio surveyed his possibilities. He needed to reform himself, to pull away from a life that could bring him harm. He was deeply ashamed, not of his love for Cloto, but of his attraction to men, which if discovered again would subject him to persecution and bring disgrace to his family. The Lamenters firmly reminded him that he could be thrown into prison or even killed. He understood that punishment for his sins and his lust was a likely outcome.

Antinio was not a religious man, and by this time there were few to be found in Havana who would publicly admit they were. On the advice of Fineo, one of his remaining friends from the University, Antinio went to see a priest at the Cathedral in Habana Vieja, the oldest part of the city. The Catholic fathers still possessed their ancient monastery, a large stone building resembling a fortress where monks were housed in small cells. He passed through the building's white marble portal, and a young acolyte directed him up the stone stairs to the Confessor on the third floor. The Confessor met Antinio at the door to his room.

"Father, can you help me change who I am?" he asked. "I love men. I have made love to men and know that this is wrong. I want to—no, I need to stop."

The Confessor looked upon the young man with compassion and put his arm around Antinio while they talked. The priest was as comforting as he was transfixed by Antinio's beauty and the musculature of his body. After listening attentively, the older man finally spoke. "We need to check whether you are working properly."

Antinio was confused, but the priest directed him, "Lie down here," and placed his hands on Antinio's body. "I need to make sure that there are no physical problems with your functioning." He began to caress Antinio's chest and loins, giving particular attention to his *pinga*. He rubbed harder.

"Don't worry, my son, I am only checking," he added as he unzipped Antinio's pants and took the young man's member into his hands. "Ah, yes, you seem to be reacting well, but let me see." He placed his mouth on Antinio's *pinga* and began to suck on it. Antinio's first reaction was to run, yet he soldiered through the priest's attention. At last, after an explosion that jerked the priest upright and released the pent-up energy Antinio had been denying for weeks, the Confessor turned to him and smiled. "Well, that tells us that you are functioning fine. Now let's see if you are able to get on your knees for me."

Without hesitation, Antinio fled through the door, fastening his pants as he ran down the stairs. The monk at the bottom smiled as Antinio hurried by, apparently having witnessed similar reactions to this test. Antinio raced out into the crowded, narrow street feeling a mixture of shame and delight, confusion and clarity. The Shriekers were horrified by what he had caused the holy man to do while Reason interjected that priests were no different than other men and wanted sex as much as anyone else. Antinio decided he would not reject sex, but that he would reject men.

Even with my lack of ability to see into the future, I knew that Antinio was unlikely to maintain this stance for very long. When it is in our nature to love and appreciate men, no matter what the brain and its voices say, the feeling of hunger will continue to reside in our phallus and *culus*. That energy must be released in a way that only another man can satisfy.

There was, however, no way I could steer him away from finding a woman. And he did not lack for women who were interested in him. Walking down *La Rampa*, women young and old would stop him and put their arm through his as they asked the time of day or directions or whatever else they could think of merely to be close to him. Gazing into his brown eyes with expectant delight, they would feel the heat of his body and flirt, wiping their breasts with a handkerchief. Within days, Antinio met Calypso, whose name, he remembered from his book *The Golden Ages*, meant "concealing the knowledge." He thought, *What a perfect name. This is exactly what I need to do.*

Antinio's Tante Avis convinced him to attend a meeting of the CDR, Comité de Defensa de la Revolución, the local Communist Party block organization that watched over every neighborhood and, more importantly, every neighbor for deviant or antirevolutionary behavior. She knew that it was always good to keep appearances up, especially when the neighbors could see that Antinio was no longer attending the University.

Calypso sat in the back of the cramped, hot meeting room simmering in her beauty and impatience, watching the proceedings with a sense of disdain. She had such a powerful seductive presence, taut and wound up ready to strike, that no one dared talk to her for fear they might make her angry. She had a reputation for practicing Santería and of being a priestess and *curandera*, a healer. Even revolutionary Cubans who eschewed all things religious were nervous in her presence. Ever since the white dove of Babalú Ayé had landed on El Comandante's shoulder while he gave his inaugural speech, all practitioners of Santería were given wide berth.

Calypso was an enchantress who could easily entrap a man by casting out her spider's web of entanglement. Usually it took no more than a glance from her dark, brooding eyes and a twitch of her lips; with a tougher candidate it might take a blown kiss; and for the hardest to snare, it might take an ambush in a dark corner. Despite his resolve to find a woman, Antinio was resistant to her spell. Calypso had never met with failure before, so she doubled her efforts. In her experience, most men had simple and predictable minds, but Antinio was unlike other men. Something in him warned her away, while a deeper force demanded she follow the intensity of her attraction. So she threw away her usual bag of tricks and incantations and simply said, "Come with me to my house. I want to become better acquainted with you and your journeys. Maybe I can help you." That invitation was enough for Antinio, and he spent his first night with her talking until late. Before he left in the morning, they made love, love that was passionate and left her wanting more.

After that, he came around to her each day. He sang love songs to her in five languages and could make her laugh with his stories, but he only tolerated her attentions, and she sensed his indifference. Even so, Calypso could not stop herself from loving him.

She could feel the forces within him, hear the ancient choruses that tormented and guided him, and, uniquely, could already see the dead spot that was starting to grow, the place where no emotion was allowed to enter, each pain being categorized, walled off, and isolated. After many months, Calypso tried to reach into that lifeless place but was repelled by Antinio, who refused to talk about or acknowledge its existence. Using her healing powers as a *santera* to penetrate deep into his body, invoking the *orishas* Babalú Ayé and Elegguá, the ones who could heal all, she could clearly see the outlines of the bullet lodged in his body, yet she could not see through or around it.

Without telling Antinio, she consulted with other *curanderas*. They spent a day drumming, eating sacred foods, and calling out to the *orishas* to possess them. In a trance they joined all of their spiritual energy and power and tried to enter that lifeless space, but every attempt failed, leaving the *santeras* with headaches and bloody noses. They had not seen a case like this and urged Calypso to leave this man for her own good. But the enchantress was herself enchanted and could not. Instead, she became Antinio's proctectoress.

She helped pave the way for Antinio to reenter the University, this time in the School of Linguistics. Whether it was the intervention of Tante Avis who knew the Dean, the work of the sub-administrator who had made Antinio's past problems disappear from written memory, or a spell Calypso cast with herbs and twigs, he started over. Calypso accompanied him to the University on his first day and met him again after class, establishing to anyone who might be spying that Antinio had a singularly beautiful woman in his life. He willingly went along with this subterfuge, knowing that real danger lurked not in dark alleyways, where he was familiar with the covert navigation of yearning and passion, but in the open corridors of the academic offices and classrooms where someone—no, worse, anyone—could report him for acts real or imagined.

Antinio could not avoid sex with men during this time. But for the first time, he was cautious about his advances. With every choice, his chorus of doubt was ready to speak their warnings—*Are sure about this one? What is he doing? Is he writing something down? Should you be doing this? Is this safe?*

Back in school, Reason flourished again in Antinio, creating a path out of the wilderness. He found an intellectual pleasure in morphology as it explained scientifically what he had known intuitively about languages since he was a child. He had always loved to trace the phonetic changes in words over time and from language to language, and now he was able to spend days learning more than he thought possible on this topic. In the evenings, he would tell Calypso about what he had learned that day.

"Did you know that certain letter pairs are really the same sound, like T and D or R and L? It makes sense when you think about it. Over time, spoken usage degrades languages, and the letters tend to soften. For example, the letter D takes over from the letter T." The next night it would be something new. "It is so interesting that what we call *guaguas* in Cuba are *autobuses* in Peru and simply *buses* in Mexico," he told her. "Yet, here we catch a *guagua* at the *estacíon de buses*. Even the simplest of things in the same language change due to location or time."

He continued his Russian studies and became fluent in French in six months. Since he could already speak and read German, he took advanced seminars in Goethe and Nietzsche and would have lengthy weekly discussions with Tante Avis. Eventually, he took the limited classes that were offered in English, the language of the despicable *yanquis*, whose radio broadcasts he could occasionally hear when they were not jammed, full of music of the Rolling Stones, Elton John, and Aretha Franklin. The more Antinio learned and the more Reason was engaged, the more the other voices in his chorus were subdued.

His biggest excitement came when he started his classes in Esperanto.

He was barely in the door when he called out, "Calypso, where are you?"

"Right here, *mi amor*. What are you so excited about?"

"Calypso, why didn't I enroll in Esperanto classes before? It is so logical and therefore so beautiful, unlike any other language that exists. Esperanto is a created language based on inspiration. Can you guess what the name means?"

Bemused, Calypso responded, "No, but I know you will tell me."

"Esperanto literally means 'one who hopes.' If you thought about it for a minute, the *espera* means he or she hopes in Spanish. What could be more fulfilling for me? My whole life is about hoping and desiring."

His excitement rose. "As a created language, it has a perfect grammar with no exceptions, a consistent spelling, and a regular means for introducing new words. As a language that hopes, it has its own culture, and the *jarlibro* (yearbook) of the Universala Esperanto-Asocio is published every year, with listings of officers for each country. I was just approved by the Dean to be elected as *vicprezidanto* for the Kubo branch."

He pulled her over to the sofa. "Come here and look at the *jarlibro* with me. It has listings of hotels where Esperantists can stay, coffee shops and restaurants where Esperanto is the *lingua franca*, and magazines that share news of the language's acceptance around the world. I would love to go to these places where I could talk to everyone even if I didn't know their native language. It would be like a spell was cast over me and everyone, and despite the differences of where we live, what type of government we live under, and our history, we could all talk together and understand each other. There are conferences every year on peace and science. As an Esperanto speaker, maybe I can travel out of the Communist bloc one year to represent Cuba. Now, that's a dream I want to believe in.

"And look, here is my real dream. There are naturist colonies, places where you never have to put on clothing, whether you are on the beach, at a restaurant, in a store, or just talking to your neighbor. If the conventions of language are shed, the next thing is to shed the conventions of clothing and political philosophies and everything else that keeps us backward. This is the future. In thirty years, Esperanto will be everywhere."

In my travels, Greek and Latin were the only two languages I would ever rely upon. My first encounter with other languages in Germania was striking. I couldn't imagine why anyone would choose not to speak the most beautiful and perfect language that already existed, Greek. I did my best to push a pan-Hellenic consciousness in the Empire, but in the lesser provinces it never caught on. At the time, I regarded this as stubbornness and ignorance.

Watching how Latin morphed into its own family of languages over the millennia, I can see how language is a living thing that changes, degrades, and syncretizes on its own. And the meanings of individual words have gone through so many twists and turns over the millennia that modern usage often appears unrelated to the origin. Earlier I mentioned that Antinio was called *puto*, a male prostitute, by Apolion. This meaning is almost the opposite of the Old Latin *putus*, meaning pure and bright, which in my time became *puttus*, a young girl. (While I could comment on virtually every word I repeat in this tale, I will reserve my thoughts to the most interesting of such words or those that are of importance to Antinio.)

Antinio began to talk animatedly again with his family, friends, and classmates. His broad smile filled his entire face, his mouth slightly open to reveal his white teeth, and his twinkling eyes reappeared, not having been seen since he had collapsed on the steps of his family home. Calypso was pleased. She could see him coming alive. "Soon my job will be done," she told her other *santera*s, "and I will be able to send him off to roam the world on his own."

One evening, after searching the city for the necessary ingredients—always a struggle since one shop might have two eggs, but it would take four additional attempts to find the third needed egg, and in the process some ripe fruit or a scrawny chicken might be found, but not any flour until one of the eggs was traded for a cup of flour from a neighbor, which meant going out and about looking for an egg again—she made him a fine meal of *fricase de pollo*, *congrí*, and *flan de mango*.

After dinner, her dark eyes moist, she took his hand as if to read his fate in its lines. She said, "Tonight, you must finally leave me and not come back. You will have other adventures, Antinio, and travel to distant and strange lands. Along the way, you will endure many hardships, yet you will be blessed. Much will come to you, life will be bountiful. You will have three great loves in your life and as much love as you can accept. However, when you find the one that you love the most, your journey will end."

He flushed and tried to interrupt, but she put her fingers to his lips. "You will recognize when it is time, and any time before then is too early. Right now, my love, all I can say is that it is time for you to leave me. I have given you all of the gifts at my disposition."

She walked him to the door, hugged him for the last time, and turned away. With the night lit by a large full moon rising over the sea, Antinio trembled as he stepped out into the void.

V

Antinio never saw Calypso again. For months he tried to go back to her home, but whether it had melted away as so many buildings did in Havana at that time or she had put a spell on him so he could not remember, he was never able to locate it again. This possibility of not remembering disconcerted him since he had an infallible memory, able to recall exact dates, times, and places of events.

It was the so-called "year without calendars"—officially, journalists reported a paper shortage precluded the printing of calendars, but most Cubans believed that the regime had decided that if there were no calendars, it could work people longer and harder since Sundays did not have to come so often. Antinio's friends and family would rely on him to remember the exact day and time of occurrences that may have happened ten years previous—not only birthdays, weddings, and graduations, but also when they had bought the rocking chair with the red seat or when his cousin got stung by a jellyfish at Santa Marta Beach.

Oddly, no one he knew seemed to specifically remember Calypso. Although she had made a big splash by accompanying Antinio on the first day of school, no one in the department or his family could describe her with any detail. They merely had an impression of a feminine presence in his life then.

A year later he graduated in the top of his class and was immediately asked by the Sugar Ministry to take a job translating for foreign technicians who had come to provide technical assistance from Eastern Europe and the Soviet Union. After the Army, the Sugar Ministry was the most important government department. Fifteen years after the Revolution, sugar was the one and only export Cuba had, not counting the soldiers who were being sent to South America and Africa to foment revolution and fight in proxy wars with the West.

It was an improbable job for Antinio, a city dweller, to be sent to a rural *ingenio*—a sugar mill. Antinio was stationed in the Cuban countryside along with his comrades (which by the way was not a Russian word but originally Spanish for one who shares the same room). These technicians had never seen sugar cane and knew nothing of the processing of it to sugar, but would nonetheless be in charge of installing machinery to make it happen. Antinio and the technicians would pile into a government truck and follow the same route through the countryside that he had once taken to the army camp. Back then there were still farmers and livestock and gardens and fields of tobacco, maize, and wheat as there had been for generations before. But all of that was gone. The only thing to be seen interspersed between the cane fields were miles of dead, dry land, the result of overcultivation.

In such an unlikely place, he met unlikely people. As difficult as life could be in Cuba, the country was paradise to Poles, Russians, East Germans, and Hungarians streaming into the country. The long tropical days, evenly measured day in and day out through the year with only a small variation, were seen as a marvelous antidote to harsh, snowy winters with five hours of light and huddling around a weak fire in the evening eating potatoes, beets, and dried mushrooms. Those willing to travel halfway around the world to this isolated island were often made of the same stuff as Antinio—men who did not fit in back in their homelands, men with expansive world views, who had ideas, who sang, drank, and wanted to enjoy life far from the tyranny and oppression of their countries. And men who enjoyed the company of other men. Antinio felt a kinship with them, perhaps since his blood was imbued with Volodya's *nostalghia*, a word that was originally an old medical diagnosis combining the meanings of "return home safely" and "grief."

Centuries before, the army I assembled for the Empire comprised explorers who were not content to stay at home on the farm or running petty businesses in small villages. These men wanted to experience more than most; they wanted to live life fully. My comrades, as they were in the literal sense, wanted to be tested for their courage, their abilities, and their prowess. And I tested them every day. Although my reign was generally peaceful, my army was always trained and at readiness. The best of my men were well rewarded by me personally.

In Cuba, the men journeyed across the island, passing though the *campo* in open trucks, six of them in the back. The next mill announced itself before they arrived by the black clouds with acrid smoke. Closer, they would be overcome by the cloying, sweet smell of crushed cane mixed with that of burnt diesel oil and the sweat of hundreds of men working in the grimy shadows. The workers who fed the maw of the mill with stalks of cane had gashes on their arms and legs from machete cuts. Their faces were blackened from sunburn and dirt. The technicians would enter this underworld with flashlights and wrenches, replacing pieces of machinery without pausing the chomping and grinding. Stopping would mean quotas not being met, and if the quotas were not met, El Comandante's punishments would be harsh. Brontes, the local mill supervisor, a giant of a man well over six feet tall with broad shoulders and huge legs, made conditions more miserable. Puffed up from domination and the prestige of his small power over his workers, he was nicknamed Cíclope since he had lost an eye when it was struck by a red-hot poker he had been hammering. The men were terrified of him. In the accident he had lost the ability to cry, and his grief was distilled into a lingering resentment toward all human beings.

Unlike these workers, Antinio and the technicians could take a break each evening. They would bring their food and supplies to the house of the chief engineer and spend the evening eating, drinking, singing, and telling stories in multiple languages. As translator, Antinio held the group together. All conversations would flow through him as he went back and forth in two or three languages, interspersing his own commentary and ideas, which themselves had to be translated.

The Russians recited poems, some classics learned in their days as schoolboys, others made up on the spot. Poems were always a challenge for Antinio since he wanted to match the right tone with the words. The Hungarians had long, involved epic stories of mountains, snow, wolves, and the rescue of lost loves. These he would embellish with incongruous details, for what did a Cuban know of snow and wolves? But he did understand lost love and could bring tears to his companions' eyes as he rendered a story into German or Russian. The Germans sang *lieder* in haunting tenor and baritone voices. These melancholic performances did not need translation.

Late at night, with lowered voices, the men shared stories of life in their countries. Despite the great distance between their native lands, they spoke of the same complaints of oppression and lack of opportunity, the deadening sameness of life, and the lack of access to new ideas. Life was not difficult so much as stifling. These were men who would not answer the question as Cloto had. To a man, they preferred short, active, adventurous times over an uneventful life.

While they made the best of what Cuba had to offer, their bodies still ached with the need for touch and release. Certain evenings, Antinio would wander off into the bush with one man, then another, then another, giving each the chance to discover what they needed from him—a special touch, a kiss, a chance to put their lips on his marvelous *pinga* (everyone learned that one Spanish word from him), or best of all, to have that marvelous organ open up their buttocks, briefly linking them together.

Occasionally several men would join in the action as a group, and eventually discretion was thrown to the wind. While there seemed little to be concerned about in the middle of nowhere, Antinio was always cautious, as Reason had taught him, searching the bushes and paying attention to strange noises he might hear. He had not forgotten his army nightmare.

One evening in September it was unnaturally quiet. The men could feel the air pressure drop as a distant storm approached. They were drinking the last of their vodka and dancing with abandon, appreciating their final night together before returning to Havana. Soon everyone had their clothes off, and hands and mouths and *pingas* probed every possible orifice. Grunts and moans of delight carried into the night and fell upon the ears of Cíclope.

He watched outside the circle of men unnoticed. He was aroused by their carrying on, and his own *pinga* was proportionate to his large size. He burst into the circle and put his giant, mottled and bruised hands on Antinio. Startled, Antinio looked up into the giant's face and saw the single red eye staring at him with a mixture of lust and disgust.

"Who are you?" Cíclope roared.

"Nobody," laughed Antinio. Cíclope quickly pushed him down to the ground, pulled out his massive *pinga*, and took aim at Antinio's buttocks. Just as the giant's massive spear would have entered him, Antinio rolled away, kicking out the monster's feet. Cíclope fell forward, wounding his head and remaining eye on a pile of rocks.

The men quickly grabbed their clothes and ran to the truck. As they left the grounds, Antinio, throwing caution to the wind, cried out, "No man dares to top Antinio."

The giant, hearing that name, roared his injustices to the heavens. Changó, the Santería *orisha* of thunder, responded by releasing a torrent of rain and winds, not only separating men and their attacker, but also changing their course. Hurricane Arges had been quickly moving over the island, but without communication, Antinio and the technicians knew nothing of its power and the massive thunderbolts, nor that it had already destroyed villages along its route. They sped away on the slippery dirt road, trying to make it to Havana some fifty miles away. As the storm increased, the men riding in the back of the open truck became soaked, uselessly trying to cover themselves with a tarpaulin. These men, as intelligent and poetic as I have described, prayed to whatever gods the Communists believed could save them.

But these men were also fools. While gods may affect the weather, they cannot prevent fate. As the truck continued up a narrow canyon, a previously dry streambed became a raging river. The driver struggled to keep the truck on the road when a thunderbolt hit the cab. In the flash, the driver mistook a tall, dark shape in the road that could have been the brother of Cíclope and jerked the wheel to avoid it. The truck tumbled off the road and into the stream, trapping several men in the water under the overturned vehicle. The rest were thrown onto the rocks and into the swirling rapids. It happened so quickly. The noise of the wind, rain, and thunder was overwhelming. Antinio was thrown from the truck along with his companions, but to his surprise, instead of being dashed against the rocks, he landed in my outstretched arms. Once again, I offered protection. Antinio fell unconscious, and I carried him to safety and laid him under a shelter near a small farm hut. For hours I stood by protecting him from the weather and fate.

For the second time, I surprised myself by saving his life, and knew I would face the wrath of the gods. When the storm abated and I knew that Antinio was safe, I kissed him good-bye. His soft lips and the very taste of him instantly carried me back to Antinous, minutes before he disappeared from me forever. Although I was not supposed to, I fell in love again. My heart sang out in joy. After two millennia of blindly searching and wandering, I had found the one.

The next morning, a young girl found Antinio and brought her parents to revive the handsome survivor. They fed and took care of him until he was strong again. The stream subsided, the road was cleared, and the Army arrived searching for victims. The bodies of the foreign technicians had been washed away; many would never be found.

Antinio was brought back to Havana and brutally questioned for three days as to the fate of his missing colleagues, and confined to a cell in the Morro Castillo. Government ministers were debating whether to put him on trial. Despite his lowly appearance, Brontes was the son of an Admiral, and he had informed his father of what had happened. According to a detailed article by an unnamed journalist in the official government newspaper, a homosexual cabal had infected the Sugar Ministry, and its members were being rounded up around the country. As was always the case, a scandal meant it was time for cleaning house. In a matter of days, the sub-ministers, their subordinates, and their subordinates' subordinates were harassed and threatened until they named names. The cycle was repeated several times until there were some 573 cabalists in the government files.

All of this coincided with a second, very small announcement buried in the same newspaper stating that this year, once again, the Sugar Ministry had failed it meet its production quotas. Seeing as it was much easier to purge the ministry of a conjured-up homosexual threat than it would be to meet crop quotas, affidavits were written up, and men were fired from their jobs or thrown in jail.

Antinio missed out on this latter fate. I had no part in this. To accuse the foreign technicians of homosexual perversion would have created too much of an international scandal for the Cuban government to endure. Despite escaping prison, Antinio was forced to face his family.

Erastus, who himself had been brought in to the local police station for questioning about his nephew, took Antinio into his room and berated him. "I want to know one thing. Do you give it or do you take it in the ass? You are my beloved nephew, and I can understand why lonely men might fuck another man, but I cannot accept you if you allow yourself to be fucked. What is your answer?"

Antinio, the macho of all macho men, homosexual or not, the man who tallied the number of *culos* he conquered monthly in his diary, understood this concept. A man can have sex with another man and still be a man. But if a man willingly lets himself be violated, he is a *maricón*, a faggot. All the poor man wanted to hear was that his nephew was a real man. But his lack of an answer was tantamount to admitting his guilt.

Antinio did not respond to his uncle for a simple reason: he never heard the question. While his uncle berated him, Antinio was trying to shut down the screams and howls that filled his ears and coursed through his body. Fear and shame had driven his internal voices into high gear, the ancient chorus accusing him of much worse crimes than those his uncle was concerned with. The screams drowned out the voice of Reason, which he needed to defend himself to his uncle. Antinio was shaking from the effort to contain the Shriekers and could barely stand upright. His uncle, who at his core had a soft heart, spit at Antinio's feet and walked out of the room. Antinio stood there for hours immobilized by the Shriekers, unable to see a path forward. Finally, he remembered Calypso's last prediction, that he would realize when his final day was facing him, and some small comfort entered him. This was not yet the time.

VI

There is no answer to whether the gods invented humans or the humans invented the gods. We have coexisted for millennia. Each requires the other. While those in the heavens may be immortal, they are as flawed as the mortals who inhabit the earth for a shorter time. As a demigod since my death, I have had the ability to speak directly with the immortals, though rarely had I strayed from those in the the Greek and Roman pantheons. But now that I found myself in Cuba following Antinio, I was required to seek those who could offer him the most assistance. Thus, I sought out the one without whom nothing is possible and who is both the beginning and end of life—Elgguá. I spotted him approaching the family house in Havana, a red kerchief tied around his head, a sheen of sweat glistening across his black chest, the staff he used to stride across the island in hand.

He nodded and came over to where I was watching Antinio. "Hadriano, as you can see, Cuba is one of my finest creations," Elegguá said. "In a perfect country with perfect people, honesty would always rule. How boring would that be?"

While Elegguá cared deeply about the integrity of his followers, many of his fellow gods argued otherwise, believing he was a trickster who did not care about anything.

"What fun is integrity?" He explained to me, "If ever there was a trick I played, it was helping to create this nation, an entire country where I can test my people's integrity and morality for my own amusement. And over and over again, they never fail me, tying themselves up in knots around the simplest moral questions.

"One must remember," Elegguá went on, "Cuba is an island with limited land mass and a relatively small population. Their friend the Soviet Union is enormous, with plenty of distant, cold and forgettable places to put their stalags and a powerful military that created the KGB in order to fill those prisons. Cuba has no such cold or far-flung places."

"I know a lot about cold, Elegguá," I answered. "I spent part of my training in Germania, and later my men and I had to traverse through the snow in Raetia to get back to Italia. The harshness of—"

"But you are only distracting me from my point," Elegguá said. "A trickster trying to trick me! We were talking about Cuba, not Raetia. Cuba is the point. Unlike its ally East Germany, El Comandante has not built walls and barbed-wire fences along its border or posted armed guards with the orders to shoot to kill. From a control perspective, Cuba is blessed by not having to import thousands of miles of wire to build fences to ring the country. The sea does that naturally."

"So there is no real need for El Comandante to erect borders," I said.

"No, no," Elegguá shook his head, his eyes rolling to the sky. "Containment is not El Comandante's most important issue; it is the control of his people's minds that is most important."

"Like the KGB."

"Again, no. The East German Stasi is a better model than the brutal, thoughtless KGB. The Stasi figured out how to infiltrate the psyche and turn integrity into spying, taking the untouched and defiling them. With a German efficiency, the Stasi eventually had note cards on everyone who was spying, everyone who was coerced into spying, and everyone who pretended to spy in order to counterspy. While the system was extremely orderly, in the end there were so few people left to be spied upon that the system turned on itself and spied on its own informers."

"So this island government has no integrity?" I said.

"What government does?" Elegguá answered. "Cuba is neither a democracy nor a theocracy. It is a revolution. This spying is the type of system that El Comandante likes. It keeps everyone on their toes, and with a minimum of physical brutality, people can be kept in order. Yet there is one constraint that neither the Soviet Union nor East Germany faces: there are not enough people in Cuba to completely eliminate the troublemakers, deviants, freethinkers, poets, artists..."

"All those people filled the most with integrity," I interrupted.

"Yes, yes. Cuba cannot afford to rid herself of them and keep the country running. So it must develop a means to rehabilitate and recycle people. One day a person could be condemned, and with the right set of connections, time, and, most importantly, needed skills, he or she could be rehabilitated the next. So, except for those prisoners of conscience, most of whom had unquestionable integrity—and I watch over them carefully—for everyone else, the offenses are usually petty and easily fixable. Stealing from a workplace, saying bad things about a neighbor or a local party functionary, listening to the Voice of America on a homemade ham radio, singing the wrong song from the past, and yes, being a homosexual can all be righted."

The bright sun had been bearing down on us, and Elegguá led me over to the shade of a banyan tree. He used his staff to lower himself to the ground and motioned for me to join him.

"So you have an interest in this young man, Antinio?" Elegguá asked.

I nodded. "It is a human quality, I admit. I am surprised myself by how much his life concerns me."

"These things happen," Elegguá answered. "Just be aware of the consequences."

He explained the challenge he had laid before the Cuban people was how to be whole and honest in a fundamentally dishonest political, economic, and social system they themselves had created. He shook his head in sadness, as few could ever manage that. And, although he thought the homosexuals would be better at remaining whole, with their single-minded focus on making their lives and their world more pleasurable, even that did not happen. The government and culture had managed to pervert the homosexuals' role, turning their very minds against themselves.

We sat and talked until the sunlight dimmed and he felt the need to continue on. Before we parted, he said, "Remind me to introduce you to Obatála. He has much to say about the more complicated topic of integrity regarding masculinity and femininity."

I made my way back to the house, stealing myself into the shadows of Antinio's room to watch over him in his sleep, just as I had spent many nights watching Antinous.

For Antinio, shame became his daily companion. After the Sugar Ministry incident, his voices were on high alert, pointing out how the fruit vendor looked at him with disdain, how his uncles refused to look him in the face, and how his mother— his blessed, dear mother—seemed to be moving further and further away from him.

The chorus sang intricate cantatas, all with the theme, *The entire world can see into your sick thoughts, and all are disgusted by you. You only cause harm to yourself, death to others, and shame to everyone in your family.* Antinio was keenly aware of loss and longing, but for what he could not fathom. When he touched the scar on his belly, it now felt lifeless and chilled him to the core even on the hottest, most humid days. The Siren song, the solo in his chorus, only intensified the loss, reminding him of desire and giving him no means to satisfy it. He had visions of draining the Russian blood from his arms to rid himself of the *nostalghia*, but was unable to physically harm himself.

The situation from his family's perspective was grave. Each of them loved the young man and would do anything to make him whole again. They talked every evening, when he was out or in his room, about what they could do. His aunts made his favorite foods and, despite the rationing, searched out mango and mamey and guanábana to make his favorite desserts. His uncles tried to engage him in the task of redesigning the house,

70

to build some additional rooms for the growing number of people living there, for although his grandmother and father had died, cousins were getting married, and nieces and nephews were starting to populate the house. Erastus would bring home any books he could find and leave them outside the door to Antinio's room (a tribute to his uniqueness, he was the only person in the house who did not have to share a room). The books in Spanish, German, and Russian were technical manuals, volumes of poetry, love stories, classic novels—whatever was available.

His mother suffered from her own depressions. She was a thin, delicate woman who had made a mistake in finding love with a man who would never treat her with sensitivity and could never match her intellectual capabilities and interests. With Antinio retreating from her (what she could see in his eyes scared her), she drifted to bed with headaches, fevers, and a listlessness that could not be cured with any of the herbal potions or medicines brought to her bedside by neighbors and the local clinic. Yet, with the little energy that she had, she tried to find a job for her son.

It was through her contacts at the school that she came home one day with a name and a phone number written on a scrap of paper. This is how Antinio met Erato and is where Antinio's needs and those of the regime coincided. If one were going to create a Ministry of Homosexuality in the most macho and revolutionary of countries, it of course would need a different name—the Ministry of Culture. Unlike some backward and lowly totalitarian states, the Communists revered the arts, especially dance and music. From the time of the Greeks, the artist was revered, his perfection seen as the representation of the highest ideals of society. Perfect artists were emblematic of the perfect society.

Every year hundreds of dance companies, orchestras, quartets, and soloists—German, Russian, Polish, Czech, Bulgarian, Ukrainian, and on special diplomatic occasions, French, Spanish, and Italian—would travel to Havana. The divas in particular needed special attention, and there were not enough people with the language abilities and the sophistication to deal with all of their needs.

Erato worked as a visa officer in the Ministry of Culture. He was in his late twenties, the same age as Antinio, but taller, thinner, and even more talkative. When Antinio first met him in his office, Erato had to restrain himself from jumping over his desk and undressing the man he wanted to become his *novio*. Fortunately, Erato's restraint needed to last only a short time until they found an empty room backstage during a tour of the Gran Teatro. Erato had met many interpreters in his interviews. In Antinio he found the person with the right skills and the smoking intensity that he knew both the women and the men coming to perform in Havana would appreciate.

Thus, Antinio's world was about to open again. But before doing anything else, Erato introduced Antinio to Circe, the woman he would eventually marry. Given the delicacy of having so many homosexuals in one ministry, marriage was almost a requirement. Married men were seen as intrinsically trustworthy. (Elegguá once commented to me that he thought this particularly comical, as even among the Santería and Greek gods, marriage had little to do with integrity.) A woman, no matter what her appearance, skills, and intellect, can rehabilitate even a member of a famed homosexual cabal. And if that woman should become pregnant, whatever records and confessions and denouncements were in a file cabinet in whatever ministry or police headquarters would be eradicated. Antinio could delay an actual marriage as long as he wanted, but having a woman connected to him would resolve most problems that could come up. Circe was a good friend of Erato's *novia*, and that connection would also give the men an excuse to be with each other often. The chorus subsided, and Antinio felt life returning to his limbs. His renewed energy would satisfy the needs of not only his *novio* and *novia*, but also a cast of others about to enter his life.

As before, the exercise of working with language brought back Reason and Antinio's interest in the world. On the first of every month, he would receive the list of artists, with their countries of origin, who were to perform in the coming weeks. He would then begin the study of whatever language he needed. With his expertise in Spanish and French, he could cover the Romance languages; with Russian, any of the Slavic variations; and German, English, and Esperanto covered the rest.

His first assignment set the stage for the next several years of his life. A Polish ballet troupe came for a month-long residency, arriving by ship. Anchored in the harbor, it was their home away from home. For the first time in his life, Antinio stepped aboard an oceangoing vessel. By world standards, it was a bit thread-worn, but by Cuban and Polish ones, it was luxurious. The individual staterooms with which he became well acquainted were lined with mahogany and brass. The built-in beds and cabinets appealed to his sense of design. The miniature sinks, bidets, and showers shoehorned into small spaces appealed to his sense of utility. In these days, a functioning toilet was a marvel in itself.

When he would go home to his family, of all the wonders he told them that he had experienced, toilets were the one that elicited the most comments. One of the indignities of city life in Cuba was the downgrading of standards for one of life's most pressing functions. In the beginning of the Revolution there was no toilet paper, and all citizens had to resort to using pieces of newspaper. However, since there was only one newspaper—*Granma*, the official newspaper—it was ordained that it could not be used for such a purpose since to desecrate El Comandante's words would be a sacrilege, a word which ironically (for a Communist regime) comes from the Latin, meaning temple robbery. By now, with no replacement toilet seats available in the stores, everyone had to make do.

Antinio escorted the troupe to the theater, arranged for food and water, helped organize the backstage crew to unpack and distribute costumes and props to the right dancers, and coordinated with the set designer to translate his orders. Antinio loved being backstage while the dancers stretched and practiced. The tall, sinewy men with strong quads and butts were his favorites. Watching them fly through the air in leaps and spins set his mind and heart soaring. He paid careful attention to how the lead dancer's butt cheeks squeezed hard in his tights as he lifted the prima ballerina in the *pas de deux*. He wondered how the men could dance with such passion without getting an erection such as he had for most of the day. He enjoyed watching the sweat drip down the men's faces and be flung like raindrops as they furiously spun around the stage. When the music stopped and the sound of heavy breathing filled the theater as the dancers struggled to catch their breath, Antinio was transported to back to his childhood, to reading *The Golden Ages* and imagining gods and goddesses coming to life. For the first time, he felt at home in his own body and in his own country. Antinio had nothing to hide and everything to live for.

During the break, he sat in the middle of the group as they drank and ate their bite-size meals. He answered their questions about his life and about Havana. They all knew which questions could be asked in public and which needed to be asked in safer places—those about politics, what was happening in the West and the U.S., and where their dreams would take them if they could escape.

The next evening would be opening night, so they continued the rehearsal. Afterwards, Antinio accompanied the troupe back to their ship to bid them good night. His heart sank when a Cuban policeman brusquely denied him from boarding. He was made to feel ashamed once more, back to being a beleaguered citizen of a repressive regime after such a delightful day where he had felt one of equals. He had scarcely turned away when a man rushed down the metal walkway and handed Antinio an invitation from the Polish Embassy to the opening night party aboard the ship. He neatly folded the invitation and placed it in his pocket, then rushed to catch the last bus back to his home.

All through the ride, Antinio kept pulling out the embossed paper in its gold-printed envelope, both to reassure himself that the invitation was real and to make sure he was not pickpocketed, as so frequently happened. When he got home, his mother was at the door. He picked her up off her feet and kissed her as they spun around. The entire family jumped up to join them. Amidst kisses and hugs, he told them of his day. These were some of the happiest days Antinio would have in his home country.

VII

Antinio had a greater familiarity with ancient Greek and Roman customs and history than he did of modern Western culture. His world contained about twelve square miles of streets, houses, buildings, and oceanfront. He had little to no exposure to unfiltered news and, since leaving the University, knew few people who had access to information beyond Cuba. By comparison, the Russians and Eastern Europeans were worldly. Traveling across borders to neighboring bloc countries and to Cuba in long voyages by sea or air stimulated their imaginations and gave them glimpses of forbidden lands.

Antinio was surrounded by artists who by their nature had liberties and freedom of expression that eluded even the highest ranking bureaucrats. Since their talents were revered by both society and government, they lived well with access to special benefits despite the supposed abolition of class differences and privileges in their countries. As long as they practiced their art safely—that is, without delving into those dangerous areas that changed from country to country and month to month and were only communicated when you crossed the line—they received encouragement to perform at their best. In the hierarchy of the classical arts, the great ballets held a special place, combining the highest forms of beauty, athleticism, and grace with approved music and themes.

The morning of the debut, Antinio spent an hour in the single bathroom of his house, having to contend with numerous bangs on the door from family members with more urgent needs. He was a vain man, as many good-looking people are, and so spent the morning attending to his face. His moustache needed to be trimmed and combed. Left to their own devices, his eyebrows would resemble black sheaves of wheat spreading across his forehead, so he had to cut them back carefully using a pair of old, rusty scissors he took from his aunt's bureau. He shaved and then examined every pore in the mirror, plucking out errant hairs and cleaning out the microscopic particles of dust, ash, and dirt that accumulated from walking the streets of this crumbling city.

After, Antinio retreated to his room to deal with the issue of what to wear. He had nothing suitable to speak of. Cuban dress standards were already on the decline as fewer and fewer imports were allowed, and what little was left of the domestic clothing industry had been converted to meet military and utilitarian needs—coveralls for street sweepers, uniforms for bus drivers, and white jackets for store clerks. He left the house and made the rounds of his friends, borrowing some shoes from one, a pair of linen pants carefully preserved over the years from another, and a *guayabera* from still another. At the theater, he found a fabric belt in the costume department that added a slight dash to his look.

That evening he watched the evening's performance of *Giselle* from the wings. Antinio's heart soared with the music, and more than once the stage manager had to shush him as he sang along a bit too loudly. He was so animated, he could barely contain himself from joining the dancers onstage. For once, the Siren's song in his head was in synch with the music arising from the orchestra, first the violins, then the cellos, followed by the flutes and French horns.

At the end of the performance, he had to pull himself back to earth to translate between the prima ballerina and the military and ministry officials present. They took little notice of this handsome Cuban who appeared to be appropriately deferential to all in attendance. For once, Antinio was able to moderate his natural ebullience and act the role he was there to perform. After the perfunctory congratulations and fawning over the prima, the visitors left. She turned to Antinio with a sigh and said, "I hate these men. They are the same everywhere. Let's get to the party."

Back at the ship's gangplank, the prima curled her arm around Antinio and they marched past the policeman who had turned him away the night before. On the main deck they entered the elegant ballroom decorated with tall, white Corinthian columns topped with flowers. There was a small orchestra, its members dressed in white robes. The waiters wore similar Greek robes, and the women had garlands in their hair. There was Polish champagne, Bulgarian wine, and Russian vodka in abundance. Tables were spread with small garnishes of vegetables and meats, *pelmini*, stuffed cabbages, caviar, and cheeses. The prima grabbed two glasses of champagne and handed one to Antinio. "*Na storovya*," she said as they downed their drinks in one gulp, as was Polish custom.

It was still early, and people were arriving one by one and in small groups. The ballerina whispered to Antinio, "Follow me. I want to change clothes and need your help." Antinio did not drink often, and the alcohol had already gone to his head. He cheerfully followed her out of the ballroom and up the narrow stairs to the next deck. Her stateroom was much bigger and more luxurious (in a thread-worn sort of way) than those he had seen. She closed the door and turned around. "Unlatch the back of my dress, *kochany czlowiek*." After he did, she slowly twirled close to him and let the dress slip off her shoulders to the floor. Antinio was hypnotized by her graceful and sultry movements. She pulled his face to her own and began the first of his sexual experiences that evening. She gasped when he pulled off his *guayabera*, exposing his muscular, hairy chest, and did a double take upon first catching sight of his ready *pinga* straining against his pants.

As the music from the ballroom downstairs filtered into her room, Antinio and the prima hastily made love on the floor. A knock on the door startled them both, but unfazed she pulled herself up to answer it. The lead dancer walked in and without a word took off his clothes and joined them.

Antinio found this dancer's *culo* magnificent—muscular, thick, strong—and while Antinio kissed him, his hands on each butt cheek, he anticipated what exploration he could do there.

I must say, Antinio's performance that evening reminded me of my youth before Trajan anointed me heir to the throne. As part of my studies, I would attend musical performances of lute and song in the finest villas in Rome. Afterward, as food and wine were served in excess, I continued my education by refining my conquests of the most handsome and virile men and even some of the beauteous women. (I soon became convinced that of the two, women had little to offer me.) I intuitively grasped the intricacies of another man's body and mind, learning positions, how to give and receive pleasure, and how pain could also be pleasurable.

I was delighted to discover that Antinio and his partners use the terms *Greek-active* and *-passive* to describe their sexual behavior. The active role befitted my status and personality, even when I was young. As Emperor, no one—not even Antinious—would expect anything else. I could never be seen giving up my power; frankly, the thought of it never occurred to me. It was simply not in my constitution to be passive with any man.

Otherwise occupied, Antinio saw little of the party and had to make up stories for his friends and family the next day. He managed to visit with the entire male corps de ballet after the prima forbade him to touch any of the other women. And, as he was leaving the ship, a particularly muscular seaman around Antinio's age took him into the engine room where, surrounded by steam and engines and valves and pipes, they added to the humidity.

The next day, the ballerina told her friends, "I lost all inhibitions last evening and threw myself on that magnificent Cuban chest, and went on my knees to pray before this god." While they knew she had few inhibitions when it came to handsome men, her friends understood. As for the lead dancer, he complained of a peculiar soreness in the gluteus maximus to the troupe's doctor and had to be replaced by an understudy for two nights.

*   *   *

The artistic world is a small one. By the time the next group came—Bulgarian folk dancers—they all knew about Antinio before dropping anchor in the Havana harbor. According to his diary, over the next two years, he engaged with 49 dancers, 5 pianists (including a world-renowned interpreter of Chopin), 3 balalaika players from two countries, 4 sopranos (including a mezzo whose arpeggios of pleasure almost got them ejected from the Hotel Nacional), 7 altos (whom he liked better for their fuller figures and butts), 23 tenors, 17 basses, one counter-tenor who definitely was not castrated (one of the few times Antinio was not the top), a pair of Russian gymnasts (hours of mutual muscle adoration), 29 guitarists (a month-long Spanish guitar festival one October boosted those numbers), 3 trombone players (the first, second, and third trombonists together from the Leningrad Philharmonic), and a clown from the Russian *cyrck* who never took off his bulbous nose and costume while having all manner of sex with Antinio.

Artistic relations between Cuba and the wider world had never been better. Erato would accompany Antinio on some of his adventures, and the same diary noted that they themselves met up on 47 occasions. Their friendship was one of deep understanding and protection. They covered for each other when necessary, like the time a minister was about to wander backstage where Antinio was performing some delicate translations between his *pinga* and the *culo* of one of the 29 guitarists and Erato diverted the minister to another part of the theater to deal with a leaking roof tile.

Antinio's diary, however, recorded only six intimate occasions with Circe, the woman who became his wife, three of those marked with an interrobang (‽). (He loved that there was a word for this punctuation mark, its etymology combining *interro* from the Latin *interogare*—to ask or question—and *bang* from the 1950s usage in comic books of the exclamation point to denote a gunshot.) He never mentioned her to any of his international visitors and never brought her to any parties at the Ministry or foreign consulates. She came to dinner at his family's home a few times, and whether that was because Antinio wanted his family to meet her or he simply wanted the neighbors to see that he had a girlfriend, the effect was the same. Family and neighbors now could say that the embarrassing episode had passed and Antinio was cured. Government records transmitted by the local neighborhood CDR indicated each of the dates that she was seen entering the house and the length of her visits.

In one regard, of course, Antinio was not okay. The trauma of being interrogated and of being the only survivor of a horrible accident remained deep in every cell of his body. He sometimes felt mini versions of these events playing out in his mitochondria, his strands of DNA unraveling and reraveling themselves in different patterns in response to the memory of these events. He learned not to show his feelings, especially around men. Although he was enthusiastically lustful in private and could be flirtatious in semi-public settings, he was always careful to cut off any deep emotional response. Antinio was sure that he could no longer be loved nor let himself love again.

One of the six times he had sex with Circe changed his future. They had discussed birth control, and he had left this up to her. A few months later, she was pregnant. Accident or not, she had no desire to get an abortion. Accident or not, Antinio felt compelled to marry her and was excited about the prospect of a boy being born in his image. After a quick signing of papers at the Ministry of Marriages and Death, Circe surreptitiously asked for copies of the necessary forms for a divorce. Antinio was busy talking to the only witnesses to the event, Erato and his girlfriend.

Between his work assignments and assignations, Antinio made preparations for the baby. He used his international connections to get bottles, baby furniture, and clothes. He tried to make sure that the mother of his child, as he referred to her, cut back on smoking and had enough to eat. The former was difficult, and the latter would have been virtually impossible without the help of his foreign visitors. Through them, he could get anything available in the stores set up for foreign diplomats (and those with access to power in the government) as well as delicacies from overseas. He wondered if his child would develop worldly tastes from Circe's eating so exotically while pregnant. As her family lived on the far end of the island near Santiago, Antinio's mother and aunts took over their role by inviting her over, making salves for her belly, and accompanying her at doctor visits.

She was getting bigger and bigger. In the fifth month the doctor informed her that she should expect multiple births. He detected at least two heartbeats and maybe a third. Cuban customs regarding twins were influenced by Santería; even the word used, *jimaguas*, was uniquely not derived from Latin as was that used in other Spanish-speaking countries, but from Yoruba, the language of the birthplace of Santería in present-day Nigeria. Twins were revered, and several of the Santería *orishas* were *jimaguas*. They were thought to bring good luck and prosperity and promised a good future. According to Santería lore, one twin is born with spiritual qualities, while the other would have worldly qualities, not unlike Castor and Pollux who were borne by Leda, a human mother, and fathered individually by the god Zeus and a human man. Only the *orishas*—not humans, not even the twins themselves—would be privy to which twin possessed which qualities.

When the time drew closer, Circe stayed at Antinio's family's home until her water broke and all of the women bustled her off to the hospital. There was no expectation in those days that men be involved in the messy affairs of birth, and Antinio was glad to have the women in his family handling all of this. That night he had to manage the lustful and dueling demands of the violist and cellist of a string quartet by suggesting that they all should have sex together. Upon having a music stand thrown at him, he quickly retreated to plan B, to provide equal time for each after starting with the one with the biggest bow.

When he arrived home late that night, none of the women had returned yet. Erastus kidded him, "This will be your last night out so late with your adventures. You are about to become a family man and will have new responsibilities to keep you home every evening."

As strange as it seems, Antinio had never really thought about his life changing in any way. In his vanity, fed by the constant attention from all the visiting artists, he only thought about how his children would resemble him, take on his characteristics and interests, and adore him as their father. Until that moment, he had never thought about what he needed to do as a father. He panicked.

He went to bed but tossed and turned, dreaming of swans and horsemen and children emerging from eggshells. In his dream, he tried to light some candles, which were immediately blown out by Changó, the *orisha* of hurricanes who had shaped Antinio's path before. Finally Yemayá, the goddess of grace, appeared. Simply by her glowing presence, the tapers relit themselves. As they burned brightly, she stood by them, keeping Changó at bay and easing Antinio's worries.

Around 5 a.m., Antinio's mother appeared. He was the father of two boys, she told him, but a third baby had died in utero. Whatever joy he felt at first was destroyed by learning of the death of the baby he would never see and who was never named. His voices held him responsible for this death, and the dream he had had earlier now seemed some sort of omen.

While *jimaguas* were a sign of good luck, what did it mean if there were three? In Santería, it is said that the second *jimagua* to emerge is really the oldest. He sends his younger sibling out first to check and see if the conditions in the world and in that particular family are propitious. If they are, both emerge; if not, only one or sometimes neither are born. Since only two of the three emerged, Antinio wondered if there was something so deeply wrong that a soul retreated back into the other world to wait for a better chance. And what of the souls of the two who emerged—did they complete the balance of spiritual and mortal, or was there something missing?

Antinio ran the five blocks to the hospital and found Circe and two surviving boys in bed. He picked up each, one at a time, and pressed their small bodies against his heart. He felt his heartbeat quicken, and theirs did the same. He could sense his *nostalghia*-tinged blood flowing between each of them and himself. Although he did not believe in any religion, Antinio made a prayer for the two boys and himself. *Never would they be parted. Never would they experience the fear aching in him at this moment and the horrors that visited him on too many occasions.*

One of nurses who had attended the birth—the one who had taken away the stillborn child, the only person to see the contorted little face and the unusual mark on the belly like a bullet wound—lit some candles and prayed to Elegguá on behalf of the family. She could see this was not going to be an easy life for any of them, no matter how much luck *jimaguas* should bring. Only Elegguá, the *orisha* of highways and paths to be traveled, and of *jimaguas* as well, could help them find their way. As I knew, he was well acquainted with Antinio. But even Elegguá had his limitations.

VIII

The trouble started immediately. Antinio and Circe battled over names for the twins, a fight that set the basis for identification and expectations of each parent. For the firstborn, she eventually chose Polideuces, a derivative of the Greek, Pollux meaning sweet, which reflected the baby's temperament. For the son born eight minutes later, Antinio chose the name Icario, meaning follower. Polideuces had all the rights of the firstborn: He was fed first, and his needs were paramount. His mother expected him to lead and to be industrious. While not generally giving much credence to the Santería stories, Antinio believed that Icario might have been the older son, the one who sent his brother to check on the world. From the day the twins were born, Antinio sensed Icario was more like him—curious and inventive. The *jimaguas* themselves, in that secret understanding that twins have from before they are born, knew that they could never be separated from each other. Although the word *jimaguas* was plural and there were, of course, two of them, they expected they would always be considered as one, indivisible.

Circe stayed in the hospital for almost two weeks. Her milk flowed amply, and both boys drank until they were sated. She noticed the smell of candles burning and whispers of prayers from someplace outside that completely permeated her hospital room, and she occasionally caught glimpses of *santeras* dressed in white smoking cigars who peered into her room with concern.

Unbeknownst to Antinio's family, who were preparing a place in the house (which seemed to have the ability to infinitely expand to meet the growing numbers of relatives), Circe summoned a friend to help find a place to for her to live with her children. One day Antinio's mother went to the hospital with some food, and all she found was an empty bed. The nursing staff had no clue as to Circe's whereabouts. Antinio contacted Erato's wife and soon tracked down Circe to a little house near the zoo and the River Almendares.

Neither she nor Antinio were vindictive people. Although she might deny it, she understood both his homosexuality and his need for a wife. What tipped her off to the former was his tenderness the few times they did have sex, a tenderness that non-homosexual men lacked. This made Antinio more exotic and, at the same time, more curious to her. The women dancers and musicians with whom Antinio had sex understood this as well and were quite satisfied with some fleeting excitement and a memory of Cuba to take back home.

Antinio, however, was blind to needs of the mother of his children and never understood her eagerness for them. For all the gentle lovingness Antinio could project, he was the one looking in the mirror while having sex, admiring his body and the power of his thrusts. The role of his partners was to complement his good looks. In the eyes of Circe, it was a trade-off—being used to cover for his real desires while she hid from him her own desire to have children by a handsome, intelligent man. By all appearances, the gene pool looked pretty good on his side, certainly better than that of the local toothless farmers in her hometown or the swine who spat and drank in her presence and wanted to live off of her earnings. So, in the larger picture of life, each got something they wanted; but their inability to communicate these things doomed to failure the unspoken bargain they struck.

Once on her own with her twins, Circe filed for divorce and tried to shut Antinio out of his new family. But she had not reckoned with Anticlea and Avis. There was no way Antinio's mother was going to part with the *jimaguas*. She had waited long enough for grandchildren. His aunts felt the same, and they all understood that these children would need as much love and care as possible. They knew that a single person could not raise children in Cuba, in that time or anytime. Grandmothers, aunts, and close friends all had to chip in with ration cards for food, to be on the alert for any needed items that might be found in shops or borrowed from neighbors. The government, with all of the scarcities self-imposed and imposed by the *yanquis*, created the impetus for the ideal Communist state at the family and neighborhood level, where there was no ownership and everything was shared. An individual did not stand a chance alone, and Circe did not need much convincing to understand the reality of the situation. So, with the intervention of the two women, a bit of intimidation, and a list of incentives, she agreed to allow Antinio and his family access to the *jimaguas*. What no one knew was how short the time would be before Antinio would disappear from their lives.

Antinio and Erato had an opportunity to go to study German for six months in East Berlin and, since both men were married, the Cuban government saw little risk of them petitioning for political asylum while overseas. Several months after Antinio's boys were born, the two men boarded an Aeroflot jet headed for Germany. Given the long flight, the limited fuel supply, and the ban from flying over certain countries like the United States, the plane would have to make a refueling stop. On the way over, it was in Gander, Newfoundland; on the way back, it would be in Madrid.

Antinio made sure he had a window seat in order to wave good-bye to his family assembled on the tarmac, his mother holding the *jimaguas*. As the plane took off bumping down the pitted runway, it quietly overcame the force of gravity and lifted up in the air. Antinio had always dreamed of flying. He remembered that Ptolemy had described the constellation of Antinous-Aquila, where the eagle carried the newly divine god in his claws to be fixed in the heavens. He watched as the plane slowly circled Havana and could pick out the long street near where he lived, 10 de Octubre, the Capitolio, the Morro Castillo, and of course the Malecón. For the first time ever, he had sight of the coastline stretching far in the distance to where it merged with the horizon. In a few minutes, the island of Cuba—the place to which he had been tethered, the place that defined his life, what he could eat, the language he spoke, how he could dress, what he could study, all that defined his very being—disappeared. He could only see the vast ocean and clouds dancing in the sky around him. This was his first inkling that another life was possible for his making.

The weight that he had been carrying since he was a young boy drafted into the Army lifted off in the thinning atmosphere. Already he knew he could never go back and would never be the same. He turned to Erato and said, "I am finally on my own Odyssey." His dreams could now take shape and become real. He could become the person he wanted to be and not how the government defined him. Despite his linguistic background, he did not know, as I did, that the name Odysseus translated as "to be grieved at," or more succinctly, "the Troubleseeker."

IX

After I gained the throne, I brought Marinus from Tyre to describe my Empire to me. He had recently developed nautical charts and was the first cartographer to include the far distant lands of China in a map. His descriptions of our lands—the mountains and rivers, the plains and deserts—and its peoples adapted to each terrain sparked my desire to leave Rome and not to come back until I had seen it all. That day in 119, I began my own Odyssey. I journeyed long and far, from Asia to Britannia, through Mauretania to Aegyptus. Traveling and movement meant I was alive. After weeks of sea journeys, on arrival at the next locale I would mount my favorite horse and take off as fast as I could, exercising us both. On my steed, with bow in hand, I felt invincible.

Antinio was glued to the airplane window and wanted to remember every second of this ride. As a child studying maps he spent hours memorizing borders and capitals, primary and secondary cities. He knew rivers, lakes, bays, inlets, mountains, hills, plains, and valleys. He could now tell you the names of countries in Spanish, English, French, Russian, German, and Esperanto. For this trip, he had memorized all the regions in both East and West Germany. He had studied the paths of the armies I had led from Rome, Greece, and Egypt; and those later on from the Ottoman Empire, Charlemagne, the Saxons, the Moors, Nazis, and Russians. He was not interested in battle tactics but in the layers of cultural, linguistic, and religious debris left by the military invaders.

It was the precise location of the boundaries that truly fascinated him. He almost expected to see dotted lines on the

earth below as the plane finally crossed the long expanse of
the Atlantic Ocean and entered Europe. Antinio had maps
but no pictures of the world's land masses. His grandfather's
collection of five decades of *National Geographic* had photos
of Paris, the Alps, the Ganges, Jerusalem, naked people from
New Guinea, and costumed dancers from Tibet. Most of the
magazines were so old, there were only a few aerial photos
showing hazy land masses and cordilleras in the distance. At
this time, in 1979, photos of the Earth were being taken from
space, but these were never shown in the Cuban press. It was
considered too dangerous to give the Cuban people any notion
of how the world was really connected.

Antinio saw how the plains stretched on, being cut
into gorges by rivers that merged into rolling hills at first
imperceptible and then, in the blink of an eye, rising higher
and taking over his field of vision. This challenged his idea
of the neatness of borders separating red, yellow, green, and
purple countries on his globe. He was relieved to recognize a
meandering river that might have formed the boundary of one
country from another, but it assaulted his logic when the river
disappeared and he knew that the border was someplace in
that jumble of hills and forests. Living so long in a country that
had no question of its borders—well, excepting Guantánamo,
which El Comandante insisted would one day return to Cuba
and bring the country back to wholeness—Antinio understood
for the first time the idea of freedom, of being unconstrained
by frontiers. To be free would mean being able to march across
those plains, to cross the valleys and hills, to go from place to
place as a citizen of the world, never again tied to one place
and one culture.

His ruminations were jarred as his plane approached
Schöenfeld Airport by the sight of a man-made physical gash
dividing this huge city of Berlin, twenty times bigger than
Havana. The Wall was brutal and ugly, dividing plazas, not
respecting the natural course of the Spree, running down the
middle of streets and creating a no-man's land where once life
had flourished. From three thousand feet in the air, he imagined

the sighs and sobs of a people torn apart and recognized the inhuman, cold decisions of those who cared not about the suffering of their own people.

I know about walls, having built one in Britannia to mark the northernmost frontier of my Empire. Antinio saw the Berlin Wall as an example of tyranny, but my wall did not divide—it conquered, separating the Romans from the barbarians. From the beginning, my wall was an object of beauty and majesty. Crossing Britannia at one of its narrowest points, the wall allowed me to manage trade and consolidate Roman power against a rebellious people. I never saw its entire length while alive, but have since walked its eighty Roman miles several times over the millennia. It is odd to see it now as a magnet for tourists.

Antinio stumbled off the plane into the vast entry hall ringed with young East German soldiers with machine guns who funneled the incoming passengers, rubbing their sleepy eyes, tired from the long trip, toward a series of gates behind which sat a row of identically uniformed officials. Antinio handed his documents to the young immigration official and began a conversation with him in German. The man, surprised by his fluency, never before having met a Cuban who could speak German, engaged him in conversation. If there was a secret test required to pass through these portals to the unknown country ahead of him, he passed it with flying colors. He received the first stamp in his pristine passport— DDR, Deutsche Demokratische Republik. Later, he would reexamine this mark with its coat of arms showing a thick, blunt sledgehammer overlain with a compass. There was a brittle coldness about this symbol of the Republik in yellow, black, and red, so unlike the Cuban coat of arms, with its sun rising over the blue ocean, a palm tree, a strange golden key, and an odd conical red hat. This hat was a Phrygian cap, and to us Romans it was a powerful symbol of liberty. In this case, the pursuit of freedom in this region of central Anatolia was against the Greeks, who naturally attributed other, less noble characteristics to the Phrygians. When he took over Cuba,

El Comandante never bothered to remove the hat from the national symbol, unconsciously reemphasizing that one man's tyranny is another man's freedom.

When Odysseus entered the Underworld, listeners of his tale might rightly have assumed that this place would be in every aspect a contrast to the world of the living. But the storyteller makes the Underworld like a town down the road—different, but not too much. Homer did not make his Greek hero very observant, in contrast to Antinio and his questioning personality. The moment he stepped outside the terminal with luggage in hand, he became aware of a difference so simple and elemental that it was frankly incomprehensible. Nothing in all of the books he had studied or in conversations with a myriad of East Germans prepared him to completely reevaluate his assumptions about the very air he had breathed since he was born. He knew that the air (or lack of it) on the moon or on Mars would be unlike anything he had experienced. So too one might imagine the air in the Underworld to be different—dank, cold, and redolent of death—although if it was, Odysseus and his poet bothered not to tell us. But the possibility that the air on Earth was not the same everywhere Antinio was unprepared to consider. His first moments in this new world challenged him to throw out everything he might have ever taken for granted.

In Cuba, it would have been meaningless to describe the air as humid and hot because all air was that way. There, a person would almost swim through the warm sea air. Even in Cuba's interior, the sun and the sea were never far away, so in contrast to the dry, cracked soil, the thick, moist air provided resistance to every movement. Here in a late afternoon in Berlin, the air lacked substantiality, a phrase Odysseus used to describe the Underworld's ghostly Shades. Antinio felt this extraordinary change immediately. Air was lighter and drier. When he walked, the air lightly tickled the hair on his forearm. A similar ten steps in Havana would have produced beads of moisture so thick, it would be impossible to tell whether it was sweat from his body or condensation from the humid air around him.

Antinio drove Erato crazy with his talking about this discovery. "Can you feel this, or is it just me?"

"Yes, of course I feel it, but why is it so important? It's only air!"

Exasperated, Antinio explained, "What if the oppressive heaviness that we feel in Cuba is no more than the air? Maybe the air itself is the cause of so many of our problems. Here, breathing is simply easier. Would I be a happier person living in place with air like this?"

"We'll find out soon enough, now that we're here."

The next day Antinio discovered that he needed to rethink other elemental constants—the sun and the sky. He woke up with sunrise at 5:30 a.m. By the time he went outside an hour later, the sun was high in a blue sky studded with fluffy cumulus clouds like the ones he had seen outside the plane window. *Could it be that even the clouds were lighter and more free to move about than in Cuba where they hung low and thick in the sky?* Through the day the sun took its time crossing the sky. It showed no signs of giving up its perch at 6 p.m., when the Cuban sun would be setting after marking a twelve-hour path across the sky. Finally, at 10:30 that evening the sun dipped below the horizon in a lingering sunset that itself took an hour to complete. If the air, sun, and sky were mutable, what other mysteries remained for Antinio to discover?

The long hours of sunlight—each day here was like a day and a half at home—made him feel like life itself had accelerated. There was so much to do that, even with his six hours of lessons, he had several hours before and eight hours after to explore in the daylight. He was to use every minute available to investigate his surroundings and relearn how to live life.

His first day out, Antinio crossed the city taking the S-bahn, studying the complicated maps. The beautiful symmetry of the original lines that circled the city had been destroyed by the frontier at the Wall. In East Berlin, the S-bahn lines ended abruptly between stations; or, in the case of Friedrichstrasse station, an East German train came in on one side of the station, and a West German one left on the opposite, neither communicating with the other. The West was so close he could see it just yards away, yet it was unreachable, unlike in his home country, which was completely separated from the outside world by miles of ocean.

He got off the train at Unter der Linden, the most famous boulevard in Berlin—its beauty had managed to survive multiple wars and both Nazi and Communist planning efforts—and walked over to Museum Island. He located and entered the Pergamon Museum right before closing. If he had thought he was in another world before, the feeling escalated when he stood before the Pergamon Altar. At over thirty meters long, it filled an entire room. It had been disassembled and shipped to Germany piece by piece in the late 1800s. Seeing an entire Greek altar, he gapsed with delight and incredulity and wished that his mother were with him to experience this magnificent piece of architecture. He walked to the steps and sat down.

"Of course you recognize this place," I said. Antinio looked up startled and noticed me standing there. It often takes great energy for those of us in the heavens to appear to mortals, but here it was easy since I had personal connection to the temple. "We were together at this place, Pergamon, not far from your home in Bithynia. We were on our way to Alexandria in the year before you died and stopped to visit the city that Attalus had bequeathed to me. You and I walked up these very stairs. I remember your beautiful, young body, so full of life and energy. Come here, do you remember this?"

We walked up the stairs to the frieze that covered the length and depth of the altar. Antinio was still dazed thinking, *Have I really been here before, or was all the reading I have been doing coming back to me?* He could not tell. At the frieze of Dionysius, I took Antinio's hand and had him trace out the connection of the marble to his own body, from the stories of men and gods long dead to the stories that were part of his bloodline and very being. Antinio stood there for a long time and thought he could feel the pulsating of blood and life in the carved frieze. He dropped his hand, startled, realizing that I was no longer there. A guard was standing next to him.

The museum was empty. It had closed a short time before. The guard, entranced by Antinio's beauty, put his finger to his mouth to indicate they should be silent and took Antinio to the left side of the altar under a small roof held up by columns. The two men kissed and quickly dropped their clothes on the marble floor. Their passionate sex consecrated and reconnected Antinio's long-lost soul to its origins. The guard, Philippides, had brought many a young man to this very spot after closing time, but already felt this encounter would be recollected with a poignant fondness for this man who seemed to almost blend in with the statuary surrounding him.

Antinio returned to the Pergamon many times afterward. There were often secret parties here where scores of men would dress in Greek costumes and meet late in the evening. The men would toast each other with wine and tell long stories of the hunt and capture, of men turned into wild animals, or of gods and mythical creatures with prodigious endowments. I was present at many of these occasions, either in spirit or flesh. The men would reenact tales in groups or would pair off under the columns and in secret rooms not open to the public. Antinio held court at these events, singing, flirting, and telling stories mixing Greek myths with Santería folklore full of double and triple entendres. He was the most exotic man there, except maybe for a Brazilian visitor who showed up one night setting off a contest between the two for who could sing the best, flirt the most, tell the funniest story, and in the end wind up with the most handsome man. They eventually dispensed with the completion and paired off together, drawing a crowd to watch these demigods at play.

Were there really that many gay men in East Berlin? At the time, neither German nor Spanish had the word "gaydar" in its vocabulary, a wonderful compound word denoting the ability to identify other homosexuals on the street, in crowds, or on a stage. Despite the lack of such a useful word, Antinio had exquisite gaydar.

Sex seemingly was available everywhere. An Esperanto pen pal who lived in a distant Berlin suburb invited Antinio to dinner one evening. The dinner ended abruptly when she caught Antinio fondling her husband under the table. Few men and fewer women had the audacity Antinio possessed. He would say, "It is a blasphemy not to respond to a person's interest. Each sexual experience teaches me and helps me to connect to other cultures." Thus, for the short time he stayed in East Germany, he continued to live this charmed life, one that, as we have seen, in Cuba could quickly turn dangerous.

His charmed life was also due to the special ability of gifted travelers to avoid trouble or to manage their way through it. Odysseus was by name a gifted Troubleseeker, and his ability to make his way through difficult circumstances made his story the fascinating tale it is. As the hero, he could count on gods, goddesses, ghosts, and other entities to help, protect, and guide him along the way.

Antinio's luck in avoiding trouble lay in both his intelligence and naiveté. One evening he walked back to his flat at 2 a.m. after a bacchanalia at a gay sauna and realized he had lost his keys. He retraced his steps, but the sauna was closed until the next afternoon. Having little money on him, he could not rent a hotel room, so he walked the streets until his landlord woke up at 7. Few Berliners would have dared to wander through the darkened precincts in the dead of night; but, as we have seen with our Greek Troubleseeker, not recognizing where you should not go is often the best way to be safe when roaming through strange parts. Antinio was mesmerized as he watched the rhythms of late-night street life change to dawn—men drunk on cheap vodka, women loud and garish (also drunk on the same vodka), prostitutes, soldiers on duty and off (duty status seemed to have no correlation with vodka consumption) changing to street cleaners, bakers, different soldiers yawning from their early rising, and teams of men and women in work clothes headed to one of the factories on the outskirts of the city. To this assortment of Berliners, the sight and sound of this stranger singing songs from *The Threepenny Opera* and plaintive *lieder* at such an odd hour as he roamed about was unnerving. Though they might sense both his fragility and strength, their own radars could not read this man, so they gave him wide berth.

By the end of his six months, he could say *Ich bin ein Berliner* and, unlike President Kennedy, was never saddled with the urban myth that he said he was a jelly donut, which was indeed called a *berliner*, but never in Berlin itself. Antinio had by then memorized the entire train system and could get from Ahrensfelde to Alexanderplatz with the minimum of difficulties, even taking into account late-night versus rush-hour trains. His German was flawless and affected a Hannoverian accent, considered the perfect German (even though in those days an East German could no longer travel to Hannover). He knew the museums inside and out and was a regular at both the Staatsopera and Komischopera.

He took pride—naively, given his past—in thinking that he managed to avoid the attentions of the Stasi and the Cuban authorities. Once again, he was wrong. The Stasi kept excellent files. It had detailed his entry into the country and every place he had stayed; reports from his German teachers—*excellent student, but questionable adherence to Marxist principles*; one description of his going to the FKK, the Freikörper-Kultur, a nudist beach where the lifeguard wrote him up for not immediately taking off his clothes when he crossed the line separating the two sides; a report from the former pen pal about him seducing her husband; dates and times of his numerous entries to the Pergamon (but, interestingly, nothing else about his visits there); and his visit to the Spanish embassy.

Antinio had convinced Erato to go with him to the Spanish Embassy to inquire about how one could ask for asylum. The men were told that it would be impossible to grant in East Germany, but that if they were in Spain, yes, asylum would be possible. Knowing their plane back to Cuba stopped in Madrid for refueling, they made a plan to run for it upon landing there.

The day of their departure, the sadness of leaving was tempered by excitement over the plan they had hatched. They would off-board with the rest of the passengers, walk nonchalantly to the terminal, and ask to use the bathroom. They knew there were not enough minders to watch everyone and that this would be their chance to slip away.

Two hours after leaving Berlin, as the plane was landing in Madrid, the captain made an announcement over the PA system that all passengers should disembark except for the two of them, whom he called out by name. As the rest of the passengers left, they all eyed the criminals, wondering what they had done. Antinio tried to talk his way out of the plane, but the guards pulled out their previously hidden guns and kept the two men in their seats. An hour later, after everyone reboarded—again with all eyes on Antinio and Erato—the plane took off.

They spent the rest of the flight whispering to each other about the trouble they had gotten themselves into and speculated on what would happen when they got back to Havana. The six months of fun and discovery crashed in Antinio's mind. He tried to keep hold of Reason, who said, *Worrying and imagining the worst will not prevent it from happening, nor will it prepare you. Each of the last days you approached as a new day, with new possibility and new adventure. This is the same.* However, even Reason started to be undermined by the voices of doubt and doom. *Why had he been so stupid to think he wasn't being watched? And what horrors would they impose on him when he arrived at home?* One of the worst things one could be was a traitor to the Revolution. It was one thing to be a traitor and never come home; the regime had nothing on you. The worst was to be a traitor coming home to face not only the punishments of jail and harassment, but also shame from family, friends, and neighbors who would have rejoiced if you had managed to get away, but will pity and shun you for being a failure.

Antinio could not isolate the voices. He knew the regime too well, and his body ached from his Army scar and his University wound and his Sugar Ministry horror and the nicks and cuts of everyday life and travail. Whether it was Reason or doom that spoke, he knew for certain that suffering was inevitable. He tried to distract himself by counting to one thousand, alternating every five numbers in a different language—*eins, zwei, drei, vier, fünf* in German; *ses, sep, ok, naŭ, dek* in Esperanto; *odinnadtsat, dvenadtsat, trinadtsat, chetyrnadtsat, pyatnadtsat* in Russian—and that helped drown out some of the voices temporarily.

In Havana, Erato and Antinio reluctantly got up to meet their fate. The rest of the passengers gave them wide berth, not wanting to be seen near them for fear of guilt by association. The two made it through immigration without any problems and entered the customs hall, both of their stomachs knotted up and hearts beating rapidly.

Fortunately, Erato's lover, an official in the Army, met them in the terminal. With a dirty look, he made it clear that he had needed to cash in a lot of chits to get these two back into the country without any problems. Together they sighed in relief, but fear had been replanted in Antinio's chest.

Homecoming is painful when you do not want to be home, and more so if you were planning never to come back. His mother was there at the airport with the rest of his family, but not Circe or the *jimaguas*. He had written long letters to Anticlea daily and weekly missives to his aunts and uncles, cousins, and friends. They already knew most of his stories, and they looked forward to hearing him retell them in person.

Everyone piled into the family car plus a neighbor's car and headed back to the house. As they drove down the darkened streets (light bulbs were on the embargo list), Antinio felt the oppressive heat and the weight of the air. He was back. Had he been aware of how short a period it would be, he would have felt much better. Trouble was about to break out on a grand scale.

X

It was the spring of 1980, and Antinio's thirty-second birthday approached. Although he continued to work at the Ministry of Culture, after being away in another world, he found it impossible to live life as he had before. He had changed, yet he was stuck in a place that did not like change. He was involved with two people: Tyro, a beautiful woman a little older than he, whom he had met in the Esperanto society and who loved the sea; and Akos, a very good-looking tall, dark Afro-Cuban man in his late twenties with striking green eyes who was a judge in one of the tribunal courts. Antinio saw them on a rotating basis, neither supposedly knowing about the other. He wanted someone special in his life, but Antinio found it impossible to emotionally connect. After the scare in Madrid, he had drifted away from Erato, remaining friends but ending their sexual relationship. As was his norm even in the most difficult of times, Antinio's sexual encounters had allowed him some sense of intimacy without sharing much depth or honesty. Then one day Tyro and Akos both were gone, as if wiped off the earth. As with Calypso before them, no one knew what had happened to them. How could they have disappeared as easily as the Shades in the Underworld?

This time the answer was more obvious. They did not trust him enough. There was little trust to go around in Havana in 1980, particularly if one was thinking about trying to leave the country. Informants lurked everywhere. There were formal groups like the Committee for Defense of the Revolution in each neighborhood, but even beyond these, there was no escaping the eyes of those who faithfully adhered to the

Communist party line and watched those who exhibited any sign of dissidence. These spies were at the workplace, at the schools, even in one's own home. Antinio's very family—aunts, uncles, cousins, their spouses—could potentially report to the officials any real or imagined disloyalty to the Revolution. Even in his own mind, Reason kept him in constant fear, shouting at him, *Stop thinking those thoughts! Someone will hear them even in your head!* He had seen the fear that drove people to inform on others who might have expressed ever so fleetingly an intention or even a desire to leave the island or a criticism about El Comandante or the Revolution. And he had seen how if you did not inform on them, they might inform on you for listening without reacting as a true revolutionary should.

Elegguá kept tabs on the mortal spies, watching with delight at each twist and turn, devising his next test of integrity for the Cuban people. It began the afternoon of April 1 (a day known as April Fool's Day in other parts of the world) when a small group of people hijacked a Havana city bus and plowed it through the gates of the Peruvian Embassy in an attempt to obtain asylum and leave the country. The Cuban guards posted at the Embassy opened fire, injuring two of the hijackers and accidentally killing one of their own. El Comandante was enraged and blamed the asylum seekers for the death of the guard. He demanded that the Peruvian diplomats return all those involved to the Cuban authorities, but the Peruvians refused. To teach them a lesson, three days later all guards were removed from the Embassy. To the surprise of El Comandante and the Army, but obviously not to the Cuban people, more than 10,000 people flooded onto the grounds of the Peruvian Embassy over the next couple of days.

Among them were Tyro and Akos. Separately, they each happened to be in Miramar on that fateful day and were swept up with the crowds as the rumor spread that freedom was to be found at the Embassy. The Revolution they had been promised for the last twenty years was finally possible.

Even when I was Emperor, with all my power and influence, such circumstances were impossible to control. Despite my attempts to forge a peace in Jerusalem, there were riots and attacks against me. I thought I could win over these people and show them how life would be better as Roman citizens, but they would not give up their ways. Despite years of Roman benevolence, the inhabitants of Judaea never forgot their identity. And so in Cuba nothing the government could do stamped out the desire for freedom.

Eventually, the Cuban authorities tried to stop the movement of people onto the Embassy grounds and posted guards to encircle the neighborhood a few blocks around the building, cordoning it off. However, the rumors that you could enter the Embassy and ask for asylum to leave the country had already spread across the island. Each day hundreds of people continued to arrive from the most distant provinces trying to get to the Embassy.

The diplomatic scuffle between Peru and Cuba continued. El Comandante was shocked that his people might turn their backs on him, with all that he had personally done for them. Surely they loved him! After all, they would stand at his rallies listening to him speak for six hours at a time. They willingly gave up title to their lands, houses, cattle, and crops because they personally trusted him to make such life-changing decisions for their own good. He was the embodiment of the will of all Cuban people, indivisible from their own hearts and desires. Since he could not possibly have done anything wrong, El Comandante was forced to admit that the people at the Embassy were not real Cubans; no, they were prostitutes, homosexuals, criminals, and other antisocial individuals.

He referred to the them as *escoria*, or scum, an old word for the residue that forms on the top of molten metal. He blamed the United States for inciting Cubans to leave the island and, in particular, the Cuban-American mafia in Miami for orchestrating it. He had nonetheless some spies among them and hinted that they could pick up their relatives in Cuba and take them to Miami if they were to send boats to the port of Mariel. The only catch was that they must also carry away the people who had taken refuge in the Peruvian Embassy.

This information was not broadcast on the nightly news where newscasters read from government-approved scripts. Instead, the rumor mill relayed the constantly changing details. Finding accurate information was made more difficult by the need to determine if the rumor teller was trustworthy or an informer enticing a listener to talk.

Elegguá was delighted by these complex layers of moral complicity, but the events were creating profound effects in Cuba. The government was allowing everyone in the Embassy compound, now numbering in the tens of thousands, to leave. And anyone claiming to be a prostitute, a homosexual, a drug addict, a former prisoner, or some other misfit could seek passage to America. Overwhelmed by the number of admissions, the processing center kept shifting locations, and those shouting "Let the scum go!" were secretly planning their own escape by transforming themselves into prostitutes and homosexuals.

Antinio tried to reason through this situation, but he could not see a clear path. Freedom was a desire he could not shake. But he was paralyzed by fear of making a move, not being allowed to leave, and then being persecuted. The Shriekers argued constantly with Reason. But it was the call of the Siren, who promised a future of a fuller life, a life without fear, and a life with love in a new land among new people, that he heard above the rest.

Antinio kept this all within his head, struggling with it day and night. As the Siren call grew louder and louder, his heart felt like it would break from the combination of desire and fear. After a sleepless night in early May, he found himself banging on the door of his friend Fineo. He opened the door and ushered Antinio in, sensing something was wrong.

"Antinio, I have not seen you so upset since that awful day when you were kicked out of the School of Architecture. This has to do with Mariel, am I not right? What other reason would you come here so early, waking me and my mother up? She is already making some tea for us, so tell me before she comes in."

"Fineo, you always divine what is going on with me before I say a word. It *is* about Mariel. I want to go, but am afraid to. But there are two things holding me back."

"You know as well as I do that I will not leave my mother behind, so I know you are not thinking of me. You mean your mother and the *jimaguas*. There cannot be anyone else."

"But should I? I need to know this." He began to weep. "My mother is sixty-four. From the moment she gave birth to me, I have been the center of her attention. Her love is the only unselfish, unconditional love that I have felt in this life. She loves me no matter what I do, even when that scares her." Antinio could feel her blood circulating in his body, her touch on his skin, and her smile on his lips. "What will happen to her...no, what will happen to me if I leave for good?"

Before he could answer, Fineo's mother walked in with the tea and mango jam and cheese. She went to the window to chase away the neighbors who had gathered underneath attracted by the loud sobs. "Go away, this is none of your business," she yelled. Knowing the men needed their time alone, she retreated to her kitchen.

Fineo addressed his friend. "Your feelings for the *jimaguas* are a mirror image of your mother's love for you. Ever since they were born, they have occupied your consistent concern, even if you were pursuing something else. Antinio, you are vain. You and I both understand this. You will always seek the pleasure of any passing handsome man, yet in your heart, I see the *jimaguas*. They are the future."

"I wonder if this is how my mother feels about me."

"It is exactly how she feels, except in your case, you live for their lives, not necessarily their love. You will always crave their love and will never be satisfied by whatever feelings they express toward you when they get older. No matter what you do or do not accomplish in this lifetime, they will live after you with the potential to do better, to live larger. When Odysseus visited Aquiles in the Underworld, what was his only question?"

"That of the fate of his son."

"With all of his accolades and achievements destined to become mere flecks of dust in the pages of history, only the possibility of his son living and loving and creating goodness in the world mattered to Aquiles."

Fineo lowered his voice and spoke somewhat enigmatically so that the nosy group outside would not hear. "You will travel much in this life. You will search for your home for a long time before you find it. I sense you are not alone in this journey. Along the way, you will encounter much love and much death," he said, "and you will die surrounded by people who do not understand you."

His kissed his friend good-bye. As he opened the door and the neighbors scurried away, he said, "We will meet again. Fear not for the gods are with you." Even though Antinio did not understand the meaning of his friend's words, he felt a deep calm and knew what to do next.

XI

The gods love to play wonderful games with humans, sometimes out of boredom, other times to teach lessons (and often they are not even sure which). Odysseus would have made it home in a few months had he not been detoured by the gods for ten years. With the invasion of the Peruvian Embassy and the Mariel boatlift, Elegguá once again made Cubans struggle with questions of integrity and identity.

After a lifetime of playing the straight man (Antinio, like many gay men, knew he was different at a young age, long before his hormones swept him into puberty), Antinio now had to play the role of a homosexual. He had decided to declare himself unfit for life under the banner of the Cuban Revolution, incapable of conforming to the moral standard of Cuba's "new man." He assumed that detailed files already existed to prove his proclivities. Ironically, he overestimated the capacity of the Cuban security apparatus and underestimated the homosexual security operation. Unnamed protectors over the years had managed to make all of those files disappear.

Working against his expulsion were two things: his marriage was enough to make him a full-blooded man; the *jimaguas* sealed the case. Homosexuals obviously could not produce *jimaguas*; doing so would be a contradiction of manhood itself. They were so special, it took a virile man to bring them forth in this world.

But his mind was made up. Antinio set about undoing the cultural conditioning that made him the man he was and who he appeared to be to others. Had he been a Santería practitioner or a follower of my Greek gods, this might have been easier for him. I needed reassurance that this was the right path for Antinio. Elegguá had promised to introduce me to Obatála, creator of the Earth and the most kind, peaceful, and loving of the *orishas*. I took this opportunity to attain broader wisdom I might need to provide Antinio. Elegguá and I found Obatála one day after a hike through the Sierra Maestra. He was dressed in white robes, brushing away insects with a horsetail whisk. Elegguá gave him a bag of meringue cookies.

"How did you guess they were my favorite?" he joked, for everyone brought him the same gift.

"My true gift to you today is Roman Emperor Hadriano, who desires to meet you. He is visiting these parts and seems to have an interest in…"

"Say no more. An interest in Antinio. A fine young man who seems to be getting himself in trouble more and more. What can I do?"

I looked into his eyes thinking I might find answers before I offered my questions. "I am trying to understand the roles homosexuals play in the world and why century after century they appear to be such a problem for society."

He laughed knowingly. "You should recognize this by now—as gods we embody the masculine and feminine yet we are neither one. My own people recognize me as a father and a mother. I have twenty-four different *caminos* or identities, some male, others female. As Oshanla I am a gentle woman, the light that infuses all. As Obanla I am also a woman, but one who rides a horse and fights with a scimitar better than anyone. You cannot ask which is me; they all are me. If I can be these things simultaneously, perhaps so can humans."

"My gods approached this a different way," I explained. "They left us stories, often about seers who through their experiences teach us. Have you heard of Tiresias?"

"His name is not familiar, but I am always in the mood to learn more. Please, Hadriano, proceed with your tale."

"Tiresias, a prophet of Apollo, was a man born to anger the gods. He stumbled on Athena bathing, and she was so angry over being seen naked that she blinded the poor man."

Elegguá laughed. "That sounds more like Oyá. She always reacts before she thinks."

"Frankly, I believe this story is a bit suspect—Athena was the goddess of wisdom, after all, but from the one time I met her I could see that her wisdom did not extend to the world of men. She remained a virgin and raised a foster son born when Hephaestus failed in an attempt to rape her, his semen falling to the earth and impregnating the soil. So, it seems more likely that Tiresias was playing with his *phallos* (as he would have called it) and did something a bit more threatening than just look at Athena. Then again, in my experience goddesses are often quite capricious (a great word, by the way, coming from *capreolus* or wild goat) with mortals, so the first story might be the right one."

Obatála roared with laughter. "Wild goat nature, Elegguá, remind me of that word next time I have to deal with one of Changó's fights."

I continued, "Tiresias was now blind. His mother intervened with Athena, who suddenly could not undo her little tantrum, so she instead cleaned his ears. While this hardly sounds like a fair trade-off, Tiresias could hear divinations and had a new job as a blind seer. The Greeks loved their seers to be blind."

"You are teaching me so much already, my intelligent friend. We don't have blind seers, but I can understand why you would want them. When our people go into a trance possession, they cannot see the same; their senses are heightened as the *orisha* mounts their body."

"The story does not end there." I realized I had assumed the role of teacher, not student, contrary to my mission to learn from Obatála. "A little time later, the poor guy came upon two copulating snakes. He could not see them, but he clearly heard their squeals of excitement. Annoyed by their pleasure and his lack thereof, he hit them with a stick. There always seemed to be a goddess following Tiresias, which apparently his divination power did not detect; nor did it allow him to foresee his own fortunes. This time it was Hera who followed him, and she became so angry that she turned him into a woman.

"Tiresias seemed to do well as a female, and in some versions of the story was a quite well-regarded prostitute—no doubt successful because, given his previous life, he knew exactly what men wanted. After seven years, upon finding some more copulating snakes smartly left alone this time, the spell was broken and she was turned back into a man who lived for seven generations."

"Such a funny story," Obatála said. "Elegguá, let's tell it to our siblings next time we are together. When our followers enter into trance possession, they embody the *orisha* completely. Men who are mounted by Yemayá will put a blue skirt around their loins and dance seductively in the manner of a woman, speak like a woman. And the opposite happens with a woman mounted by a male manifestation of an *orisha*."

"Are you saying that humans should embody both sexes?" I asked Obatála.

His eyes met mine. "Not necessarily, because that would be too limiting. Humans have all of these energies. The problem exists when they cannot recognize them. We created homosexuals to show other humans how they can do this every day, not only when possessed. But too few humans understand that."

For a moment, my eyes locked with Obatála's and I had a vision of Antinio's future. But then he turned away.

"Thank you for visiting me," he said. "It has been an honor to meet you. Elegguá will take you down the path so you don't get lost. Your friend Antinio might need your help soon." And with those words, I found myself back in Havana.

*   *   *

Antinio figured he could learn how to act like homosexual scum, which meant acting like a man acting like a woman, or in his case, being a homosexual who acted like a man acting like a man acting like a woman. Short of being struck by a goddess and converted into a womanly type of man, he knew this would take an extreme amount of concentrated effort and practice since at the root of Antinio's homosexuality was his masculinity.

This wonderful contradiction lies at the heart of both internalized and external homophobia: the man who flounces around or wears a dress can be identified and categorized as the other, while the strong, confident man standing upright and exuding sexuality clearly is sending different signals. Or is he? Antinio was very careful about how he acted and presented himself. He had honed his abilities such that even the goddesses would not perceive which side he was on. He could walk through a room raising the temperature of the women and men, find his prey, and walk out with a man eagerly trailing him to some darkened corner. He would be horrified to think that a non-homosexual man could identify his desires. Like many such men, Antinio had learned early on that outward appearances are what get you in trouble.

He concentrated his transformation on the walk. I have already referred to the flounce. In English, there are a bevy of names describing this style of moving one's body—swish, mince, prance, nancy—none of which is used in a complimentary fashion when describing men. For hours he rehearsed in front of a mirror, trying to move across the floor in an effeminate manner. With over thirty years of practice making sure he did not flounce, he was quite inept at making it happen now. He tried one way then the other with his hips, shoulders, and *culo* moving in divergent directions. The effect was comedic not sultry, but he realized that the Cuban officials and police would not understand such subtlety. The more clownish he appeared, the more real it would look to them.

The most recent rumors said that one had to report oneself at the local police station. Antinio made his way to the station a few blocks away, unable to swish in public, saving it for his entry. He dressed in the most feminine way he could with very tight jeans, a shirt half-buttoned and pulled up to show his waist, and a tight belt borrowed from his mother's closet. In sum, he looked like most Cuban men dressing up for a night out. He did wear his one pair of *calzoncitos atléticos*, bikini-style underwear that had been given to him by a Spanish flamenco dancer as a good-bye present. Before stepping into the police station, he pulled out a marker since cosmetics were not available in Cuba and painted his eyelids a dark blue. As he entered, he made an effort to sashay conspicuously and convincingly as rehearsed in front of the mirror. He needed to come across as a *maricón*, a faggot, an effeminate, repulsive being so they would send him to Mariel.

The scene was not what he expected. Quite a few people were there talking to the police, obviously for the same purpose, including two men with long eyelashes and heavy green paint for eye shadow who looked like they could be men pretending to be women or women pretending to be men. There were a few unsavory characters apparently recently released from prison. One wore a very tight, dirty tank top from which thousands of tattooed images stuck out in all directions, including a crudely drawn Virgen de la Caridad with a knife in her right hand stabbing a bleeding heart. Antinio joined the long line of these curiosities, potential scum in the making, all trying to prove themselves unfit to remain in Cuba.

When he made it to the front of the line, he modulated his voice and flirted with the policeman by batting his eyes. The officer was cute, making the flirtation more real, although it clearly was not the way he would normally approach a man. He was told to drop his pants, and when he did, the policeman remarked to his associates, "She must be a *maricón*, she is wearing *atlánticos*."

Antinio corrected him in the snappiest way possible: "*Atléticos*, not *atlánticos*! Don't you know the difference? One is the ocean and the other is sexy underwear." His point was made. They brought Antinio in front of a clerk who opened a case against him—he was accused of public scandal for wearing makeup in public, taunting clothing, and lewd underwear. It included a citation for a hearing. They gave him a copy of the completed document and ordered him to present the citation to the president of the local CDR.

The president of the CDR was a good friend of his aunt's, the same person who the previous year testified that Antinio was a good revolutionary and a married man so he could travel to East Germany. This was the person Antinio had to meet next. Crestfallen, he slunk out the door. One of the policemen sneered as he left, "You're not going to leave this country, *maricón*! You're going to rot in jail!"

He had come full circle. Antinio had spent his life avoiding the topic and confided in no one except for Fineo; he had not even talked to his first lover, Cloto, about being a homosexual. They both knew and had no reason to talk about what it meant. Now, to fulfill his destiny, Antinio had to talk to his aunt's best friend, a woman who had been protecting him for longer than he knew.

I had summoned Elegguá to watch this meeting. As he arrived at my side, he said, "Cubans are specialists in not talking about dangerous or uncomfortable things."

"Why do you say that?"

"It is very simple. If you do not talk about something, then it does not exist. It is unknowable. This in itself opens up many additional subterfuges."

"What other rules are there for me to learn?"

"You will need to understand a lot more if you are to watch over this Cuban for his entire life. The next variation is if something is so obvious, then there is no need to talk about it, especially if doing so could cause harm."

"So, I shouldn't talk about something because doing so might prove it exists or might reveal something I am not supposed to know or, even crazier, because it is so obvious that anyone would know about it. Am I getting this right?"

"Yes, my centurion friend. The overriding rule is to never talk about politics or anything the regime does not want you to talk about."

The next thing Antinio did was truly amazing—he told the truth for the first time.

Elegguá and I followed as he walked to the little third-floor apartment a half-block from his family's house, where the President of the Comité lived with her son. Her name was Alethia, a most beautiful Greek name that means "unforgettingness," and in English, "truth." He climbed the stairs and knocked on her door. She answered with a surprised and knowing smile. The following comes from notes she submitted to CDR headquarters later that day:

> Antinio, a former true revolutionary and well-respected son of Anticlea, sister of Avis, former District 57c CDR President, came to see me. He told me that he was a homosexual and wanted to leave this country. Although I had no previous awareness of the circumstances, he declared that he was expelled from the University, fired from the Sugar Ministry, and harassed many times by State Security for being a homosexual. Before he came to see me, he presented himself at the police station to be taken to Mariel and filled out the papers there. He asked to be put on the list of scum who should be let go from this country. Although I previously thought that he was upstanding, he cried in front of me, showing the weakness of his moral character. That he would embarrass his distinguished family, who have shown their support of the Revolution through multiple acts of allegiance and sacrifice, further signifies to his degenerate character. The Cuban people and El Comandante would be best served to have this scum removed immediately before his deviant behavior infects anyone else.

Their actual conversation reflected the conflict and pain they both felt from his declaration. Antinio had asked Alethia, "Will my renunciation and departure have any repercussions on my family and the *jimaguas*?"

"I don't think so," she replied. "Most of the attacks are directly on the *escoria* themselves. Your family has a good enough revolutionary pedigree to be left alone."

"That's a relief. I don't want to hurt them." Antinio asked what would happen next.

"I can't speak about the logistics of leaving, since officially no process exists for an act that no one can commit—to leave the country, to go to a place with which the government has no relationship, let alone any legal passage. What is crystal clear is that you should not go to work again. Last week a teacher was killed by his own high school students after they found out he was leaving. I'm saddened to hear things like that happening, Antinio. Stay inside and do not venture out of your house for any reason."

She kissed him good-bye on both cheeks and gave him a hug. As he left, she said, "I will watch over your mother. Her condition is delicate, but inside she is strong. She survived your father for the years they were married, and she will survive your departure."

Before sitting down to write her report, Alethia cried. She had watched that family for years and, like everyone in Havana, had her own secret thoughts about living away from the hard life of this country. No one had ever talked to her as freely as Antinio did that afternoon. His heartfelt honesty moved her. Honesty was such a precious commodity in Cuba, she herself wanted to hold on to it for a while before writing the letter she needed to submit. She was never so aware of the truth hidden by lies, but wrote what was required in the hope that Antinio's passage could be secured and that one day he would return to help those he had left behind.

On the street, Antinio looked at the houses with their fading paint, worn entryways, and terrazzo patios. The street had last been paved fifteen years ago and was pockmarked with potholes and ruts. Dusty brown dirt came through where the asphalt was worn away. The light grew dim as the sun set. The few streetlights with bulbs flickered on, and the neighborhood children were playing ball and yelling happily. A radio playing an old cha-cha-cha could be heard from open windows, the melody pouring through his body—*Where are you going, where are you going, my love? When will I see you again?*

He watched as if from outside himself as he walked into his house like it was normal. Avis was sitting on the porch in an old wooden rocking chair, and Antinio gave her a kiss. The strength that had carried him to the police station a few hours ago (*Was it only hours and not days?* he thought) and to Alethia's house was exhausted. He lay in his bed for a few minutes trying to stay calm, trying not to cry out loud. He then went to his mother's room. She was lying in bed with her eyes closed. He kissed her on the cheek, and she opened her eyes and whispered, "Oh, my son!" He kissed her again without a word.

He had never felt the need to explain himself to Anticlea, and they never openly talked about the traumatic events that had occurred in his life. He remembered the day when, sitting side-by-side on the sofa, his arm around her, breathing together, his arms so strong and her thin little arms so cool to the touch, she turned to him and said, "*Mijito*, nothing seems to come easy to you in life." Nothing else was ever said. He assumed that she knew about his problems simply by osmosis, as he knew the pains and concerns of her life.

But, as much as a mother can ascertain, there was much she did not and would never know. And by never talking about the things that affected him, his mother's worry about her son deepened. During these times, she was being treated by a psychiatrist at the Quinta de Dependientes, a hospital near their house where Antinio had been born almost thirty-two years earlier. Her stamina was weak, and Antinio was cautious not to give her anything else to worry about.

That Monday he did not go to work and knew he could never go there again. His supervisor called to say the director wanted Antinio to come to the office and "clarify" his situation. Based on Alethia's warning, he knew how dangerous that could be and hid at home. At first his family did not ask what was going on, but tensions built. He yearned to go out in the tropical sun, walk by the Malecón, and smell the ocean breeze, but he dared not.

Eight days into his self-imprisonment, a bus full of people from the Ministry of Culture pulled up in front of his house. It emptied out with people carrying signs and stones, tomatoes, eggs, and other projectiles to be hurled at the house. At this moment, the same scene was repeating itself all over Havana as people were bused in to repudiate the *escoria* trying to leave. In a perverse way, this was a good sign. (According to Elegguá, perversity was a synonym for Cuba as everything here was other than it seemed.) It meant that Antinio's petition was moving through the channels. If he survived this confrontation, he might be able to leave soon. He had remained strong during this waiting period. Even though doubts would creep in, the Shriekers and Lamenters were still. Only the Siren calling him to a new and better life sang to him each day, filling him with hope and fortitude. Even with the agitated group mobilizing outside, readying their chants and getting out paint to scrawl slogans on the house, he was calmly alert.

Alethia came down the stairs of her apartment, the badge of the CDR star pinned to her breast. Antinio's heart sank. The crowd parted to make way for this short, determined woman. She stood on the stairs to his house. The crowd cheered and started chanting, "Death to the scum." She signaled for them to be silent.

"How dare you enter this District without my approval and approval of the local Comité! How dare you assemble here in front of the house of a local member of the Communist party and a family of revolutionaries." A man started to argue, but she shut him up. "You have no right to stage such an act at the house of a party member. I demand you to leave or I will have you all arrested."

Some members of the group were noticeably upset by this turn of events, but an observer could see the sense of relief on most of them. Antinio was well liked, and given that most of the men were themselves homosexuals and envied him for this bravery or pitied him for his stupidity, they wished him no harm. Some wished they had the courage to take control of their own lives. The bus took off and disappeared around the corner toward the main street, leaving clouds of exhaust floating in the air.

Alethia came into the house shaken from the confrontation. She talked to Antinio and Avis. (Anticlea had been recently hospitalized.) Alethia warned them, "Things are getting difficult in the city. The ire of the government is increasing as the list of citizens braving their lives to renounce their citizenship and leave the country is growing by thousands each week. There is no sign of it slowing down."

Antinio tried to keep out of the way, but it was a small house. The mob scene frightened his family, and they had their own lives to worry about. At work they were under pressure to inform on him, but even by telling the truth as they knew it, there was not much to say. Erastus confronted Antinio in the hallway where everyone could hear him. "How can you possibly leave and abandon the *jimaguas* and your mother? Aren't you ashamed of yourself? You deserve what has happened to you. You are a pervert who sleeps with men, a *maricón*, a *pájaro*."

He could not say anything to his uncle. The unforgettingness answer—the truth—was that Antinio was indeed a homosexual. He would not back down from that now. He did not answer Erastus, and the conversation ended with the last words he heard from his beloved uncle, "I am not sorry for you. You are no longer my nephew."

This interaction destroyed Antinio's hope that this uncle in particular would support him. He felt wounded, not by the words but by the actual rejection of the man who had raised him so lovingly, that he so admired and tried to emulate. He lay in bed that night unable to sleep, turning over and over the events of the past week. He was not ashamed of being a homosexual. He was angry at the Cuban government—and El Comandante in particular, since all policies originated from him—for destroying his life and dreams.

About 1 a.m., there was a loud banging on the front door, and the whole household was awakened. Tante Avis entered

Antinio's room and said someone was looking for him. He knew his time had come, and his heart beat strongly as he quickly dressed. In the living room stood a policeman surrounded by half-dazed aunts, uncles, and cousins, silent with their eyes downcast. The policeman told him to be at the gathering center for Mariel on Calzada de Palatino in two hours, no later than 3 a.m., and left the house.

Despite having spent weeks in hiding, he had not packed a bag, partly because he had been told that all possessions would be confiscated upon arriving at El Mosquito, the tent camp in Mariel where one waited to be put on a boat. He filled a small cloth bag with fifty pesos to pay for food, an old aluminum drinking cup, an extra pair of underwear (he was a homosexual, after all, and could not be expected to wear the same pair for days at a time), a second shirt, and the by now worn book held together by glue and tape, *The Golden Ages.*

While packing these few things, he could hear his aunts weeping in the living room. When he walked in with his bag, each of them rushed up to hug and hold him, afraid he might not survive the dangerous trip or ever be able to return. His little cousins were frightened by the situation they did not understand and clung to his legs begging him to stay. Antinio gently pulled each one off and told them that he loved and would come back to them. He asked Avis to say goodbye to the *jimaguas* and to take care of them. He also asked her to tell his mother that he was going on a very long trip for work and would write her from East Germany. One of his uncles hugged him and slipped him twenty pesos. Erastus was not to be seen.

Antinio faltered for a second as he walked down the steps, not sure if his legs would carry him away. Yet they did. He saw the neighbors discreetly looking out their windows and a light on in Alethia's apartment. He turned to wave good-bye and take a last look at his home, a place he thought he might never see again. He noticed Erastus looking out a window, and Antinio thought he saw him nod.

By two in the morning, Antinio was on his way through the dark streets of Santo Suárez to the gathering center. He tried to burn all he could see in his memory as he walked along Avenida Lacret past apartment buildings and old houses with peeling paint and broken columns that precariously supported the roofs of what used to be elegant verandas. He crossed Juan Delgado and saw the boarded-up façade of the old Mara movie theater where his mother and uncle took him as a child. He saw the school from which he departed to join the Army. He passed another abandoned theater, this one with a tree growing out of its crumpled façade. Once a cosmopolitan city with many such theaters showing films of dreamed-of faraway places, most of the screens in Havana had been shuttered. Everyone in Cuba had lost dreams by now, and too many lacked dreams completely.

Antinio picked up his pace—he still had a long walk ahead. The Siren song was at once sweet and brassy. He was in a parade marching into the unknown with his unseen fellow marchers streaming in from all parts of the city at this odd hour. For the first time in his life Antinio was marching ahead with no more looks back. Nothing else could be heard but the sound of his footsteps in the night under the watchful eye of Elegguá, who served double duty as the god of pathways.

XII

Elegguá had advised me to speak with Yemayá if Antinio sought a path beyond Cuba, saying that I would find her on the Malecón watching over her followers. She stood on the seawall with her hands across her chest.

"You would think that being the mother of all living things was enough responsibility for me," she told me, "but no, I am also the mother of all *orishas*, and that is a Herculean task. As if that were not enough, when the *orishas* divided up the known universe, the waters were left over. They turned to me and said, 'You should be in charge of these also.' It is so like men to do that."

"Is this a burden?" I asked.

"Motherhood is a privilege and a joy, Hadriano, but with it comes never-ending responsibility."

Her long, flowing blue dress undulated like the waves as she talked. "When I was in Yorubaland, being in charge of waters was pretty easy. We had a large, slow-running river and a couple of lakes. I could attend to these while rocking my babies, singing lullabies, and attending to *jimaguas*, which were popping out all over the place. Are you aware that *jimaguas* were my best labor-saving device? Why deal with individual babies when by doubling them up, I could have fewer individual mothers to watch over, right? With my efforts, the Yoruba became known by demographers to have the highest birthrate of twins of any ethnic group in the world. So much easier on me and the mothers alike!

"Then one day the slave-trader kidnappers came into our land, bringing an evil that no amount of incantations and slaughtered goats could stop. With my people being hauled away in chains, I had no choice but to follow them downriver, where I had never ventured before. At the end of the river, I discovered the ocean. Once my people were packed away like sardines on the ships, I was called to be with them through the Middle Passage. The vast, unfathomable seas were now my responsibility."

"How strange that must have been to see the ocean for the first time," I said. "We were seafarers from birth with the Mare Internum connecting most of our lands. In the west, it flowed into the Oceanus, which had no other name since we thought it surrounded our entire continent."

"It was unimaginable is what it was—the salty environment, the massive currents, the size of the ships, the vast distances. Forget about coordination with Changó and my sister Oyá over the winds, hurricanes, and thunder—those two need an *orisha* to keep them in line. The ocean was a far cry from the river to which I was accustomed." As emotion grew in Yemayá, the waves crashed more forcefully against the wall of the Malecón. "People always assume gods can see and anticipate everything," she said. "I lost tens of thousands of human lives in those voyages. I finally called on Poseidon and got some pointers on how he managed."

"You've met Poseidon?"

"We all know each other. Each pantheon of gods tries not to interfere with the others, but at key times we cooperate." For a moment she was quiet, reflective, her eyes darting to the anxious Cubans around us.

"Where was I before you interrupted me? Oh yes, survival of my people. For those who survived and arrived on the islands, the only thing I could do was to make sure they did not try to embark on the oceans again. I consulted with Elegguá, Changó, and Obatála, creator of the Earth. We decided together to implant in the collective human subconscious a fear of the sea. We did what we could to erase the painful memories of the Passage from their minds, as no person could live with such trauma. Still, for many years afterward, no *jimaguas* emerged, frightened as they were of the evils of people.

"Until the current day, our plan had worked. Cuban cuisine is noted for pork, not fish. I made sure the sea was seen as dangerous and unpredictable. Oyá constantly buffets the island with winds and storms, while yearly hurricanes did their best to show the power of Changó. I heard your friend Antinio had a run-in with Changó. Such a disagreeable man. He was my husband at one time. In fact, most of them were my husbands at one time or other. Currently, my sister Oyá is with him. 'Good luck with that,' I told her. But she never listens to me. Have you noticed the storms' greater and greater intensity the last few years? That's the two of them going at it. Don't expect the situation to get any better. As usual, no one else has the *cojones*—look that one up in your etymology book, Mister Latin Authority—to intervene but me.

"We made sure that the ninety-mile straits between Key West and Havana had strong currents, dangerous *tiburones*, sharks that would chew swimmers and fishermen into small pieces of tender human flesh, and jellyfish that would cling to the body and sting it mercilessly. Using a hint from Poseidon, I spread stories of whirlpools and dangerous shoals even though we don't have anything like that around here."

"Do you advise against this exodus?" I asked. Waves were crashing over the Malecón, and I was dripping with sweat and sea water.

"Human will is often greater than any powers of the gods," she said. "Your young man desires freedom. If he doesn't obtain it now, he would only seek it another way."

"Is there a way to make the passage safer?"

She answered, "Only if I make the journey too."

*   *   *

When Antinio arrived at the gathering center, he found hundreds of people in lines, moving from one place to another before getting on buses and being driven away. For the first time in his life, he witnessed the Cuban government working efficiently. Even the Army was not this well coordinated.

He slowly moved up in line to a table at which three men were sitting. He gave them his name. They checked it off and sent him to another place to wait. It was dark, but he recognized a student from one of his Esperanto classes who seemed shocked to see his former teacher there. There were a few families with children and, surprisingly to him, some elderly, single men. The majority of people he could see were homosexual men or men pretending to be homosexuals. As they were herded into brand new microbuses, he thought what an irony it was to be leaving this country of ancient vehicles and Russian Ladas riding in the nicest vehicle he had ever seen.

Quickly this irony would change to absurdity. The Cuban government had two days before accepted this load of Yugoslavian vehicles but had not yet discovered the severe mechanical flaw that would cause their engines to burn up. The next day, El Comandante transported visiting international dignitaries to Cienfuegos. In the middle of the countryside the engines seized up and the entire fleet collapsed at once causing crashes, numerous broken bones, and a public relations fiasco. El Comandante immediately blamed the homosexual scum who had used their mechanical abilities to secretly alter the engines while in Mariel. In an unintended outcome of El Comandante's prevarications (and with some game-playing by Elegguá who could never resist tweaking the morally flexible Cubans), there soon appeared employment ads in the Miami Spanish papers asking for *maricones* to work at car repair shops all over the city, a boon to all of the men pretending to be homosexual, who found instant employment.

It was 4:15 a.m. on the first day of June 1980. The bus carrying Antinio and dozens of others passed formerly exclusive neighborhoods that now contained deteriorated mansions with wooden scaffolding straining to keep the roofs from caving in. They made their way through Marianao, passing close to the Peruvian Embassy where everything had started, and by the beach resorts of Miramar. Antinio saw the amusement park Coney Island and, behind it, La Concha Beach, where he had spent many a weekend with his family enjoying the warm waters of the ocean while Benny Moré sang through loudspeakers.

Antinio would get on a boat in Mariel and travel across the shark-infested Straits of Florida. He had never learned to swim well, had not been in the sea for longer than fifteen minutes at any given time, and had never been on a boat in the sea. His nightly excursions to the vessels in the port did not prepare him for this next experience. Although he did rock the boat many a time, he would soon come to see what that phrase really meant. It was still dark, but he could see the whitecaps hitting the rocky shore and splashing high in the air. For a quiet morning, the waters looked ominous.

They arrived in Mariel at dawn and were dropped at the tent camp, El Mosquito, which lived up to its name every evening at sunset. As they filed through the gate the guards took away their identity cards, the internal passport every Cuban must carry at all times. They also took the pesos Antinio had brought and rummaged through his bag to see if there was anything else of value. They flipped through the pages of *The Golden Ages* and, with a snort of derision, flung the book back at him.

The sun started to come up on the eastern horizon as they were assigned to large tents that each held thirty people; here they would stay until being put on a boat. Yemayá conferred with Oko, the *orisha* of food, to make sure they were fed twice a day. The weather was hot but bearable, the gentle trade winds blowing from the sea keeping the camp cooler than it would have been in the city. A nervous excitement tinged with fear permeated the camp colony. For a movement predicated on the perverted leadership of homosexuals and prostitutes, there appeared to be very few of either in Antinio's group. The pretend homosexuals from the night before seemed to have converted themselves back into regular Cuban men. The strain of waiting tamped down whatever lust Antinio would have acted upon any other day by the shore. His mind grew uncharacteristically quiet while waiting. The Siren sang, but in the background. He could not hear the words, but he was comforted. The Siren always wanted him to feel safe; that was the only way it knew to lure him into danger.

Before sunrise the next day, Antinio and his neighbors were awakened and asked to follow a camp guard to the port. They marched in the cool, damp morning for about forty minutes. Just as the sun began to peek over the sea, they arrived at a rusting, hangar-like warehouse. They were told that officials were waiting for the weather to calm down so they could navigate safely across. "They are probably waiting for the weather to get as bad as possible before sending us off so that the boat will sink before getting to Key West," the man next to Antinio commented.

Among the crowd waiting in that Mariel warehouse were a few children, including a baby no more than six months old. The oldest was a man who was eighty-three who said he wanted to leave Cuba to die in a free country. The reserve that everyone had maintained until this point broke with the realization that their moment was coming—they soon would be leaving.

A soldier appeared and called them to the piers where a shrimp boat was waiting. Antinio had been hoping to get on one of the yachts or sailing boats that he heard had been coming down from Miami. He followed a couple with two small children onto the *Andrea*. No one was allowed to enter any of the boat's cabins. They were directed to stay outside at all times. Antinio found a place to sit on the rough deck, which smelled fishy ("shrimpy" might have been more accurate, but he was not clear on the difference, having never seen nor eaten a shrimp in his life). Within minutes, he was crushed into a smaller and smaller space as people crowded onboard. He tried to count but could not easily see, and later was told that 153 were aboard the boat approved for 23.

It was 7:10 a.m. on June 2, 1980—the time and date were burnt into Antinio's memory, as if it were a moment of rebirth.

He tried to push aside all thoughts of his past traumas as the boat moved toward the center of the Bay of Mariel, past dozens of ships of all types and sizes moored there waiting to leave with their human cargo. When they reached the open sea, Antinio gained some solace in seeing that they were part of a long line of boats heading north. Ahead was a large steamship with a Panamanian flag, preceded by several smaller vessels flying the American flag; behind was an impressively beautiful yacht (*Oh, if I had just stalled for ten more minutes, my fate would have been different!*) followed by boats large and small, fancy and rickety. Yemayá was there as Antinio filled his lungs with the utterly wild and expansive sea air that had not touched land but was nurtured by thousands of miles of open sea.

Farther from shore, the sea became choppier, and the waves grew larger. The sun disappeared behind a bank of large white and grey clouds.

XIII

The boat was owned by a Cuban-American woman. Those words rolled around Antinio's tongue. *Cuban-American, Cubano-Americano. Will I become Cuban-American? If so, how will that happen? What action creates that hyphen? Am I Cuban-Russian because Volodya's blood is in me?* Yemayá nodded *Yes* on hearing Antinio's questions. *Creation is creation.*

Antinio found the boat owner and thanked her. "I have two brothers in Cuba," she told him, "but the Cuban government allowed me to take back only one with his wife and son, under the condition that I accommodate another 150 people from the Peruvian Embassy." In the camp Antinio had not met anyone who had been on the Embassy grounds. "I'll have to come back with the boat to get my second brother and another shipload of Embassy people. I'm nervous about some of these people, but for the love of my family, I am trapped into doing what El Comandante wants. So far, everyone seems to be behaving." She added, "Normally this trip would take three to five hours, but this is an old boat and it is overloaded. The journey could take us as long as fifteen hours."

She asked Antinio for help. "I don't have much food available for all the people here, merely a single saltine cracker with a very thin slice of ham. *Puede ayudarme, por favor?* Can you help me by giving these out to everyone? I have so much to do."

"*Sí, como no,*" Antinio responded. It was barely a bite, but the snack tasted delicious since none of them had eaten since the previous evening. Everyone seemed in good spirits as Antinio walked around the boat and talked to a few of his fellow travelers. One of the first he approached was a muscular man with a scar across his face, a large black moustache, and a tattoo of an elaborate cross on his right arm.

"How did you get here?" Antinio asked.

"I'd been in the Combinado del Este."

"The prison outside Havana?"

"Been locked up since I was twenty-two. Thirteen years. About six years ago, my cellmate inked this arm to honor Changó. Changó, he gave me strength to put up with the rats, the crappy food, and the screams."

Antinio nodded. The whitewashed buildings were infamous for locking up both common criminals and dissidents against the government.

"Three days ago, one of the bastard guards come up to my cell. He tells me, 'You have a choice, but I need an immediate answer. Do you want to remain locked up for ten more years or go to Miami and be a free man?' I looked at him like he's nuts. Pissed off, I said, 'Why are you playing with me like this?' 'I'm not,' he told me, 'this is a serious offer. You have ten seconds to give me your answer.' What a choice, right? So, here I am. And *mira*, look what they give me—a passport with a letter saying that I'd been in the Peruvian Embassy. I never learned to read. Can you look at it? What a *chingada* country. I'm glad I'm getting out of there."

He pulled out a shiny new Cuban passport with his photo and a letter from his back pocket and handed them to Antinio. The letter was printed on good white paper and declared him an asylum seeker from the Peruvian Embassy.

The prisoner was not the only one with a new passport. Next to him, a grizzled old man told Antinio his story. "I might not live very long. Last Thursday, the night nurse came to my room in Mazorra, the psychiatric hospital, and told me I could be released if I agreed to get on a boat headed for Miami. My son and daughter have not visited me in over two years, and I was tired of the dirty sheets and the disgusting food. They treated you like you were less than human, like you were a piece of shit, *pura mierda*. First I said no because I thought I was too old, and then I thought about it, and finally I told the nurse that I would go. When I left they also gave me a passport! I still wonder if this is real or if I am seeing things in my head. I've been pinching myself so much to make sure I am awake that my arm is bloody. The world is turning upside down when crazy people like me get to go to America and all of the sane ones are stuck in Cuba to suffer."

The old man started laughing loudly, uncontrollably, and it turned into a cough. Everyone nearby stepped aside as the old man hobbled over to the railing and choked up some phlegm and spit it out into the sea. He kept coughing and laughing. At moments it seemed like he might be crying. He said he felt seasick and vomited over the railing and was still vomiting when a wave hit the side of the boat, drenching him up to his neck.

Antinio was worried. He had no passport, no papers at all; even his identification card had been taken away. He could say he was anyone or no one. The last time he told someone he was nobody (to Cíclope) it unleashed an incident he did not want to repeat. But he had already decided that when he arrived in Key West, he would state his name proudly. He knew things were different in the United States—one of the Spanish dancers had given him a copy of an American magazine having a cover headline, "How Gay is Gay?: Homosexuality in America"—and Antinio would inform the officials that he was seeking asylum because he was oppressed in Cuba for being gay. This would be the first time he would use that word—not *maricón*, not *pajaro*, not even "homosexual," but the American word "gay."

The waves became bigger and more threatening, and the boat rocked heavily from side to side. At this point no one wanted any crackers, so Antinio found a spot near a small opening close to the bow, between two very seasick men. He thought he would be fine, but by late afternoon he too was vomiting uncontrollably. All 153 passengers would spend some time at the railing, unable to prevent the wind from tossing the fetid bile back on top of the unlucky ones nearby with no means to wash off the gooey, repulsive mess.

With grey clouds filling the sky, it grew dark without a sunset. The boat began shaking violently and hitting each wave with a loud thud. Antinio hugged an older woman sitting by him who was in tears. A small group of women prayed softly in the back of the boat, "Yemayá, Nuestra Señora de Regla, hear our prayers." Changó and Oyá had been fighting all day because Ochún, Changó's jealous wife and Yemayá's other sister, was stirring up trouble. Ochún felt her Cubans should remain in their own land and seek to change the ways of El Comandante, a revolution against a revolution, while Oyá, a staunch warrior for the force of change, wanted her believers to have the opportunity to seek their own paths, make their own decisions to leave their homeland. So the waters tossed and swelled, shifting back and forth, and Changó was forced to keep the two women in balance, unable to overpower one another. It was Yemayá who heard the prayers of her people seeking exile—she always does, no matter where they are—and she convinced Ochún that the Cubans were no different from any explorer seeking new knowledge. The refugees were lucky. Without Yemayá's intervention, this fight might have brewed up a hurricane.

It was pitch black out, darker than Antinio had ever seen the night, darker than his most Stygian dreams. Waves slammed hard against the bow, and he was soaked. Only a few on the deck slept. Most prayed softly to any of the gods they thought might help. Others sobbed. A young boy not older than five stepped over bellies and limbs searching for his parents. As the bow started to creak even more loudly, Antinio imagined the boat cracking in half and sinking, *tiburones* circling the wreckage searching for an easy meal. It had been hours since they had seen any other ship. Perhaps they were lost. He was seasick, hungry, and drenched, numb and cold in spite of the mild temperature. He did not have energy enough to even move. Even the Siren had left him. His mind fell quiet as he floated between states of consciousness.

I watched over Antinio as best I could on this voyage, sending him into a dream that he was on one of my mighty ships, in my cabin with silk bedding and a soft pillow for his head. I lay beside him naked, softly stroking his body, speaking his name over and over. Holding him tightly, I gave him a long, deep kiss, a kiss so he would realize how much I loved him and that I would continue to be beside him. We did not speak. Words were not needed. Antinio understood that he was safe for now and would survive this ordeal.

And so it happened. Shortly before midnight, someone shouted, "*¡Una luz! ¡Una luz!*" There was a light on the horizon, barely visible. People started screaming and laughing and crying. Some continued vomiting, and the child who had been walking about started to dance. The light grew brighter and was joined by other lights on the left, and then to the right. Yemayá breathed a sigh and turned her attention to the next boatload of wayfarers.

At 12:45 a.m. on June 3, 1980, the shrimp boat *Andrea* entered a marina on the southern shore of Key West at an old naval base where hundreds of boats had preceded them. Bright floodlights illuminated the cement pier where the boat docked, and the joyous, nervous mass of refugees pushed and shoved their way off the deck. The shouts of joy and prayers energized Antinio. As his foot touched the ground, Changó released a bolt of lightning that coursed through his body. Everyone around him was dancing. Floodlights cast streams of light and shadow as he felt the unwavering solidity of the ground beneath him and watched how the leaves of a large tree in one corner glistened. His heart stopped beating, his blood stopped flowing, his ears stopped hearing, and his lungs stopped breathing as his brain ticked off these scenes and inscribed them into his memory.

Antinio's body surged with life again. At this very same moment, thousands of miles away, two different men were also stung by Changó's bolt and filled with longing and desire that only Antinio would fulfill. Changó turned to his sister-in-law. "Antinio's fate is set and his journey will continue," he said.

Antinio gasped as American air filled his lungs. It was softer than the Havana air, slightly bittersweet. A woman in an American Navy uniform appeared before him with a big, toothy American smile, welcomed him to the United States, and like in an old, prerevolutionary television commercial from his youth, handed him a soda. Canned drinks were an invention that had not yet made it to Cuba. Antinio took the welcoming talisman and did what any adventurer in a new land would do when offered hospitality—he said, "Thank you, ma'am" in his best English.

The generosity of this new land continued with more food in a little cafeteria. As he stepped into the room, the smell of food cooking almost knocked him over. He was served a cheeseburger and an apple. The cheese was a curious yellow color, almost orange, and had a tangy taste unlike any cheese available in Cuba. After a whole day of no food and vomiting, Antinio was hungry and wanted more.

XIV

The refugees were led to large buses with cushioned, high-back seats. As his bus passed through the gates of the base, Antinio noticed that someone had painted in big letters on the wall, "*EL ÚLTIMO QUE SALGA DE CUBA, POR FAVOR, APAGUE LA LUZ*" (The last person leaving Cuba, please turn off the lights). It was still dark when the buses rolled through the nearly empty streets of Key West. One of the Cuban newcomers shouted out the window when he saw an American, "*¡Viva Presidente Carter!*" but instead of a positive reaction, he got the finger. Antinio had not considered that the American public might not welcome the Marielitos, as they were now being called, with open arms. Already the media was filled with reports of Cuban prisons and mental hospitals being emptied out, thieves, prostitutes, and homosexuals being rounded up to be sent to the U.S. Political pressure was building to send these undesirables back home.

Antinio was mesmerized by the fleeting glimpses of houses, traffic signals, lampposts, sidewalks, trees, billboards, and stores. Even his time in East Germany did not prepare him for the abundance that he saw on this first night in America. *Am I still dreaming? Has a spell been cast over me? What type of world am I entering into?* A short time later, the buses arrived at the United States Naval Air Station. The refugees disembarked at a hangar where hundreds of cots were neatly lined up close to each other. Antinio was assigned one and fell asleep immediately. Given the tumult of the trip and the new sights, sounds, and foods of the past few hours, it was surprising that his dreams were so peaceful.

After a quick breakfast of a banana, yogurt, a piece of toast with butter, and a strange, very weak coffee that tasted like dirty water, Antinio and his compatriots were told to return to the hangar to wait. A little later, the families, women, and children were taken away on buses; only the single men remained. Being the only one there who knew any English, Antinio made himself useful working alongside some Navy airmen unloading goods.

At 2 p.m. the men were called one by one to the tarmac to board a plane bearing a pine green Evergreen Airlines logo. The line of men climbing the stairs to the plane were a motley crew: many were scantily clothed, some bare-chested, several went barefoot, and a few wore shorts that looked like hand-me-downs, raggedy, stained, and wrinkled. Antinio had changed to his second pair of underwear and a clean shirt that morning after spending fifteen minutes at a sink trying to wash himself clean.

Yemayá had spent the past weeks accounting for her people and was not entirely pleased by what she discovered in America. "I assumed when I got here that I could pass them on to the care of some other goddesses."

"Goddesses, why goddesses?" I naively asked.

"Don't get me started. Who else can I ask but the goddesses, since the males would only mess things up for everyone. We do all the work and then Obatála comes down in his female form and gets the credit. Did you know that the United States does not have any goddesses? I saw a genie on the television, but this mortal woman has no powers. They seem to have a god, but he is of no use. First of all, what god are you familiar with that insists on a capital G? Secondly, he is a male and would not even acknowledge me. I was ready to show my bad-girl attitude, like that time I nearly flooded the earth when the other *orishas* neglected to invite me to their party. Obatála came down hard on me for that one. Where was I?"

"This capital-G god..."

"Right. Capital G has no direct interest in or consciousness of the people under his realm. He doesn't intervene in their lives and does nothing more than sit up in his heaven pontificating. No wonder these people are so white—they've had the blood taken out of them, and this god did nothing to prevent that!"

"Why don't you abandon them?" I asked her. "And then they could forget you."

"Only a man would ask that question. They are my people. How could I ever leave them?" Yemayá answered. "It's my responsibility to watch over them wherever they are. I did it before, and I will do it again. But I don't like it. This place Antinio is being sent has lots of water, but for half the year it is frozen solid. What can you do with solid water? I might as well be the goddess of rocks."

Once all the men were seated in the plane, the captain announced that they were flying to La Crosse, Wisconsin. Antinio alone understood the announcement, and he translated it for the man seated next to him, and the news was passed around the cabin. From his geography study, he knew that Wisconsin was in the north-central part of the United States, but to all of the other Cubans sitting on that plane, the captain could have said that they were flying to Saudi Arabia; they would not have known the difference. The men coming from prisons and mental hospitals found the name of the place, La Cruce, intriguing, religious-sounding, even hopeful. I, of course, was filled with foreboding, for in my times *crux* was synonymous with misery and torture, for it was the stake on which criminals were impaled.

Most of the men were exhausted and slept throughout the flight, but Antinio was too curious about where he was going. He asked the stewardess about the plane's route, trying to imagine the line the aircraft drew over the globe. He had been as far north—in fact, further north—when he was in East Germany, so he imagined that La Crosse might be like a small Berlin. He still had no idea what was going to happen to him. The authorities he had met so far only directed him to eat, sleep, and get on buses. Since the night he left home, Antinio had been at the mercy of others. He felt more alone than ever. If he died in a plane crash at that moment, someplace over the middle of this country, his family might never find out. His only identification was his carefully printed name on the *ex libris* sticker inside the front cover of *The Golden Ages*.

He wondered if his mother knew he was no longer in Cuba. It was likely that his family would not tell her until she came home from the hospital. And the *jimaguas*, barely two years old, would not know anything. Cuba seemed so far away, far from this modern plane, far from what looked like fields stretching to the horizon, far from the modest, starched blouse and pressed skirt that the stewardess wore. *And what will it mean to be here*, he pondered, *wherever in the U.S. that "here" will be?* In spite of all this haunting uncertainty, Antinio finally fell asleep like his fellow voyagers.

He woke when the plane was landing. La Crosse had a tiny airport surrounded by fields of crops and cows. Three yellow buses with the words "Sparta High School" stenciled on the side waited on the tarmac. As he was herded from plane to bus, his name checked off another list, he had a sudden realization that his life so far was no different than it had been in Cuba. He had imagined he would be free in the U.S., but so far, it appeared that he was a prisoner.

The buses took off through a flat land with rolling hills in the distance. The sun was high, and the sky a deep blue. The air felt warm but dry. So different from Cuba and Germany—he could smell green in the air, redolent of lush and vibrant plant life. The young crops were growing. It looked like maize, he thought, in straight lines that maintained their straightness even as they rose over and back down hills. Antinio was not a country person; he was certain he had never seen anything like this before. *How do they get plants to grow so orderly?* The trees were brilliantly green, some lighter and some darker, with big leaves that waved lazily. He worried a bit about becoming trapped in this vast, green land and waited impatiently to see the grand city of La Crosse. He could not wait to get back to a city, to walk the streets and find adventure in the dark alleys.

For Elegguá, who had never been this far away in the U.S. either, the most impressive thing was the highway itself. "For all the paths and roadways that I have guided humans along, this one—a long, continuous ribbon consisting of two lanes in each direction, with a very large green area between, so large that sometimes those lanes were not even all visible at once—this was finally a road for a god."

Antinio, for his part, noticed how smooth it was, without potholes, which allowed vehicles to travel fast. Occasionally, large but relatively modest houses could be seen nestled between the slope of a hill and the edge of the highway, with a car or two parked in front. Antinio wondered what type of people lived here. The few he saw did not look like any type of *campesino* he had known before. It was all so exciting yet eerie. The landscape was huge, spreading out as far as he could see; yet, along this highway, he saw hardly any people. This place made him nervous.

They never entered any cities or towns while on this highway, although he saw signs with names in white letters on a green background: Onalaska, Viroqua, Sparta. He felt some kinship with Sparta, but the other two names made no sense in any of the languages he knew. The bus turned at the sign for Sparta then drove through the small town. There seemed to be nothing Greek about this place—there was a white, steepled church (he would have to look up the name for this structure later, it puzzled him so); some houses with trees and bushes, children's toys on the lawn, and usually two cars in a driveway; some small shops, their windows filled with goods and neon signs advertising their wares. At one point, the road they traveled on—small in comparison to the highway, but bigger and nicer than any road that existed in Cuba—entered a forest of tall, dark green pine trees blacking out the late afternoon sun. On the other side of this forest were fields with cows, huge black-and-white cows with udders that hung down practically to the ground, bearing no relation to the few scrawny cows with flies circling them remaining in the Cuban countryside.

As evening approached, the sky took on a profound indigo hue and started to darken slowly. The sky was so different here—in some ways similar to East Germany, but Antinio had spent all of his time there in the city. He had never experienced such vastness without buildings to limit the view. Soon it was pitch black outside, as dark as it had been on the sea. It seemed as if light had never existed; that was how Odysseus described the Underworld. *How could such a place, so light and green by day, turn so dark?* More curious was that in this darkness, he saw tiny flickering lights that seemed to move. Antinio thought he might be hallucinating from his travels. He knew nothing of fireflies.

The yellow bus passed through a gate manned by soldiers. After exchanging some documents, the men were admitted to the Fort McCoy U.S. Army Base Mariel Refugee Holding Center. This would be Antinio's home for the next several months. The bus stopped outside a large building, and not until everyone got off did the Cubans realize how cold it was. The half-naked men shivered in the Wisconsin air, colder than the coldest winter day any of them had experienced. In spite of the chill, Antinio stayed outside for a few minutes marveling at the sky, at the brightness of the Milky Way and the myriad stars so clearly visible. He picked out Orion low in the sky, Ursa Major and Minor, and finally the constellation of his namesake, part of Aquila. He felt expansive and free, despite his awareness that he was not free at all, trapped in this cold, fierce place until they (whoever "they" were) would let him go. He hoped it would be soon, and he ran inside to get warm.

XV

"This country is more beautiful than I imagined," Yemayá told me a few days later. "From the sky even the lakes appear to be flowers. I like Minneapolis the best. It is filled with lakes and surrounded by two rivers, the Mississippi and the Minnesota. And there are the *Jimaguas*, a baseball team that, despite their marginal success, brought blessings to the region with their name alone. I've met some of the gods of the original inhabitants, the Lakota. It's nice to see they share my love of water."

"If *polis* is Greek for city, does *minne* means water?" I asked.

She nodded. "You've always enjoyed being the linguist, Hadriano. *Sota* means cloudy, so the Minnesota is cloudy water."

"And the Mississippi?"

"Its name is from another tribe, the Ojibwa, and means big river."

"I haven't noticed these gods. Are they still powerful?"

"There is a sad truth about gods: as much as we direct the lives and control the fate of humans, we depend on their love, too, their veneration and sacrifices for our existence. When they forget us, we are diminished. We never die, of course, but we are as good as dead if we are not remembered."

"I always wondered why the Greek gods are still so powerful when those from Germania have almost disappeared."

"The Greeks were very smart. They led humans to exalt the arts almost as if it were a religion. Art was created to last an eternity like the marble statues of your beloved Antinous.

Architects built temples that still stand in remembrance. Homer's tales became part of the human consciousness. These gods have been remembered, and their names are repeated in many cultures. They have been the most successful of all the pantheons in keeping themselves alive and active."

"But why do I then continue to exist? All of the Roman emperors were deified upon their death, but I seem to be the only one still roaming this earth."

"My dear Hadriano, if I may call you that. I have made fun of you and been annoyed by you, but that's how I act to keep my men in line. You don't understand why you are here? The answer is in front of your face, as clear as your big Roman nose. Your love for Antinous is legendary. In creating a legend, you have created a love and veneration that keeps you alive. Yet you should recognize that as a demigod there are limitations."

"Limitations? I am aware that I cannot see the outcome of human lives, even ones like Antinio's that I follow closely. And I don't have a special realm with particular powers over that realm. Is there something else I do not comprehend?"

She looked at me long and hard. "I have said too much already. Anyway, we were talking not about you but about the people who live here. Most of them have forgotten their old ways, and their gods are now weak. Their gods see their people who have been dislocated from the lands that sustained them and suffered from diseases brought from European settlers. Many of the tribal children were taken away from their parents and brought to special schools where they could only address the American god and were not allowed to practice their old ways.

"Your Antinio may be in good stead," she said. "The local gods talked about what they call two-spirit people, the ones who encompass both male and female energies in one body and soul."

"Obatála talked about that when he discussed his many *caminos*. This sounds the same."

"It is the same, and I wish that Changó, among others, would gain a bit of this two-spirit quality. Let me show who may help Antinio." She flattened her fingers and turned her palms skyward. In the cup of her hands was a vision of a road and many trucks. "Another journey will begin."

* * *

Yemayá directed me to a group of men and women who might be able to take in some of the refugees from the camp. They called themselves Gay Liberation Minnesota, and they had read that El Comandante blamed gay people for the entirety of the riots at the embassy and the boatlift. The unofficial leader of this group was Laquesio, a striking thirty-year-old man with long, curly brown hair and a large moustache, who worked at the railroad. His politics, spiritual beliefs, and ethical principles were malleable and indefinable yet dependent on possessing an open sexuality. He believed in sex as a powerful connector between men and that being gay was a gift to be widely shared. Although he spoke of his experience as a man, he recognized that lesbian women had similar experiences. Any attempt to repress these impulses was by nature evil in his view, and Laquesio was born to fight that evil.

I learned that five men from the organization planned to visit the camp where the Marielitos were being kept. They would bring along the local reporter for the gay newspaper as well as a doctor, two translators, a lawyer, and ten bags of donated clothes.

By now, Antinio had been in Fort McCoy for five weeks. As in Key West, he was one of the few people who knew English. He had by now increased his fluency to the point of becoming an informal translator. He talked to the various guards, young Army men who came from all parts of the U.S., and learned to differentiate Midwest patterns of speech from the Southern drawl (the hardest to understand), the New York accent (the funniest to his ear), and the Bostonian patois, which, like his own Cuban Spanish, dropped any number of consonants when spoken. He often found himself changing his own patterns of speech like a chameleon depending on whom he talked to, which endeared him to the Americans even more. The men brought him gum and candy and shared with him the cookies or other treats their mothers had sent. In turn, Antinio regaled them with stories from his own army experience, telling about the anti-aircraft guns searching for the *yanqui* bombers that never came. He made these stories funny and played upon the irony of it all. "Who would ever have thought that I would go from fighting the *yanqui* imperialists to being on one of their Army bases?" he laughed.

Antinio discovered that he felt relief from the pain of his experiences. The more he told the stories, the funnier he could make them, the more the pain receded. What he did not perceive was that the pain was traveling inward, bundling itself like a tightly coiled spring at the center of his being.

Antinio learned that he would need a sponsor to get out of the camp. He wrote to some cousins of his father in Miami whose names had been given to him by his aunt before he left. Eventually a letter arrived with a phone number to call. Excitedly, he waited for his turn at the one phone in the camp that the refugees were allowed to use.

"*Migulito, como estas?*" he asked his cousin.

"*Bien, y tu?*"

"I am doing as well as I can here in this camp."

"Yes, we have been reading about it in the paper, *ay, dios mio*, what a mess this Mariel is for us decent people. El Comandante is releasing prisoners and rapists and mental patients and putting them on the boats. It's awful. Even worse, we hear that he is sending over all of Cuba's homosexuals, prostitutes, and perverts."

"Well, *primo*, since when do you believe everything that El Comandante says?"

"I don't need to believe him. I look out on Calle 14 and I can see what type of *escoria* there is. We are afraid our reputation as good Cubans will be damaged."

"Tia Avis gave me your address when I left Havana and said you might be able to help me. I need a sponsor to get out of this prison camp."

"It's a prison camp, you say? Have you been in prison?"

"No, of course not."

"Sorry if I offended you. *Mira*, Antinio, I have never met you or members of your branch of the family. Friends of mine got a call like this, claiming to come from an uncle, and when they brought him here to Miami, it turns out he was an imposter. I'd like to help you, but our house is already full with other relatives on my mother's side."

"There isn't anyone else. I promise not to be a burden. I am a great storyteller and can entertain you and your children. As soon as I can, I will get my own place. Please, I don't have any other way out."

"We all have our hands full. Maybe you should find a church to sponsor you. I hear that they are doing that. Sorry I can't do more for you. *Adios*." He hung up.

Antinio wandered the base alone. I tried to breathe joy into him, tried to shape hopefulness into his dreams, but his desolation and loneliness in this new land were deeper than the powers I contained. He had seen so many people leave at this point, some in joyful family reunions, others with a plane ticket from relatives to fly to Miami, Houston, or New York. Some of the other gay men had left to be united with their "uncles," former lovers or friends who had left Cuba earlier and would vouch for them. He heard about other sponsorships that made him nervous (since he could understand English and heard the side conversations between so-called sponsors). There were the tentative introductions from doing-God's-work church members who sponsored people in order to bring God to Communist heathens. Equally bad were the brutish-looking men recruiting laborers to work at dirty, difficult jobs that no American would do.

After his cousin declined to help, Antinio knew he would have to find a sponsor. His day to report to the large office building in the middle of the camp to meet with the immigration officials finally came. He had been waiting for this opportunity, knowing that sometimes they would help find a sponsor. With his English skills, Antinio thought maybe he could be matched with just the right person.

He opened the screen door and walked into the plain room. Several men sat at wooden desks all in a line, each with a chair in front with a Marielito sitting in it talking. Behind the desks were large, open windows through which he could see a big, spreading—he knew the name now—elm tree. His name was called by a balding, bespectacled man, and Antinio took the chair in front of him.

"Good afternoon, my name is Antinio."

"Oh, you speak some English. I am Mr. Archon."

"I studied English in the University of Havana and have been practicing the entire time I have been in the U.S. It is a very interesting language, with its roots from all over Europe."

"You're well educated. That's good to know. So many of these people here can't speak English. I don't even know if they went to school. It's good to find someone different."

"I have always believed that learning is important, and I can't wait to have a chance to really experience life in America. I want my boys..."

"You have boys. So do I. Mine are six and ten. My wife and children and I live on the farm where I grew up myself, just a few miles down the road. They are good boys, always running around and exploring the farm and the woods near our house. How old are yours?"

"I have twins, and they are two years old right now. I miss them so much."

"Wait until they grow up, then you will see how much fun it is to have boys. There are so many things they learn from their dad. You seem to be a good man. Hopefully you can be out of here soon and reunited with your family. I don't get to see enough of mine these days. With so many people here to be processed, I have been working long hours. But your case sounds easy." Archon, who had been writing many things down, then asked, "So, why did you leave Cuba?"

He expected one of the standard replies, *To make more money* or *To be free*, either of which would have given Antinio his permit to stay in the country, to be released once a sponsor could be found.

This was the question Antinio had prepared for. "I was oppressed in Cuba. I was kicked out of the university and later lost my job because I was gay."

Archon looked at Antinio. "What did you say?"

Thinking that he had not been understood, Antinio replied, "A homosexual. They oppressed me for being a homosexual."

Archon nodded at the clarification and then spat out the words, "So, do you take it up the ass?" Every hair on Antinio's body rose up in alert. A screaming started in his head, accompanied by deep moans of pain. Antinio recognized this question and knew the outcome would not be good.

"I don't understand what you are asking me. I am married and have two twin boys that we were talking about only a few minutes ago. Remember, you were telling me how much yours learned from you."

"Listen, faggot, I don't want some illegal Communist pervert talking about my kids. Maybe I asked you the wrong question. How long have you been sticking your dick up men? What else do you do? I am so tired of you lying, sick Cubans who try to make up stories. For once, someone told me the disgusting truth that all of you hide."

"But wh—"

"No more talking. Sign this affidavit acknowledging that you told the truth. The interview is over, and I will refer the case to my superior. For your part, you should prepare to be sent back to Cuba where people like you belong." Archon could see the shock in Antinio's face. He even felt some sorrow for Antinio—he was a nice guy, after all, very well spoken. "The law is the law. Homosexuality is an excludable disease, and thank God those infected with it are not permitted in the country."

Antinio could barely walk out of the room, his head was pounding so hard from the Shriekers' accusations: *You are so stupid. You are perverted and the epitome of evilness. Everyone can see this in you.* There was no place to run and be alone in the camp. He could not let out any emotions without drawing unwanted attention. He had to swallow the bile rising up in his stomach and find a way to stuff this all away. He imagined a vise in his head getting tighter and tighter, squeezing the voices to make them fainter, compressing them until they were barely audible. As he did, the Siren, who had not stopped singing since he left Cuba, became apparent. Antinio remembered that Odysseus had himself tied up so he could hear the Siren's song but not be lured by it. Antinio had been so mesmerized by the song for all these weeks, he had forgotten that the Siren was never to be trusted. The Siren had led him here and given him false confidence. He would learn this lesson. *From this point on, anytime I feel confident, I will remember that this is the false song of the Siren luring me to doom. Confidence is a false illusion. I have no reason to feel confident as it only brings me suffering.* He did not notice that the Siren was singing a victory song. She had planted the seeds of doubt and knew that time would make them grow and make the song all the more strong.

XVI

Antinio's misery grew. In Cuba, he had his family. He had his few books and clothes. And he had a sense of belonging. It was home, with the familiar smells of beans and pork, the chipped paint, the dated markings of his height on the closet doorway; home, where the television was always on, loud and brassy, with ill-groomed men and women reading the news, never daring to vary from their scripts. Even when confined, Antinio had been able to hear the playful screams of children in the neighborhood and the music blaring, a mixture of songs, some wistful, some happy, with rumba, merengue, and ballads.

The worst place to suffer is a strange place where people either do not understand you or make no attempt to. Flipping through the only book he owned, he wondered how Odysseus had managed. After ten years away, he had started his journey home only to be kept captive by Calypso on her island for seven years. Reading it this time, Antinio could only focus on the seven years. *What did Odysseus do all that time? Did he miss his son, Telemachus, who was growing up without him? Did the pain of being stuck in a place he did not want to be eat at him daily, reminding him that the only thing he desired—to leave— was forbidden?* When Odysseus finally left Calypso's clutches, his next stop was the land of the Lotus eaters, where his men ate the narcotic fruit that made them forget their reason for going home. *Could anything make me forget my home?*

Antinio decided to go for a walk. By now he was familiar with every inch of the camp, and he usually walked around the perimeter fence several times a day. The outside world was scarcely inches away, yet like a caged animal he could only pace back and forth along the fence gazing at what he could not reach. It reminded him of the Berlin Wall randomly cutting off parts of the city, this simple chain-link fence separating him from everything else on the entire planet.

*　　*　　*

I was also frustrated because time moved so slowly. I had paced the perimeter of the refugee camp for the hundredth time that day when a ball rolled up to my feet.

"And what will be the fate of this ball, Hadriano?"

I turned around and there was Elegguá, smiling with a cigar in his mouth.

"Is this another one of your tricks? A ball has no fate."

"There is a path for everything. This ball can remain here, or it can be picked up and moved. It can bring great joy or tragic sorrow or simply be forgotten."

"Elegguá, do you ever take anything seriously?"

"I take all things seriously, Hadriano, including sharpening my wit. I would have thought you had learned some things during your centuries with the gods. Loosen up. You have eternity, so have some fun. And remember your place. You crave to see Antinio's fate, yet you don't even realize yours, do you?"

"My fate is to be a demigod. Is there more to that?"

"No, my friend, that is your path. You as well as all humans have a fate. I am surprised that no one has told you this. Of course, beyond this I cannot tell you more."

"You are playing with me, saying I have to deal with fate."

"I am deadly serious, Hadriano, so listen to me carefully and do not doubt my words. Your fate did not stop the day you mounted the throne. It did not stop when Antinous died, and it did not stop when you died. As Yemayá tried to point out to you—and you can appreciate how much it bothers me to have to say she is right—you have a special role that you are yet to discover. Mark my words today."

Elegguá said, "I can tell you want to talk about Antinio."

"I fear being caught up in his life is subjecting me to human emotions, emotions I have not felt for almost two millennia. I don't want him to be hurt. At the same time, something is happening to me."

"Hadriano, the transformations you are experiencing are of your fate."

Elegguá kicked the ball at my feet, and we watched it bounce against a fence and roll into a ditch and disappear from our sight.

"What I will say to you is that two different paths will coincide to release Antinio from his captivity," he said. "The first pathway is bureaucratic. Despite our young friend's honesty, which would normally be enough to remove him from this country, there exist countervailing forces. Among all immigrants to the U.S., Cubans have special status. Once they step foot on American soil, by law they are given immediate rights to stay. They can only be expelled if they break some law while in the country or lie during the naturalization process. Oddly enough, Antinio's unforgettingness will make it difficult to say that he hid anything. Now, here is a nation that oddly respects integrity yet seems to act like a trickster at the same time.

"The U.S. government cannot deport any of the Cuban refugees because El Comandante will not accept them back, and no other country will be likely to accept them either. The fate of any particular refugee is not determined by immigration officials at Camp McCoy—that is why this place is called a processing center—but by the courts. So, much as the officials would have had an open-and-shut case against Antinio were he a citizen of any other country trying to enter the U.S., they have no real choice but to let him go once he finds a sponsor and afterwards let the courts do their job."

"You said there is a second pathway, no?"

"There are always alternatives, but let's see how this one unfolds."

*   *   *

The activists from Gay Liberation Minnesota arrived with a truckload of urgently needed supplies. Upon entering the inner ring of Camp McCoy, the group set out to distribute the clothes they had collected. Antinio, curious about anything new, wandered over and introduced himself.

"Do you want to help us unload?" one of the men asked. "You can have first choice."

"Sure, all I have is what I am wearing, and I am sick of these clothes." As he helped to unload the truck, Antinio noticed some nice shirts that might fit.

"Go ahead, try it on," one of the men encouraged him.

Antinio unbuttoned the shirt he wore and slipped it off. Barechested, he lifted a shirt out of a bin, aware the men he was helping were watching his every move.

"That fits you perfectly," a man said. "Shows off your great pecs."

"Pecks, like a bird does? I don't understand."

The man laughed. "Pecs are pectoral muscles." He put his hand on Antinio's chest.

"I'm Boreas, an immigaration lawyer. Let me introduce you to the group. That's Ale and Ajax. The guy with the curly hair is Laquesio, and last but not least is Theron. He's a journalist."

Theron stepped forward and shook Antinio's hand. "How long have you been here? Do you know any gay people here in the camp?"

Antinio recoiled from the man who posed such direct questions. Determined not to make the same mistake twice, he tried to get away before the guards saw him. But the man persisted.

"Don't go," Theron said. "I am a writer and editor for the Minneapolis gay newspaper."

Antinio could not comprehend how those two words could go together. *What would a gay newspaper possibly be like?*

"We are all part of GLM—Gay Liberation Minnesota," Theron added. "All of us are obviously gay, and we want to help sponsor men out of the camp. We understand that there are a lot of gay Marielitos. Do you know of any that might need our help? We will be here today and tomorrow morning."

Antinio could not trust these men. He continued to talk for a short time more while he picked through the clothes as more of the refugees crowded around the visitors. Uncharacteristically, Antinio revealed nothing about himself. When the activists finished distributing clothes, Antinio gathered up his bundle of clothing and found Theron. "I will see if there are any people at the camp that might fit the bill," he said, "and will let you know tomorrow."

In that first encounter, Antinio and Laquesio did not talk, yet each was aware of the other. Antinio thought that it was not just his nicely shaped *culo* outlined in his tight cut-off jeans, but something more fundamental. He felt deep down that he already knew this man.

That night in a small restaurant in Sparta, Laquesio told his companions about a strange event that had occurred about two months prior. "It was a little before midnight on June 2, and I was settling in my bed when out of the blue my body seized up like I had been hit by a lightening bolt. And since that day, I have noticed an unusual arousal or energy in me. I can't even describe it well, but I know it's there." His friends laughed because they knew Laquesio liked to make up stories and that he also enjoyed ingesting hallucinogenic mushrooms.

"No," he said, "I had not done any drugs for days before. This afternoon when I saw that man Antinio, I felt the same sensation again. It's bizarre."

That night at the camp, Antinio struggled with what to do. Freedom was a complicated path. He wanted to trust these people, but what might they want from him? He was desperate to leave. This might be his only chance. He guessed that he was in as much trouble as he could be with the U.S. government, so even if he told the truth to these people, what more could happen to him?

I was watching Antinio when I noticed Yemayá was watching me.

"These people and their ideas!" she laughed. "Humans are constantly inventing things that do not exist and then spend their lives trying to make such things real. The *orishas* and the gods have laid out the world, and the humans only have to do their part. There are rituals and incantations, and we even made it fun for humans to carry these out—they get to dance, sing, wear funny costumes and makeup, and eat special foods at certain times. Their lives would be empty and boring without our rituals. And all they need to do is follow these rules and they would be fine. But no, humans perpetually struggle and act like they are missing something from their lives. I will never understand my own people..."

"Just as they ultimately never understand the gods," I finished off. "But as a god, you have never been confined to a camp or an island or a human body that would get old and die. The gods have a limitless canvas to draw upon, one day inventing hurricanes and the next pestilence. I have been around long enough now to see that with every human generation, the gods invent new and more extreme horrors. Will this ever end?"

"These are bigger questions for Elegguá and Obatalá. Let me reiterate, it's the humans who create the horrors. Each human has its own false idea of what is confining and controlling him or herself. And with that false conception, they invent the false solution—freedom. Until he arrived in the U.S., your Antinio had been absolutely certain that the Cuban government and El Comandante himself personally were the cause of all his misery. Therefore, to him, freedom equaled the absence of that government and its ideology. He naively assumed that escaping from Cuba would solve all of his problems. His time in East Germany was the happiest he had experienced only because he was not there long enough. Had he stuck around, his troubleseeking would have created eventual problems. But that was not his fate."

And with that she disappeared.

*　　*　　*

When Antinio met the gay activists the next morning, he opened up and revealed his story, from his first experiences in the Army and his rape (he had never used that term before), the desperation he felt to get away, and his gunshot. He told them about Cloto, his first and only true love, and how he had been kicked out of the University for his love. He talked about the Sugar Ministry scandal, his time in the Ministry of Culture, and being thwarted in gaining asylum in Madrid; and he told of the degradation he went through to leave on the boatlift, the dangers of the trip, and his arrival in Key West. Last, he told them about the interview, the question that the immigration official had asked, and his concern that something was very wrong and he would never leave the camp. This was the first time Antinio had ever told his whole story to anyone.

The activists had a million questions at once about his life, his plans, and what the group could do for him. Laquesio announced, "Theron is willing to sponsor you to get you out of the camp. Boreas, our lawyer, will start on the necessary release paperwork, and I will see about getting you a job. This will take a few weeks to arrange, but if you agree, we will make it happen. What do you say?"

"Yes, yes, and yes," he replied without hesitation. "You're saving my life. How can I ever thank you?"

Everyone gave him a hug. When Laquesio approached, their embrace seemed to linger timelessly, igniting a desire that each longed to fulfill. Only reluctantly did they part.

*   *   *

The weeks passed quickly for Antinio, and near the end of August he was released. While freed from the confines of the camp, the camp officials made it clear that his freedom was provisional and would likely be revoked, and he would never be granted citizenship. Until the process worked its way through the courts, though, Antinio had his temporary green card, given only reluctantly under pressure from Boreas and the other immigration lawyers the GLM had found to work on his case.

Antinio jumped in the front seat of the pickup truck Laquesio drove, and Theron took the window seat. It was a hot summer day, and the truck had no air conditioning. The windows were rolled down, and the smell of green fields mixed with heady smells of the three sweating men. Antinio loved the feeling of Theron's thigh rubbing against his while Laquesio's arm and shoulder touched him on the other side. Surrounded by two handsome, sexy men driving down long country roads past beautiful lakes and forests—this, finally, was the freedom he had dreamed of. Each bump jolted them together, laughing as their arms became entwined. Antinio burst into song, Cuban songs he missed and the few American ones he had learned over time. Laquesio and Theron corrected mondegreens Antinio had invented and taught him new songs popular on the radio.

Arriving in the Twin Cities—*Las Ciudades Jimaguas*— Antinio thought to himself, *Where are my boys right at this moment?* With the difficulties of the last months, Antinio had barely thought about them. As they drove past the State Capitol in St. Paul, Antinio told his companions about the Capitolio in Havana and how it had been modeled after the U.S. Capitol. They arrived at last at Theron's house in Minneapolis, a Victorian with a wide porch. A huge oak tree shaded the street, and a green lawn surrounded the house. It looked elegant and unlike anything that existed in Cuba. Laquesio dropped them off and said he would see Antinio the next day.

"It's already late," Theron said. "Let me show you around the house. There is only one bedroom, so, Antinio, you can either sleep with me in my bed or on the sofa in the living room."

Under normal circumstances, Antinio never missed an opportunity to sleep with a handsome man. But, this being his first night as a free man—at least in his evolving definition of what that meant—he did not want to make any decision that could commit him to anyone. And he did not want Theron or anyone else to think that because they had freed him, he would pay them back with sex. No, if he had to pay back anything, he would figure how to do that later. "Thanks for your generosity. It is late and I think I will sleep on the sofa. I don't want to put you out."

"It won't be putting me out, and the sofa is not too comfortable. Come on, don't be shy and sleep with me."

"I think it will be better if I sleep by myself tonight."

Theron left the room and came back with a pillow and some sheets that he threw on the sofa. "Good night then" were has last words as he slammed the door shut to his bedroom.

The house never got completely quiet. All night long, Antinio heard insects chirping in unison, getting louder and softer. He could not imagine where they were or what they looked like. It was a beautiful, comforting sound, if you could get the idea out of your head that they were bugs. A soft, warm breeze came through the open windows. Occasionally a car would rumble down the street. There was a sense of peace in the air. For the first time since he had arrived in the U.S., there was no one sleeping next to him. Maybe this was also why Antinio rejected Theron's offer.

When he awoke Theron was already up. He served Antinio breakfast and talked while Antinio was eating. "After breakfast, I am headed for work and will be back in the afternoon. Laquesio said he would come by later this morning. Just down the street, a few blocks east of here, is Lake Harriet. It's a beautiful walk. I think you might enjoy seeing one the lakes Minneapolis is famous for."

Antinio thanked him. After Theron left, he explored the house and the backyard, another new concept. His family's house had only a narrow alley and a wall separating it from the neighbors. He then ventured over to the lake. It was an incredible sight—a big, wide lake surrounded by a walking path, with trees and beaches, park benches, joggers, women pushing baby carriages, old people sitting, kids on bicycles, and sailboats in the middle. It all seemed so safe and peaceful and calm. People smiled at Antinio when he walked by, and he smiled back. Yes, this was freedom.

When he got back, Laquesio was waiting for him at the front door. The moment they walked in, the two men turned and kissed, a passionate kiss that had been waiting for not just the three weeks since they had met, but for their entire lifetimes, a kiss that reverberated back to Changó himself and that made Yemayá smile. She loved the moment that humans separated by birth or circumstances connected. Although they did not know it, these two had been waiting for their story to unfold.

Their kiss opened a door. For the next several hours, they explored new territory that they created together, beyond physical, beyond emotional. Antinio and Laquesio traveled far and wide in those hours. In the end, they knew every inch of each other's bodies and glimpsed the synapses of their minds. It felt as if the two were really one person to begin with, and so it could be said that they explored each other or that they explored the separate parts of themselves. Maybe this was freedom. Maybe it was fate.

And in this first meeting, a group of tiny beings made their escape from Laquesio to Antinio. Neither was aware of this, and no humans knew anything about them.

Exhausted, having measured the length and breadth of Antinio's life, they lay together on Theron's bed, having already christened, rubbed, and anointed every other part of his house including the kitchen pantry and the hallway closet. The door opened and Theron walked in. Caught but not captured, there was nothing they could explain, nothing that would take away the violation that Theron felt.

"Get the hell out of here, both of you."

And that is how Antinio came to live with Laquesio.

XVII

I found Yemayá at Lake Harriet hovering above the water with a smile on her face. When she saw me waving, she waded toward the shore without making a single wave.

"Isn't it beautiful here? And the women here appear to be very strong. I suppose everyone must be to survive what they call the winter. What brings you to me this day, my friend Hadriano?"

"I have been thinking about our last conversation. It raised more questions than it answered."

"I would not be an *orisha* if that did not happen," she laughed. "Very little is straightforward, and yet it is all clear. You were once a human, so answer me: why do humans obsess about what they think are opposites—freedom and fate?"

I was about to answer, but I knew the goddess well enough by now to recognize a rhetorical question and that she would not even give me the space to respond. Indeed, that was true.

"The gods—not merely ours, but all of the other pantheons too—have always been very clear with humans that their fate was etched out before they were born. Humans, unlike the gods, were born so that one day they would die. Nothing will ever change that. The challenge of life is to maintain a sense of one's own self knowing that death cannot be avoided. Of all the humans I have run into, I always thought the Buddha was the only one who understood that life's suffering came from the unwillingness to accept aging, sickness, and death."

"Even in my days as Emperor of Rome, I knew of the Buddha and his followers," I replied. "But the Buddha accepted his fate. Can a human ever do anything that might change their fate? Can people tempt fate, as they say?"

She laughed heartily. "There is nothing to tempt. Humans have to live within the boundaries of their fate and not take the rare but not impossible actions that could bring on their fate earlier than ordained. When a human goes beyond what they deserve in life and tries to take or make or be more, they cross the rules of fate and bring on destruction. Odysseus always teetered on the edge of creating massive universal trouble, which unbeknownst to him would have created too many imbalances in his known world, causing even more destruction than the Trojan War. The gods, goddesses, and oracles kept a constant eye on him, continually intervening in his course in one direction or another. This sort of large-scale, intensive meddling by the deities is extremely rare."

"As a demigod, I bridge the gap between being a man and a god," I said. "One of the dubious benefits of being an emperor was deification after death, although in my case, the politics of the Senate tried to prevent this from happening. You have already told me about the limitation of my powers, and I can see already that we demigods do not have the same family connections as those born of the couplings of gods and humans.

"For a few centuries, while there were people who remembered me for good or bad, I enjoyed my special existence. The old gods treated me well but never would tell me what I could expect. I've had a much longer existence than other demigods. As I saw others of my type disappear, I realized that my existence was temporary compared to the endless life of the gods, yet it would be eons compared to other demigods and humans. I began to wonder about my fate and ultimately dropped that question as answerless. However, at my core there is a burning, a human shame that I cannot rid myself of. I can never relieve myself of the guilt for the death of my Antinous.

"Yemayá, your powers of perception are enormous and far outweigh mine. Most people think that emperors are free to make decisions, free to live their lives as they desire, but we too live in the human world. My power relied on the support of some key senators and of the army. However, my love for Antinous went beyond what was traditional, and soon there were whispers around me. I tried to protect him as best I could, but I feared for his life, which made me cling that much more closely to him.

"In my human life, an oracle said that I must lose that which I loved the most in order to become the most powerful emperor ever, but I was blinded by my power to not realize that Antinous's life was at stake. I thought if I became the most powerful man on earth, I would not be reliant on any person, any god, or any oracle. As the most powerful, I could be with Antinous as I wanted to be. Alas, I never saw the contradiction until his wet and swollen body was brought to me."

Yemayá was respectfully silent for a moment, her gown billowing around her like a stream. Then she said, "What you're saying is that you did not realize how your own fate was to be carried out. But even if you somehow could know, you still had to suffer."

"Suffer I did. I wept like a woman as the records show. I was not ashamed. I deified him and thought that after my own deification we would be eternal lovers."

"But you found out that was impossible. A human cannot deify another human and later join them after death in the heavens. You found that out when you were deified. You were never destined to join Antinous in the afterlife."

"I carry the blame and the loss in me today. In Greek the word 'blame' meant to speak amiss of sacred things. It took me centuries to realize that my pride of my own power was a way of speaking amiss of the sacred bond Antinous and I had. It appears that the purpose of my life in this intermediate world between eternal and human form is to atone for my responsibility in the death of the one I held most dear. That is why Antinio is so important now. In the beginning, I thought this would be an easy job, but I am discovering the limitations that demigods have. Two times already I have saved his life, and

I can feel my own powers draining from me. I am beginning to feel what it is to be human and face death again. And like humans, I cannot foretell when or where that will be."

"I see you do understand. We are not allowed to tell demigods about the limits of their power. Frankly, the reason that most of your fellow emperors are gone from the heavens is that they stupidly used their powers right away to help family members or friends. You, however, have waited. There are so few of your type around, we have all been watching you for centuries. Of course, we do not know your fate. But each time you intervene in Antinio's life, more of your own life force will leave you until..." Here she paused. "I'll say no more about that."

As she always seemed to do, she disappeared leaving me with more questions.

*　　*　　*

Antinio settled in quickly with Laquesio, the first man he ever lived with outside his family. The house was full of sounds: TVs, radios, kitchen appliances, Laquesio's practicing on his grand piano, and his dancing along to songs that blasted out of giant stereo speakers. In Cuba, Antinio had learned to focus his concentration, blocking out distractions, and he used this skill to devour the books and magazines Laquesio harbored in the rooms. Every day there was a new wave of information—*Time*, *Newsweek*, and other magazines left in the mailbox; the daily newspaper tossed onto the front step; the *New York Times* and *Wall Street Journal* found in the public library; and, in gay bars, gay newspapers and magazines with covers of shirtless men, full of lists and ads announcing where gay life flourished.

New rhythms were established to accommodate Laquesio's work schedule. Each of them was a great teacher to the other, and both were intuitive and motivated learners. They spent the mornings together, often in bed experimenting with new acts, positions, roles, and ways of being. They reveled in sex and were not parsimonious in sharing it with others, individually or together. When Laquesio was away at work, Antinio explored the gay bars and bathhouses, discovering that gay men in America introduced themselves through sex and only later opened up about their lives. He found many new friendships this way.

Of the GLM activists he had met at the refugee camp, he saw Boreas the most. Six-foot tall, with blond hair, piercing blue eyes, and a sharp chin, Boreas looked like he had come right off the farm where his family still lived. He met with Antinio and Laquesio frequently in his downtown office to discuss Antinio's legal case and to understand the differences between gay life in Cuba and America.

"How can I take my gay experiences out of my life? It is all one, the same," Antinio told his lawyer.

"Then how do you compare your experiences as a gay man in each place?" Boreas asked.

"Civil and legal rights are much stronger for the individual here. I will have more freedoms once I am a citizen. But gay rights do not seem to be better here than they were in Cuba."

"That asshole in the camp certainly demonstrated that discrimination and oppression were the same in both countries," interjected Laquesio. "With Reagan in the White House, things are not likely to get better."

"The biggest difference you will never understand is the constant presence of El Comandante. His secret police are everywhere. I could never have this conversation in Cuba, and if I did we would be whispering for fear of being overheard. I appreciate the greater openness of America. Here in Minneapolis I feel like I can create a life as a gay man. I am excited that gay people are trying to claim their freedoms even amidst prejudice and oppression. On the other hand, I am too Cuban, too much a product of a police state to imagine that gay people or any people could create a communal effort to change their lives. After all of my conversations with you two and the others in the GLM, it is still hard for me to imagine what that would really be like."

As a leader on the cusp of the gay rights movement, Laquesio had to jump in. "Legal equality and social acceptance of gays are still in their infancy in the U.S., especially here in Minnesota. However, we have created the bubble of the gay community where we can live life semi-freely."

"You mean we can live normal lives compared to the way things are in Cuba," Boreas added.

"Normal? Who wants a normal life?" Laquesio answered. "If you mean acting like straight people, I'd rather be dead. Paternalistic, straitlaced, religious, straight-dominant culture is a dead end, and gays should have no part of it. We don't want to imitate the dominant culture. The last thing we need are failing institutions like marriage, the military, 'looking straight,' or conforming to puritanical mores.

"The gift of being gay," he went on, "is that we bring a different spirit and sensibility that is neither feminine nor masculine, but a combination of both energies, in itself a new energy. Gays were never meant to be monogamous and by nature are meant to share their energy through sex. The sex act itself is the center of gay identity. It was not meant for procreation, but rather for the creation of a bond between its participants."

"I am not sure about everything you said, Laquesio, but I can agree about the sex part. Despite my experiences in Cuba and in the camp, I never believed that sex was wrong. The problem was that sex with men got me in trouble and I was punished for it. I think all sex is good, even sex with women."

Boreas jumped in. "I can't agree with that last statement. To be gay, you have to reject sex with women. Otherwise you are hiding and going back into the closet."

"I agree," said Laquesio. "Any gay male that has sex with a woman is trying to gain straight male privileges. You have to be gay or straight. You can't be both."

"Maybe that's true for you, Laquesio. And maybe as the leader of the GLM you have to say that. But for me to limit myself to just one gender reduces the possibilities of life experience. And being so recent to arrive here in the U.S., I need to learn about all communities and all people before I can make any commitments. You both take everything for granted. For me everything is new, like I am on another planet. The house, the way people look, the weather, the air, the lakes— anything I see, feel, and smell is different. I don't think that I understand anything yet, let alone that there can be a gay culture. What can gay culture be? Isn't all culture gay in the first place?"

Laquesio answered, "Antinio, what I mean by gay culture is how we live, act out our lives, and dream together as a community. Our experience as gay men and lesbians changes our experience of politics, religion, the arts, literature, and even science. When our gay voices are heard, we create an alternative to society that is much freer, with all the rights we need."

"Speaking of rights, let's get back to the legal aspects of your case," Boreas said. "You have some legal advantages as a Cuban refugee over other immigrants. And U.S. immigration law, while not protecting gay people, sets high legal standards for everyone. But as your experience shows, the laws here are little different from those in Cuba regarding gay rights. There are virtually no legal protections for gays in any part of our lives. We are discriminated against in jobs and housing and cannot openly participate in many social institutions and are excluded by most religions. Gay bashings happen frequently, and police not only offer no protection, but often are instigators themselves. America is no icon of freedom for gay people."

"This is why we each individually and as a group must stand up and claim our rights no matter what the laws are," Laquesio said. "We must be outspoken and risk exposing our lives to non-gay people—this is the only way that things will change."

"Laquesio, my heart agrees with you, but I need to be more practically oriented than you and Boreas," Antinio said. "As a born citizen you have many privileges that are denied to me. It is easy for you to rail against what you call the prevailing culture since you grew up in it, are steeped in it, and can make your way through and around it. I, on the other hand, need to get a job soon to support myself and to gain citizenship. I did not have a chance to share with you, Boreas, what happened the other day."

"Tell me. You were meeting with that Cuban-American you were referred to who works for an international medical company in St. Paul..."

"Yes. We met in his office and hit it off pretty well at first. We chatted in Spanish and right away discovered that we grew up a short distance from each other in Havana and as kids went to the same *dulcería* to get candies."

"Sounds good so far. I told you how Americans start interviews with small talk before the serious questioning begins."

"Right. Things were going fine until he asked me, 'When did you get here?' His family came in 1959, at the start of the Revolution. When I told him, he spit out, '*Un Marielto, no me molestes*, don't bother me. You Marielitos are damaged goods that bring down the image of good immigrants.' He called me *escoria*, can you believe that? No one has ever called me that to my face. By this point, he started shouting, 'You people will ruin everything good, upstanding Cubans have done in this country. And don't bother anyone else in the Cuban-American community here.' As he showed me to the door, he said, 'No one will help you. Go back to where you came from!'"

"Did you have any idea that would happen?"

"Of course not," Antinio said, "or I never would have talked to him. It appears that I can't ever be honest with my own countrymen, even here in the United States."

* * *

In Cuba, Antinio had always been assigned jobs. He had never gone through interviews and competed against others for a position. With additional coaching from Boreas, he was soon offered a job in one of the first companies to work on computer-based educational materials. Expecting large markets in Europe and South America, the company needed someone who could speak, read, and write in English, French, and Spanish. This job would be the first step toward Antinio gaining citizenship.

Laquesio prophesized that joining corporate American could be a misstep. "Your gay spirit will be ground down by the indignities of the corporate world," he warned.

In a picture taken on his first day of work, Antinio was at his cubicle talking to someone outside the picture, a broad smile on his face. With his wavy dark hair and thick moustache, he resembled the movie star Burt Reynolds. He wore the new shirt, tie, and jacket he had bought over the weekend with money Laquesio loaned him. Antinio loved the modern office décor, so clean and expensive and sleek. He had a computer terminal sitting on his own desk, connected to a mainframe.

He took to computers quickly, understanding their requirements for logic and reason devoid of emotion. While he could be a voluble, upbeat man around people he knew, Antinio never bared the darker, difficult moments; these he kept winding tighter and tighter in a ball within his body. Computers were the ideal interlocutors. If there was a problem, it meant that his reason and logic were incorrect. It was never the computer's fault. When there were difficulties communicating with the machine, those had nothing to do with him personally. His life at work focused on discovering logical answers to questions presented.

He wished the rest of his life could be like this. When he could depend on Reason, Antinio seemed to be on safe ground. He was wary of most emotions, their voices in his mind, and the pain they caused his body. Love could be let in only as it was connected to sex. Passion, excitement, and deep connection from sex were feelings he encouraged. His relationship with Laquesio was sexual and intellectual. He bonded with him yet never shared the fears that inhabited his body. He simply did not have the capacity to do so despite the profound love that he maintained. He did not realize that Reason, when not balanced by the heart and emotions, was not enough and could steer him wrong. But, at least in his workplace surrounded by other people interacting with computers, Reason worked well enough.

Over the next two years, he would explore this new life and grow to feel like he had a home. Antinio's circle of friends and sexual partners grew. His job responsibilities expanded, and he was delighted when his job grew to include editing and correcting the written English documents of his coworkers. While this brought grumbling from a few of them, they all realized that Antinio had an unparalleled talent for languages. He still spoke with an accent, but his grammar, spelling, and punctuation were excellent. He took night courses at the University of Minnesota, eventually earning a baccalaureate in computer science. His field of work held unlimited opportunities, and his company actively supported his path to citizenship. Unfortunately, no one could forsee the tsunami that was about to wash ashore.

XVIII

I was content to be a witness to the evolving relationship of Antinio and Laquesio. Each, I felt, was in good hands with the other, learning, adapting, sharing. Then, shortly after celebrating his first anniversary in the U.S., in July 1981, Antinio noticed a small article in the *New York Times* about a new, strange disease being seen in gay men in New York and California.

When he finished the article, he gave it to Laquesio to read. "Antinio, what if I have this disease? I've had a feeling that something was wrong inside me."

The two men stood quietly looking into each other's eyes. Antinio wanted to convince Laquesio that he was wrong, but no one knew what course this new disease would take. The disease soon acquired a name, GRID—Gay-Related Immune Deficiency. A year later, it was renamed AIDS, for Acquired Immune Deficiency Syndrome, an improvement over GRID, once it was found to be not limited to gay men, but to include an odd combination of fellow travelers—Haitians, among the poorest people on earth, who had their own panicked diaspora to the U.S.; and intravenous drug users, among others.

Laquesio, true to his prediction, soon fell ill. One day he was fine, and the next he could not breathe. Antinio rushed him to the hospital and waited outside the emergency room.

After two hours, a doctor came out. "Are you Antinio?"

"Yes. How is Laquesio?"

"He should be fine. I'm Dr. Paean. I have been Laquesio's doctor for many years. He has pneumonia. That's all we know right now. He's very weak. It is unusual for pneumonia to develop so quickly, but he should be better soon."

That was not to be the case. The doctors soon noticed that Laquesio did not respond to antibiotics. As his condition worsened, they did more tests. Several days later, Dr. Paean called Antinio. "The testing shows that Laquesio has PCP—*Pneumocystis carinii* pneumonia. It's a rare and serious opportunistic infection that attacks those with compromised immune systems. None of us here has ever seen a case before; we've only read about it in textbooks. That's why it took us so long to identify it. The bad news is, we don't have any protocols to treat this disease."

"Can I visit him?"

"No, I am afraid you can't. He's under quarantine, and we can't let others be exposed to him. There's another thing I want to tell you."

"What is that, doctor?"

"In doing our research, we found there are groups of gay men coming down with PCP in New York and San Francisco. This appears to be a precursor of what they are calling AIDS. Have you heard of this new disease? Do you have any reason to believe that he could be infected with it?"

Antinio was silent.

"I think I know the answer," Dr. Paean replied. "I've known Laquesio for a long time, and he has always been open with me about his sexuality. And he knows I'm also gay. I know he loves you and you're the most important person in his life. Normally, as a doctor, I wouldn't be talking this way to someone who was just a friend. But you are not just a friend to him, and you have my confidence."

"Thank you, doctor. I was afraid to say anything. I wasn't afraid for me, but for him. We have talked about this disease, and Laquesio thought he might have it. What happens now?"

"We'll treat him the best we can. I'll talk to my colleagues in San Francisco to see how they are treating PCP. Meanwhile, stay healthy yourself. He will need your help when he gets out."

Three difficult weeks passed with little change. But Laquesio had been a healthy man, and eventually the right combination of medications helped him survive. He emerged from the hospital greatly debilitated, with difficulty breathing and gaunt from weight loss. When Antinio picked him up, he was shocked by the changes.

At home, Laquesio tried to regain his weight, but discovered it was impossible. In a few weeks, his once muscular, trim body grew thin and gaunt from the loss of body fat and muscle. He cried when he looked in the mirror. The thirty-five-year-old man suddenly looked seventy.

He was not alone in his suffering. Friend after friend began to have the same symptoms. Although Antinio sensed it was likely he was also infected, he showed no symptoms and was able to take care of Laquesio.

*   *   *

Even in the heavens it was impossible to remain detached from events on earth. Stunned by the quick new wave of mass illness and death of humans, Yemayá was the first *orisha* to confront Babalu Ayé, *orisha* of both the spread and the curing of disease, much like the Greek god Apollo in my time. Babalú Ayé specialized in the care and nurturing of all bacteria, viruses, germs, and parasites. He had a special fondness for the smallest ones, viruses, a Latin word meaning poison or slimly liquid.

"I expected you sooner," Babalu Ayé told Yemayá when she found him in a forest collecting herbs that he might fashion later into potions. He was dressed in dark robes, a hood covering his deeply scarred face.

"I questioned you before about smallpox, Babalú Ayé," she said, "if such misery was necessary. Now I must ask it again. Why?"

"You accuse me as though you were a human yourself, Yemayá," Babalú Ayé replied, "when you are not immune to such accusations yourself. I am not responsible for all of your floods."

"You don't have to be so touchy."

"And you know very well I cannot answer your question, *Why?* None of the *orishas* appreciate what I do. While the rest of you are doing big things with oceans and thunder and pathways, I am simply paying attention to my beings. I don't need a big canvas to work on, all I need is one little cell in a plant or animal to grow and reproduce my beings. Soon they create colonies and cities where generation after generation they increase and mutate. They develop defense systems to repel attackers and adapt their armor as necessary to send out legions of new armies to spread their version of the gospel. In the smallest space in a body I can recreate what you do in entire continents. My tiny beings vastly outnumber anything that you or the others are in charge of."

"You forget that I know all about your tiny beings. I am the mother of all beings, yours included."

"But yet you come to me to complain."

"I'm sorry, Babalú Ayé. My purpose is to worry."

"That is true, yet you still come to me. The history of my beings is unrecorded except by me. I love to watch as they affect the world around them. No time or place exists where they have not changed the course of the histories of plants, beasts, and humans."

"Tell me about this new set of things you have been so secretive about. We had an agreement that you would tell me about these things before they get out of hand."

"Not things, beings. That's why I don't tell you anything, because you never respect them. I need to protect them from you."

"I am sorry, I meant to say beings. I understand that their lives are no different than the lives of others in this world. So tell me more about them, my dear Babalú Ayé."

"As with many of the beings under my care, they don't have a name for themselves. They do have names for their hosts, names based on a vast cosmology of types of movement, smell, taste, touch, location, and a myriad of other functions only known to them. Over time, this virus decided that it wanted to leave the confines of the jungles where it had been living in chimpanzees. Looking around at possible carriers, they investigated birds since they fly long distances and antelope because they were fast runners before finally choosing humans, a species noted for its restlessness."

"Restlessness, why restlessness? That is odd."

"You really should pay more attention and try to think like my little ones. No single virus or even existing community of viruses would experience much of the odyssey they were to embark on; they understood that the migration would encompass millions of generations. Therefore, speed or distance carried were not as important as restlessness. Restlessness would get them across hot dusty plains, over snowcapped mountains, through windswept seas, and into every zone on earth."

"That makes lots of sense. I would call them wily, but you will probably get mad if I do, so I will say they are very intelligent."

"When they got to North America a few decades later, talk about intelligent, they split up into groups to test three pathways to see which would be most successful in spreading their colonies. One group infected the intravenous drug users, who had short lives but steady habits that would allow the viruses to penetrate across all groups regardless of social status.

"The second group chose the Haitians, since they would not notice one more injury in their poor, assaulted bodies that had endured century after century of pain and degradation.

"The gays represented the viruses' most inspired choice of hosts, as this branch of the viral community wanted their efforts to be recognized by the hosts themselves. Gays are the most restless of all humans, constantly searching, bumping into each other in dark corners and performing large on the stage of life. Importantly, gays are invisible to most people, so can go places that others cannot."

"Babalú Ayé, this is not the first time you have watched your beings develop an ego. Your smallpox virus had to be transmitted from face to face; they thought they would be unique by being so open about their transmission. I remember you telling us they were so happy when they got a human name. But once there is a name for a disease, humans set about trying to get rid of the agents that cause it."

"Please don't remind me. Just like you with your humans, Yemayá, I can only watch when viruses make decisions of this nature."

"I appreciate you telling me this story. Be prepared. In all likelihood the rest of us will be called to do something."

"I must come to understand the complexities of these new tiny beings before I can help find a treatment. This will get worse before it gets better."

*   *   *

The illness did not stop Laquesio from being an activist. As more and more men became ill and the medical establishment had no answers or treatments, panic spread. One local politician proposed to lock up all gay people and send them to special camps where they could not infect others. Laquesio called an emergency meeting of the GLM, and the room was packed. A few months previous, gay men and lesbians were feeling confident about the future as they took to the streets and began to come out at home and at work. This disease was met with a combination of skepticism, fear, and suspicion in the gay community.

That night Laquesio declared, "I am not about to allow myself or our community to be stigmatized by a disease that attaches its name to gays. We fought to remove being gay from the list of mental disorders and won that battle just two years ago. Now we are told there is a new disease that is described as a disease of gay men, blamed on gay men, a disease that will give straight society an excuse to further discriminate against and punish us. This disease, whatever it is, will not put me back in the closet. We have fought too long for our rights, and I refuse to be shipped to a camp or anywhere." The crowd cheered. "I will organize, I will protest, and I will fight until I can't any longer, and then fight some more. Tomorrow we will meet on the steps of City Hall to demand answers and not discrimination."

Despite the wild enthusiasm, the next day only seven brave men and women showed up, the rest afraid of being associated with AIDS in any public way. As TV news cameras appeared, so did a religious leader who castigated the group, preaching about God's punishment. I was so angry, had I Changó's thunderbolt, I would have smote him on the spot. Yemayá, watching with me, muttered, "As usual Capital G doesn't even show his face and lets his ill-begotten minion step in to spout this ignorance in the guise of religion. I suppose I should let him have it right now."

Thirty policemen wearing thick, yellow rubber gloves appeared on the scene standing with handcuffs ready. Despite the seriousness of the situation, Laquesio started chanting at the police, "We will see you on the news. Your gloves don't match your shoes." The small group took up the chant in solidarity. The police, embarrassed and confused, not to mention quite nervous themselves about contracting this disease, backed off. Yemayá smiled. "This is why I love my gay people. No one else would have laughed in the face of danger as they did today. Bravo!"

News of the demonstration spread. At the next one, over fifty people joined, followed by another with two hundred and a fourth with five hundred. The gay community found their voice.

This initial group led by Laquesio started the Minnesota AIDS Health Group to provide information to other gay men. It was part support group and part book club, as reading scientific articles became a requirement for gay men everywhere. Anything and everything in print was gobbled up and dissected in hope that a cure or at least some relief could be found.

The next blow for Laquesio was to develop red, purple, and black lesions over his legs and genitals. A previously rare cancer soon to become all too common—Kaposi's sarcoma, KS—eventually covered his face, a final affront to this handsome gay man. He slowly retreated from public view, both because he did not want to be seen and, frankly, because people did not want to see him. He was too vivid a reminder of AIDS, suffering, death, and the unknown .

Antinio, a few friends, and GLM stalwarts took care of Laquesio as did his mother, who came over frequently. Selflessly she tended her son and helped model to the others what needed to be done. She befriended his friends, particularly Antinio, who could not communicate directly with his own mother. Babalú Ayé appreciated the role of mothers teaching others how to care for the ill. This was one of the few areas of agreement between Yemayá and Babalú Ayé. They were already seeing too many mothers and families unable to accept their child's gayness and therefore rejecting them completely when this frightening sickness engulfed them.

The following year, 1983, Laquesio was frequently in and out of the hospital with bouts of PCP becoming increasingly resistant to the drug treatments. The routine treatment for KS, radiation, lowered his resistance further and made him vulnerable to other illnesses. He became weaker and less able to get around. He lived with IV tubes in his arms, bottles of medications, and reams of worsening test results. Antinio would come home from work and find Laquesio sitting propped up against a wall because he had fallen and could not raise himself up again.

Long before this, their lovemaking had ended. Antinio was afraid to share a bed with Laquesio, and Laquesio did not want to see the fear on Antinio's face every evening. Exhausted by all of the insults placed on his rapidly declining body, Laquesio had little desire or energy for sex. Yet, despite the many questions about transmission of the disease, Antinio would still meet men at the gym or on the bus on the way home and go off with them before returning to his house. Laquesio, ever alert for the special smells of semen or sweat mixed with another man's scent, would temporarily perk up and ask for the details. Antinio freely shared his stories. These seemed to make his partner happy for some short moments. On occasions when Laquesio felt strong enough, Antinio would help him masturbate while telling him the intimate details of the most recent encounter.

Of course, Antinio worried about his own health. Every morning he would look at his face to see if he could detect any microscopic changes that might have started during the night. He would examine his body closely looking for any sign of lesions, using a hand mirror to examine his buttocks and the back of his legs. He increased his daily gym workout, confident that a physically strong body could keep the disease away. If he caught a cold, he would worry. Worry was his constant companion.

One morning Laquesio awoke and could not remember his own name. Antinio joked about it and reminded him of the story when he responded to Cíclope, "I am Nobody." They laughed, but both men were scared by this. When Laquesio lost the ability to read, Antinio would read to him from *The Golden Ages*, which was torn and pockmarked from its own adventures.

Another day, Laquesio started screaming, "There's a monster in my room. He's over there, he's over there. What is he doing here? Help me, please!"

Antinio came running. "There's nothing here. What are you seeing?"

"Why can't you see him? It's some sort of man with a long, scarred face from disease. He looks at me and smiles. Chase him out of here, please. He scares me."

"I'm here with you and you'll be okay. Drink some water and I can get you one of your sleeping pills." He left and returned with the medicine. "Here, take this and try to rest."

He took the pill and Antinio left the room. Laquesio calmed down and asked directly, "Who are you and why are you here?"

"You don't know me, and my name is Babalú Ayé."

"Babalú, weren't you on the Ricky Ricardo show?"

The *orisha* laughed loudly. "I forget that the only thing Americans know about Cuba comes from that television show with the funny redheaded lady. Yes, Ricky was a *santero* practitioner, and when he played the song you call *Babalú* and drummed so wildly, he was calling me in a trance. I am the god of viruses."

"What is the god of viruses doing in my room? I really must be crazy. Antinio is right, I am hallucinating. I don't believe in God, and I don't believe in religion or screwed up ideas like that. Religion and gods were invented as means to promulgate blame and shame. I have had enough of that for one lifetime, and I don't need a god coming here expecting me to convert. But if you are a god and I am actually talking to you, then answer this: What did I do to make this happen?"

"What if I said this is not about you? You happen to be the host for some millions of viruses that are living in your body. It is but a disease. You recognize that, and eventually your misguided government and even the religious people will begin to understand that. They will soon understand that this disease has a viral cause and has nothing to do with moral character, sexual orientation, or any other ridiculous factor. My job is to watch over my viruses. Since you are one the first of the gay ones that they infected so badly, I want to see who you are and how they are affecting you."

"Do you hate us as well and blame us for being different, for loving the wrong type of person?"

"Why do you humans have such a need to create blame where none exists? You should have named yourselves *Homo blasphemeinus*, as this seems to be your universal tendency." This made Laquesio laugh and nod in agreement. "While the gods so enjoy observing the creativity of you gay people, we cannot understand your ability to turn creativity into destruction when you project your inadequacies onto yourselves. As my ex-wife Yemayá says, 'There's no such thing as god's punishment.' Gods do not need to punish. We let humans do that to themselves.

"Go to sleep and rest. I see my little beings in you are getting anxious. Don't mistrust yourself, and we will talk again."

As the weeks went on, Laquesio's demeanor worsened. His determination and drive turned to anger, and he began to lash out. He accused Antinio, his mother, and anyone else who might be around of abusing and torturing him. While he no longer remembered his lover's name, he intuited that he had an important connection with Antinio and therefore saved the worst abuse for him.

"Why are you are trying to poison me? I tried to help you out, and now you are killing me in return."

Then, just as suddenly, Laquesio would get calm and recognize his lover again. "Antinio, I never told you this before, but I love you. From the first day we met, we had a special connection unlike any I have had with any other man. You know I don't believe in love. And here I am admitting that I love you. If you love me, please help me die. The suffering is too much for me. Call Dr. Paean and ask him to help. Please, only you can do this for me."

Antinio was reaching a breaking point. He had continued to work as normally as possible, but there was no one there he could confide in about Laquesio's state of health.

He called Dr. Paean. "Laquesio doesn't think he can stand the pain any longer. You mentioned that you could help when we get to this point."

"I did, Antinio. The problem is that dementia has already kicked in. Even though he has some lucid days, the opportunity to make a rational decision has passed. I can't ethically prescribe anything for him any longer. I'm sorry. You will just have to see this through to the end."

Soon enough, Laquesio's mother and Antinio could no longer provide enough care for Laquesio, and he was moved to a bed in a special, sealed-off section of the county hospital. They could visit only if dressed in special suits that prevented all physical contact and that could be safely destroyed after use.

They took turns sitting by his bed, unable to touch Laquesio's skinny arms and withered face. He was under sedation for his outbursts, the dementia not controllable in any other way. He lost most bodily functions and wore a diaper that constantly smelled of urine and feces. Antinio walked through the paces of being a human as best he could at the bedside, but his emotions compacted around the bullet in his belly. He felt the dead weight there merge with the other dead weights he carried inside.

On Laquesio's last evening, his mother sat on the bed singing him a song from his childhood. He opened his eyes one final time and, despite the respirator in his mouth, called for Antinio and in a strange language blessed him—or at least that is what she understood he did. Laquesio then smiled at his mother, sighed, and let out his last breath. By the time Antinio reached the hospital a short time later, the body was gone, taken to the morgue to be cremated. He was alone. And for a second time, his love was over.

XIX

Antinio found, as others have in the midst of a plague, there is little time to grieve. The living require all of the energy and attention they can muster to survive. Much as he hated to do it, Antinio stripped the house bare of Laquesio's clothing, linens, and anything that might carry this disease. The house once so alive with sound was now mostly silent, making way in Antinio's consciousness for the Shriekers, now so full of doubt. While scientists focused more on learning about the viral cause of AIDS, there was still plenty of confusion about the means of transmission. It appeared to be borne in blood and semen, though it was not yet clear if saliva, sweat, coughing, or even touching could be other pathways for the virus. Everything Antinio touched in these days caused him to question his own health. He kept only the few of Laquesio's books that he could not bear to part with. His mother took the piano and other mementos. All else was discarded. Much of it was burned.

Antinio redoubled his gym efforts. His diary shows that he spent up to three hours there at a stretch, increasing the specific exercises for his legs, arms, and butt. He was especially worried about his *culo*, having watched Laquesio's melt away to skin on bones. He hoped to build up as much muscle as possible as a bulwark against the wasting syndrome that had become the most obvious outwardly visible AIDS symptom. He talked things over with Dr. Paean, the only one in the city willing to work with gay men coming down with this illness. The doctor advised Antinio to keep doing things that would keep him healthy, which was really no advice at all. Impotence, frustration, and fear reigned as both the physician and the patient were reduced to waiting for something to happen. With no known cause, AIDS had no prevention and no cure.

Questions swirled in Antinio's head. *What do I do now that my lover is gone? What do I do when my lover dies from a disease never seen before and from which everyone dies? What do I do when it is likely he has given me this disease? Who can even answer these questions? Why is this happening to me?*

This last question was one humans often asked directly to Babalú Ayé. They made this dangerous query, Yemayá and Babalú Ayé noticed, only when times were most difficult. "If they asked this during good times, they might come up with a useful answer," Yemayá said. "But they don't, so their answers are tinged with fault and shame."

Babalú Ayé agreed. "The human mind is so simplistic, it's hard not to laugh at these nonsensical conclusions. Right now, Antinio is telling himself, 'If I had not left Cuba, this would never have happened.' What he doesn't know is that the first AIDS case in Cuba has been diagnosed, and El Comandante is considering remote quarantine camps for homosexuals, regardless of whether they are symptomatic."

"*Ay, dios mio,*" Yemayá added. "This absurdity always ends in pain. Antinio's questions are evolving. 'If I had not left my mother, this would not have happened. Why did I leave my mother behind?' Mothers never have that much power, no matter what their children think. Next, it will be self-judgmental. 'If only I had been a more careful person, I would be fine.' How can he even think that, this human who prides himself on Reason? There is a complete absence of logic here. A person only can say 'more careful' retroactively, when they already know the outcome. Even we cannot see this outcome."

Babalú Ayé understood the special role of gays in the world, and if he had the ability to feel sorrow, which he did not, it would be because his viruses had caused crisis on many levels—political, social, and medical. "Antinio's next thought will be his most absurd one," Babalú Ayé said. "'If I wasn't gay, then everything would be normal.' Why do gay people even say that, Yemayá? Don't they see how crazy straight people are? Their marriages are a mess, they are always looking for people in their lives other than the ones they are with, they have children for the wrong reasons, ultimately are unhappy. And they dress badly, to top it off."

Antinio wrote his mother that he was now living in the U.S. His aunts had told her that he was living in East Germany. He had devised a scheme to enclose letters to his mother with those he mailed to his friend Philippides in Berlin, who would resend them along to Antinio's mother in Cuba. Anticlea would write back to the address in Germany, and Philippides would forward the letters to Antinio. He was relieved to drop the subterfuge and be able to describe more of his new life to his mother, though he omitted the details of his love for and the death of Laquesio. There were often dried teardrops and smeared ink in the long, neatly written letters Antinio would receive, and not too infrequently in the ones she got back from him.

He learned that Anticlea visited the *jimaguas* as often as she could, taking the long, bumpy bus ride out of the city and back each time. She did her best to create for them a memory of their *papá*, since like Telemachus, they had been too young when he left on his journey to have their own memories of him. The longer he was gone, the more distant he was becoming to them. In her letters filled with news of her grandsons, she also helped to fill the gap in Antinio's life with memories of his boys.

Reading his mother's letters, a wistful Antinio dreamed of holding his sons in his arms and telling them his own story. He had written a lullaby for them in Esperanto and used to sing it to them right after they were born. On Antinio's last birthday, Laquesio had given him a guitar, and to quell the rising voices in his mind, he would pick it up and sing, trying to imagine the *jimaguas* growing up as they turned three, then four, five, and now six years old. Much is made of the mother-child bond, both by the gods and humans, but the bonds between fathers and their children are no weaker. From the moment they were born, Antinio's boys occupied a space in his mind and heart. Perhaps because of the journey that the sperm must travel to fertilize the egg, a father's bond is more in the nature of seeking, whereas the mother's bond comes from nurturing this embryo. If Antinio had continued to live with or near the *jimaguas*, he would have been the one to swing them in his arms, explore new territory with them, and discover the ways of the ants and insects in the grounds around the house. He would have taught them new words and songs. Together they would have discovered the world and uncovered the secrets of life, love, and ideas. With the *jimaguas*, his soul could have opened further, which in time could have counteracted the pain he stored. But this was not to be.

I never had children of my own and never wanted any. We did have a tradition of adopting sons for the purpose of choosing our rightful heir to the throne. That is what Trajan did when my parents died and what I did when I neared the end of my life. But these are political machinations, not familial ones. At first, my love for Antinous was as a father, elder, and teacher, but very soon it changed into one of a partner and an equal. This is what bothered my critics so. After Antinous died, my heart was closed to emotions. Although I lived another eight years as a human, those were years of solitude and emptiness. Watching Antinio, I grieved with him and wanted to make him whole again.

His legal case sputtered on. Boreas submitted all the necessary paperwork to the Immigration and Naturalization Service. At each step, the reaction was negative. Boreas became convinced that there was some middle-level official blocking Antinio's case, but despite meticulous research and many contacts within the INS, he could not discover where. The Ninth Circuit Court in California had ruled recently that a gay person had the right to citizenship, and Boreas thought that this precedent might help. They had to simultaneously push forward and remain patient.

In 1985 the first test to detect antibodies to HIV, the virus responsible for AIDS, became available. Another test measured

T cells in the blood, an indicator of the extent to which the immune system was compromised. Dr. Paean advised Antinio, "I don't recommend that you get these tests. None of my patients are."

"But why?" Antinio asked. "Information is power. Every day, my work demonstrates that data is neutral, neither right nor wrong. We make our decisions by interpreting data. Living without factual information when it is available is a sacrilege, a theft of the natural order of things."

"But if the result shows that you have HIV, it is likely that you will die. We know so little about this virus and can only treat the complications that arise from it. We don't know how low the T-cell count can go or how T-cell levels correlate with health outcomes."

"But this information could help order my life in one direction or another. I think it's important to be tested and to know the outcome."

The doctor drew Antinio's blood into several vials. Like this virus that could linger in pockets of cells quietly but steadily reproducing itself unknown to the rest of the body, Antinio still felt the *nostalghia* of Volodya in his blood coupled with a sad restlessness that now permeated all of his body, having entered into every cell and mitochondrion. If this virus was within him, it would enter the *nostalghia* itself.

The weeks spent waiting for the test results were punctuated with bouts of doubt. Many times, the voices ridiculed Antinio's decision to be tested, and he thought of calling the doctor to destroy the vials of blood. *They are an ill omen forecasting the pain and agony of a death alone without your family or anyone around to take care of you.* But if Calypso's prophesy was to be believed, he was still to have another lover.

"Antinio, your test results are mixed but inconclusive," Dr. Paean told him. "You tested positive for HIV antibodies, meaning you are infected. But I do have good news—your T-cell count is over a thousand. You have the virus, but it apparently is not yet affecting you."

"So I should be more hopeful than scared?"

"Each case I have had is different," the doctor said. "You are not Laquesio. His suffering was unspeakable. That may not be your path."

The two talked more as the doctor wrote some notes and scheduled a follow-up appointment. Dr. Paean left the exam room, leaving the chart on the door to be picked up by his assistant. Antinio took the test results and notes and slipped them into his briefcase. When he got to the office, he put them through the paper shredder and watched as the handwritten words and printed numbers were reduced to confetti. He imagined writing a computer program to reassemble those pieces back into a document again, but it would take years of work to input each single letter or number or period or blank space contained in every tiny scrap.

Antinio felt safe once more—by hiding this information not from himself, but from the INS. In the midst of AIDS hysteria, the U.S. Congress banned anyone with the disease from entering the country and made its diagnosis an exclusion from citizenship. As a gay man, Antinio was automatically suspected of having this disease. In the public's eye, "gay" meant "AIDS," which in turn meant "death." When the INS subpoenaed his medical records, as was the norm in immigration cases, they would not find a trail of evidence to hold against him. His doctor also knew this to be true, so he purposely left the records behind for Antinio to cleanse, always feigning surprise when he could not find past records each time his patient came for a consultation.

Antinio's next test, a few months later, showed that his T-cell count had dropped below 700. This confirmed what he had been feeling. Although Dr. Paean counseled against jumping to any conclusions, he was himself preparing to lose another patient.

XX

Estranged from his homeland and alienated from his own body, Antinio wondered how he had happened upon this land of everlasting winter. He enjoyed the contrast of the seasons, yet by the end of March he longed for sultry sea breezes that never arrived, scorching rays of the sun that never appeared overhead, and the sweet smell of frangipani, unknown in these parts. He discovered one oasis during that long, lingering winter, the Como Park Conservatory. It was a bitter cold day when he first walked though its large doors, and Antinio was shocked by the warm, humid climate inside the large glass building. He was pleased to find a Cuban Royal Palm stately presiding over the pure jungle of sights and smells. Everywhere large fronds of tropical plants, orchids, and flowers he had forgotten and now remembered brought back feelings of desire. Slowly walking around, ducking under low-hanging branches, eyeing some papayas growing from the trunk of a small tree, he met a blond-haired man his age with a firmly shaped *culo* similarly seeking refuge from the winter's remaining blasts. They moved underneath the foliage to a secluded spot and soon added to the humidity and fecundity that this building celebrated.

This brief break from Minnesota winter reminded him how he had never really adapted to the northern region. He had lived here for years but never felt part of this land. For centuries I have watched the meanderings of people as they search for new homelands. Maybe immigrants are no different from adventurers and Troubleseekers like Odysseus and Antinio. They are searching for the home that they left behind. The Finns, Swedes, and Norwegians who traveled across the

United States could have lived anywhere but were not content until they arrived at the northern reaches of Minnesota, where both the extreme climate and rocky soil signaled this was home.

Antinio had not chosen Minnesota as his landing spot. Eventually, his journey would continue in search of a place where birds of paradise and hibiscus could bloom unfettered in the open.

Adrift and rootless, he had several affairs with women. Yemayá could only shake her head at these vain attempts.

"What does he think he is doing?" she asked me one day. As usual, she replied to her own question. "He is trying to hide from his true nature. This is not right. He says that he could be in love with anyone, but he could say he was an elephant and that would not make it true. Women love gay men. I certainly do. Gay men are more attentive to our feelings and bodies than other men. They want to please us and, unlike any straight man, they notice our clothes, shoes, and new hairdos without prompting. They are interested in our work and what we think, whether it is about music, literature, movies, social issues, or politics. They especially like strong-minded women as their equals. I have been married to about six—or was it seven?— orishas. Anyway, too many of them, including that bullheaded Babalú Ayé. Getting any particular one of them to pay attention is nearly impossible. I'd love to marry a gay orisha for once, but then in the end he would ditch me for a male."

True enough, several women offered to marry Antinio once they heard about his immigration woes. And he thought about it each time, making plans, meeting families, once even spending Christmas on a farm with a redheaded cello player named Euterpa. Her mother and father adored him, and when he told stories about the jimaguas, their hearts yearned in unison with his for reunion. Though that relationship was short-lived, Euterpa's parents still asked about him years later. Everyone loved the idea of Antinio, seeing his playfulness, enjoying his singing that now included all of the popular songs of the time, and admiring his language abilities and his devotion to the family from which he was separated. Few saw his fears and inability to connect to his emotions, and none ever saw the depth of his traumas.

They took to his tales as parables of bravery, of vanquishing foes, of meeting enemies and outwitting them. The scope of his journey he had honed into his own epic poem, just as Odysseus spends a good part of Homer's epic relating his tales for different audiences who react by granting him advice and help. As Odysseus realized, his homebound listeners lived vicariously through his travel stories chronicling experiences they themselves were too timid so seek out. In telling the tale, the storyteller shaped it to show himself at his best. Naturally, he hid not only the parts that he wanted hidden, but also the parts to which he could not admit. Only when he talked about his mother or the *jimaguas* did Antinio begin to express real feeling. In quiet moments with one or two people, he might come close to revealing more, but he never did.

Antinio was still cautious about proclaiming he was gay. He had little trust in the legal system and, unlike Laquesio, did not feel like he could directly confront the world as openly gay. Despite the fight with the INS that hinged on his homosexuality, Antinio acted gay only around gay people. He was neither completely closeted nor completely open. The freedom of the moment of unforgettingness, of telling the truth with Alethia that day in Cuba, died with the unforgettingness that he experienced with the agent at Fort McCoy. As Eleggua often reminded me, truth can be dangerous to one's life, but the lack of internal truth destroys one's soul.

One day Antinio talked to Fineo on a static-filled line for a few moments, hoping that he could help Antinio assimilate the events of his life. "Everything that has happened to me opened new wounds, which are compounded by additional, more intense assaults on my soul. Is the problem our Cuban instinct not to tell the truth? Or do you think a gene passed down in my family is causing my introspection, depression, and paralysis?" His mother's problems made Antinio lean toward that theory.

"I realize this sounds strange, unlogical, but maybe it is my own fate that is at the root of my problems."

Fineo responded, but only a few words made it through the long-distance lines—*don't fret ...fate is soon...trust...you will when...*—before the line went dead.

Antinio's legal case moved on. Records subpoenaed under the Freedom of Information Act revealed that the original doctors at Fort McCoy "did not detect any homosexual deviation in his medical exam." At least that was true honesty. To have said otherwise would have been a travesty against the Hippocratic Oath. Without this determination, the government had no right to exclude him. This piece of information was enough to keep legal briefs flying back and forth. Antinio's status eventually moved from temporary to permanent alien resident.

Yet, each step forward was met with attacks and assaults. The government was now fighting against his application for citizenship. The INS did not bend in its opposition despite additional interviews, proof of child support to the *jimaguas*, and affidavits of support from the vice president of the company where Antinio worked. The unknown entities in that battle pushed back harder as the final hurdle was now in sight. The INS continued to refuse to grant Antinio citizenship because of his initial interview at Fort McCoy. INS practice had changed quite a bit through case law by then, and they did not normally get involved in cases of so-called "private, consensual activity." However, for whatever reason, officials continued to assert that Antinio had willingly talked about his "perversion" in the interview. An INS legal brief was leaked to the public around the same time referring to gay men as "faggots," showing that homophobia was still prevalent among local agents. For nine long years now, Antinio had desired to add that "hyphen-American" to his nationality. It seemed to him that he would be forever in limbo, keeping his means of livelihood and his health and health insurance in continued doubt.

Finally Boreas petitioned for a citizenship hearing before the U.S. District Court. "This is an extraordinary action," he explained, "but the only one that will force the INS to make a decision. It is risky while being our best chance at forcing their hand."

Antinio had received bad news from his doctor days before the petition was filed. The latest tests found unexplained elevated enzymes—something apparently was eating away his liver. In the ancient times before I roamed the earth as a man, it was understood that liver disease was caused by what our doctors called the melancholic emotions of anger, resentment, and jealousy. The blood transfusion from Volodya had given Antinio something in addition to *nostalghia*: hepatitis C. But that was not the worst news. Dr. Paean sat Antinio down with a grim look on his face. "Your T cells—or, more accurately, your CD4+ T cells—are down to 489. There is no doubt that you are progressing to full-blown AIDS."

Although Babalú Ayé's then-nameless beings had entered Antinio's body the first time he and Laquesio had sex together, Antinio continued to have no major symptoms. But he felt depleted and exhausted and was starting to lose weight. "What do you suggest?"

"The currently available drugs are so toxic, let's follow the suggested protocol and wait until your count drops lower or you start showing symptoms."

Within weeks, his CD4+ count dropped to 65, and the doctor started him on AZT for the HIV and an aerosol of pentamidine to forestall PCP. He suggested that Antinio read up on the side effects. "These are difficult drugs to live with, and you should know what you are in for."

For Antinio and others diagnosed with AIDS, "side effects" was soon understood to be a euphemism, that word derived from the ancient Greek word from religious ceremonies, the superstitious avoidance of words of ill omen.

The Greek names of the side effects fascinated Antinio. I too was surprised by how well I could understand this modern medical terminology: nephrotoxicity, azotemia, hypotension, arrhythmias, hypoglycemia, hepatomegaly, hepatitis, leukopenia, thrombocytopenia, splenomegaly, hypocalcemia, cardiomyopathy, and neuralgia. Antinio would look up these names in medical textbooks and the etymologies in Greek dictionaries in the library and take down long notes in the diaries that he continued to keep.

More surprising were other words whose meanings had not changed since Antinous and I traveled from Mauretania to Aegyptus by sea—"nausea," literally, sickness from the sea; and "diarrhea," a word coined by Hippocrates himself. Antinio puzzled over what it meant for both humans and linguistics that these two words would be in continual, ongoing use for over two thousand years.

Then there were the plain, ordinary English words for side effects with no hidden meanings: upset stomach, heartburn, headache, light sleeping, loss of appetite, faint discoloration of fingernails and toenails, mood elevation, occasional tingling or transient numbness of the hands or feet, dizziness, confusion, and hallucinations. He loved the irony of adding hallucinations to the list of otherwise normal, everyday aches and pains of life. He wondered what harm hallucinations could possibly bring when he was already living a life with AIDS. *Would hallucinations make me believe that I was normal without my Greek infected body? Or perhaps they would make me dream again of a life without pain, without counting T cells, to believe that I would live. Were thoughts such as these hallucinations?*

At his sickest, when he felt the worst, I would appear, bringing him comfort that no mortal was ever able to provide. We would lie together and I would soothe him, whisper in his ear, and kiss his cheek. Antinio would lie astride my muscular body and let his fears and desires and inhibitions melt away. As he let himself go, he would look into my grey eyes while my phallus entered into and pulsated within his body until our two hearts beat together. Our sexual and spiritual joining reminded him of the love and acceptance he had experienced with Cloto and Laquesio. These momentary glimpses of respite from pain and suffering allowed him to imagine a future love might be waiting for him.

On the day of the hearing, Antinio had trouble calming his nerves. The Shriekers, this time in the voice of a wailing infant, revved up his fears. *Everything that you earned will be lost and you will be set adrift to sea away from this country and away from all countries. In the end you will wind up rotting in a Cuban prison until you die.*

Boreas ushered him into the hearing room. Antinio's boss, who volunteered to testify on his behalf, was already waiting for them. The judge was annoyed when he read the case documents to discover that the INS had not followed its own procedures. Rather than torture himself listening to their excuses, he asked a few questions of the INS attorneys and then immediately overturned the ruling and welcomed Antinio as a U.S. citizen. The hearing lasted less than an hour. After so many years of setbacks, doubts, and worries, Antinio did not react immediately. A broad smile crept across his face as Boreas, his boss, Theron, and his friends from the GLM hugged and congratulated Antinio.

"This is the happiest day of my life. I am finally a Cuban-American, *Cubano-Americano*! My travails are finally over. I finally belong somewhere." No one could kick him out of the country; he had the right to stay. "I am a citizen!" he exclaimed. "I can work and vote. I am finally home." Now he had less to hide.

Also in the room was the blond man, Pothos, that Antinio had met at the Conservatory almost a year before. After their brief tropical dalliance, they had exchanged phone numbers. Recently, Antinio found the slip of paper and out of the blue called him up. Pothos remembered and invited him over that evening. He opened the door, kissed Antinio, and led him to his bedroom while exchanging a few charged words of lust. After, they chatted and followed up with a second course of sex, breakfast in the morning, and then the ritual post-breakfast sex that happened with any successful date. The two men started seeing each other, working out together, going out to eat, and continuing to have sex. Some nights they would vary this with a movie or a play or a walk around the lake.

This romance provided routine for Antinio during an unstable time.

XXI

Babalú Ayé watched the progress of the disease. Whereas most of his viruses were quite simple and merely had to get beyond the body's defense systems, this group of retroviruses created a new behavior that scientists had never seen before, having developed a complex means for turning the human body against itself.

I have seen diseases come and go for the eons I have watched human civilization on earth. In previous plagues, bodies were quickly buried or burned to prevent further contagion. Some palliative care might have been given by families, but they knew well enough that if one person was dying, so would several more in the same household. Any doctors who looked into the disease did so quietly, trying not to draw any attention to their transgression of examining the body parts of corpses. The Venetians conceived the word "quarantine" from Latin words *quarantina giorni*, the forty days' time that ships from plague-stricken countries in the late 14th century had to moor their ships outside of Venice before they could enter.

But AIDS had taken a strange turn. People were not hiding behind shuttered doors. Gay men were demanding that they themselves be studied and given access to experimental treatments. Eleggua was in awe of the gay community, of activists who clamored for a multiplicity of treatment options and the sharing of results and information. "How noble that these men were willing to use their deaths to try to prevent others from sharing the same outcome."

But I felt helpless, not knowing how to guide or intercede in Antinio's life, a life punctuated by side effects. At first he refused to take any new drugs due to their possibile toxicity. But in a single year, 1990, he was on AZT, pentamidine, 3TC, Bactrim, Diflucan, and Biaxin. His T-cell counts continued to decline, and the disease became indistinguishable from the side effects. Indeed, his lethargy and tiredness were listed both as AIDS symptoms and side effects from the drugs. The Lamenters became especially active. *These medicines are killing you. It is not the disease but the medications that are causing your face to become so gaunt and the awful lesions in your mouth to grow.* The Siren, masquerading as Reason, also took up this plaint and planted it firmly in his head—he assumed every drug he took was likely to harm him.

Yet, he needed a cure to live. AZT helped slow the illness's progress, so instead of quickly running through the stages as Laquesio had done, Antinio experienced his changes in slow motion. He watched his T-cell count drop until it hit seven. Dr. Paean told Antinio that he was unlikely to see the end of the year. Was this bad bedside manner or the unforgettingness, truth? Odysseus never lacked for excitement in his epic tale. Whenever attention flagged, a new monster, enticer, or god would appear, throwing the hero in one direction or another. If things quieted down, Homer would dispose of years, cut to the chase, and start the story anew. With a disease that slowly destroyed one's immune system, the day-to-day drama was diminished. A heart attack or stroke by its name implied action—a quickening of pace, rushing to the hospital, preparations, scurrying around, the emergency room, surgical stations, clamps, scalpels, sutures, heart monitors beeping incessantly, machines that breathe and others that pump vital fluids and drugs. While the person with AIDS was likely have the same tubes and machinery eventually hooked up to him, the dramatic elements of any good tale and the ending with a heroic cure against all odds simply had not been written yet.

Antinio's oracle was the CD4+ cell count—today seven; a month later, twelve. These were magical numbers, and he divined the meaning of them. *How did the twelve feel different from the seven? It was 71.428571...% more.* Each time he did the math, Antinio wanted to follow that division out as far as possible as if extending his own life. With the numbers irrational, his spirits were buoyed. *If the numbers never end, this is a sign that I will continue as well,* he thought. If they were rational, he would count out the digits to determine his life expectancy. Whole numbers meant a short life; with each decimal place, some indeterminate additional time would be added to his life. He charted the rising and falling of the counts on a graph that, for all the minor ups and downs these days, hardly changed at all.

The miracle was that he continued to live. There existed a few cases of people who were infected with HIV and never became symptomatic. When discovered, scientists would poke, prod, and draw whatever fluids they could in search of the secret elixir, a Latin word for the material that alchemists in my day believed would change metals into gold; or, more relevant to our discussion, something that would cure disease and prolong life. Antinio, however, was not one of these people. He was affected and was suffering.

Watching him, I became worried about the complications my interventions may have caused in his life. In preventing that bullet from killing the young Antinio, did I create his ultimate demise in another form? Was he really born to suffer so, or by saving his life did I accidentally create new, even more difficult and hurtful forms of suffering for him? Unintended consequences two millennia ago caused my original grief. And now I wonder if I will only continue to cause grief going forward. Am I the Troubleseeker? To make matters worse, I could feel the limited powers granted me as a demigod waning as Yemayá foretold.

At each key point in his story, Odysseus would be advised directly by the gods or through some emissary. Antinio, not believing in gods, could not hear such information directly. His infrequent encounters with me he accepted as fever dreams, results of a vivid imagination when he was sick or overwrought. The sensations of love and protection that he felt he never directly connected to me since I did not exist for him in any shape or form. My love was one-sided. Reason would not allow Antinio to see gods even when they tried to show their faces to him. If we wanted him to understand something, we would guide him to stumble across what he had to learn next.

Such was the case about a week after Antinio was told he had less than a year to live. Distraught, he tried to hide away at home, pushing away Pothos, their Labrador named Dionysius (a breed of dog developed by the gods to bring energy, endless love, and prodigious amounts of drool to humans), and anyone who came to see him. The Lamenters sang dirges and chanted hymns of his coming death. Reason had little good to add, only that the facts were lining up to portend the end of his life. By then Antinio had recorded in his diary the deaths of seventy-three friends, number one on the list being Laquesio. All gay men at the time were learning of the ways of death, joining their antecedents who had been through the Holocaust, wars, or other genocides.

However much death he had experienced, it did not guarantee him a willingness or ability to grasp his own. He was forced to admit that death was real—certainly it was for the seventy-three and for the thousands more that died every year from this disease. But for him, death was something to fight back, push away, and run from.

On this morning, Antinio was alone in the house with Dionysius (who could never imagine such a thing as death). Living up to his nature, the dog kept planting his panting, smiling face wherever Antinio went in the house and pulling out his leash, hoping his owner would take the hint. Finally, he succumbed and took Dionysius, now jumping out of pure delight of the moment, out for a walk around the lake. The clear, cool day with the last of the red and gold leaves falling from the trees reminded Antinio that he had never figured out how to explain autumn to his mother in his letters. She lived in a place that had no seasons, where the weather changed from wetter to drier, windy to still; but it was always hot, always humid, and the plants in response were continually growing.

This strange land where he had lived now for a decade had this time when plants died off en masse, dropping their foliage while the temperature plunged lower with each passing day. How did one explain the feeling of living with this onslaught of death and dying all around? Everything that Antinio had taken for granted that first summer in Minnesota—the lushness of the grass, flowers, and trees—one day started to die off and disappear. He remembered being concerned, and his American friends had laughed and said it would all come back. And in the springtime, it all did.

But this cycle of birth, growth, death, and rebirth was only for plants, not for humans like Antinio or for his dog. It could not be called a cycle if it ended with death. *How do you live if you know you are dying? How do you live knowing that death is the end?* He walked and walked (and Dionysius bounded and bounded alongside), pondering these questions. Tired, he found a bench under a giant elm that had been growing by this lake for over a hundred years. It was not only losing its leaves, but also had holes drilled into its trunk with tubes running back to a large attached tank. At the same time gay men were dying, so were the elms of the Upper Midwest to Dutch elm disease. Another type of Babalú Ayé's little beings at work. This disease also had no cure, and this vain, experimental attempt to prevent the death of the urban forest seemed too familiar to men like Antinio who themselves were having drugs pumped into their bodies, hoping against hope that they would survive to see another season.

Antinio sat with Dionysius curled up at his feet. He sat and sat and sat, listening as Reason and the Lamenters continued their drone. He tried to put them aside, but they kept coming back to torment him and remind him of his impending death, of everything and everyone he was missing and who would miss him when he was gone; to remind him of his suffering and the suffering of others around him and of his inability to stop this. The torment was relentless. He felt immobilized under this tree, sitting all day and night as the voices attacked with everything they had. But he never moved and never gave up, drawing on strength that I had bequeathed.

Then, out of nowhere, a new set of voices was heard:

I am of the nature to sicken. I am not beyond sickness.

I am of the nature to die. I am not beyond dying.

All that is mine, beloved, and pleasing will become separated from me.

I am the owner of my actions. Whatever actions I shall do, for good or for ill, of those I will be the heir.

Reason pounced on these thoughts. *That's it! That makes sense. Yes, I am sick; yes, I will die; and yes, everything I have will become separated from me. I have already seen this. The moment I left Cuba, I started experiencing this. In fact, in that moment, I died upon the sea, literally throwing up the last remnants of the food that nourished me in Cuba, leaving behind my mother, my belongings, and my past life. And on that pier in Key West, I was reborn, practically naked in my shorts and T-shirt, and fed new foods listening to a new language in a new place, being struck by a bolt of lightning and understanding. So the cycles of life do pertain to me as a human. What I am experiencing is life itself. I do not have to be a slave to death and dying, waiting for my last gasp of air, looking pitiful as others surround my bedside. I have a journey to continue, and I accept that I do not know how long it will be. I am ready to continue on that journey.*

This time it was Antinio who bounded home, with Dionysius sleepily following him. Antinio never noticed the sign for the Zen Center of the Lakes behind where he had been sitting or the chanting monks reciting Buddha's five reflections. Yemayá, watching this scene with me, turned and said, "Did you notice that Antinio managed not to hear the first reflection, 'I am of the nature to age. I am not beyond aging'? This will cause his future troubles," she sighed. "He is so like Odysseus, the original Troubleseeker, never taking in the full message that the gods gave him."

But Antinio had purpose again. Life was to be lived until it was gone. And, before that, who knew how many times he might be reborn in the life he had?

XXII

His first U.S. passport arrived in the mail. Eleven years after he had left, Antinio was finally permitted to visit Cuba as a U.S. citizen, and as part of the first group of *escoria* allowed to do so. This was less about reuniting a long-lost people and more about the new state of affairs in Cuba.

Cuba was in the Special Period in 1991. Even Yemayá liked the sound of that when she first heard it. "I always guide young girls through that process of becoming a woman."

Elegguá laughed. "No, this is a special time for trying out new privileges and getting rid of the crazy, distasteful rules that bother everyone."

As wise as the *orishas* were, the moment that the Cuban public heard the evening news broadcasters announce the Special Period, they knew that they were in for trouble.

The Soviet Union had collapsed the year before and took the Cuban economy with it on the way out. The socialist economic miracle that El Comandante bragged about so much turned out to be entirely dependent on the largess of the Soviets who, in turn, only cared about bothering the *yanquis* ninety miles away. The Cuban people had always appreciated the friendship of the Soviets and the entire Eastern Bloc, their only contacts with the outer world. They brought petroleum; the smoky and noisy Lada cars, which broke down instantaneously but gave Cuban mechanic jobs for life; steel, iron, and cement; and curiously designed consumer products whose styles never changed in thirty years, all in strange shades of brown, yellow, and pale green.

The Special Period did change life in Cuba. A country that had never experienced widespread hunger discovered it. A country that relied on the automobile soon saw its people walking, bringing back horses and donkeys to big cities and enduring three-hour waits for so-called buses, the most famous of which were the "camels," flatbed trucks with improvised metal covers that could seat 300 people at a time. A country that had one of the best medical systems in the Western Hemisphere found their doctors being traded for oil from Angola or Venezuela and the hospitals and pharmacies being depleted of drugs, medical supplies, even aspirin.

The only thing the government could not take away was sex. In fact, they were so supportive of sex, they allowed it to be sold on the streets again. That the same revolutionary government that had swept to power in 1959 and closed the casinos, kicked out the mobsters, and shut down the prostitution rings would in the 1990s allow, even promote, prostitution would have been too great an irony if any of its citizens had any capacity for irony left. In the mid-sixties, the government had sent young city dwellers, Antinio and his cousin included, to the sugar fields to participate in the five-year-plan harvests. The unofficial new five-year plan was to let women and men sell their bodies to the influx of Western European tourists coming to see the island for the first time. These were times of desperation, and the streets around the Hotel Nacional and up to Coppelia were filled with men and women, young and old, soliciting anyone that looked like they had some money.

As part of the search for dollars to support the economy, the Cuban government began a rapprochement with the Marielitos. They permitted "study tours," a euphemism meaning that the Cubans lectured their visitors and forced them to tour sugar mills in which they had no interest in order to earn some free time to visit with their families and friends.

Antinio had just two days to see his mother, aunts and uncles, and the *jimaguas*. The boys were now twelve and were curious to know more about the father who had been sending them gifts once or twice a year. Family photos from this trip show two skinny, blond boys smiling with identical new blue-and-white-striped American-made shirts, Anticlea looking up at her son's face in adoration, the aunts and uncles also in new clothes, and Antinio in the middle with his arms outstretched trying to encompass the entire family in his embrace. His own face is smiling and shows his cheekbones, which were in fashion in Cuba with the food supplies shrinking, meat and eggs becoming a memory, and bread starting to taste a bit like it was made with sawdust instead of flour.

His time with the *jimaguas* was awkward. What could he do or say to make up for the missing years? Despite their curiosity, they were shy and not very talkative. The three of them walked from Parque Coppelia where they had ice cream to the University a few blocks away. As they walked up the broad stairway to the campus, Icario got up the courage to ask him why he had left.

"It was hard for me in Cuba in those days," he said. "I can't really explain it to you, but life was different, harder than even today. I had the chance to escape, and I did. I never fit in here. I wanted to have a life that was freer than it ever can be here."

Polideuces asked, "But why did you leave us here?" and Icario continued his brother's thought. "*Mamá* said it was because you were selfish and didn't care about us."

"*Mis hijos queridos*, please don't think of me that way. I could not take you with me. You both were just babies. The voyage was dangerous, and I could not risk your lives. When I left, I did not know if I would survive the trip and where I would be taken. The things I have seen and have lived through so far are not things that I ever want you to experience. I think about you all the time and what I have sacrificed to get away from this island.

"Life is never what you expect it will be... Oh, your mother is here to take you back home. I love you both and hope that I will be with you again soon." He reached to hug them but they squirmed away and ran into their mother's arms. With their heads lowered, they waved good-bye. His own face frozen in sadness, Antinio waved back as they left the plaza under their mother's watchful eyes.

Seeing the rest of his family and the family home was a comfort yet disconcerting. The familiarity only served to remind him that he lived in a different place and was dealing with different problems than anyone here. By outward appearances, time had stopped in Havana somewhere in the mid-sixties. The furniture, the pictures on the wall—including El Comandante, who was in everyone's home—the books, the television, the light fixtures, the bedding, and the rocking chairs on the veranda had barely changed. One not insignificant change was that the rocking chairs had chains around their legs. In the Special Period something special that had all but disappeared from Havana reappeared—petty theft and crime. Workers always stole from their workplace—that was considered a major unspoken benefit of any job—but it was extremely rare to violate the sanctity of a home until the Special Period ushered in such hunger and poverty, it created a demand for the old-fashioned skills of thievery.

Anticlea had been recently diagnosed with terminal colon cancer after suffering debilitating symptoms for months. Cuban doctors never told their patients such bad news. Instead, the doctor would share it with family members and leave it to them to decide what to say or what not to. So far, no one had said anything to her. Antinio wondered if this would be the last time he would see his mother.

Neither of them discussed their illnesses. Those were not conversations that could be had. Never told that she was dying, Anticlea did notice how tender her brother and in-laws had become toward her in these last months. For Antinio to tell any of them about AIDS would open issues too complicated and difficult to ever speak about with his family. He hid the pills he had to take every day. He had not been seen by his family for so long, they did not notice the wasting away that he catalogued daily.

Despite her condition, Anticlea insisted on making some of Antinio's favorite meals. With the dollars he brought, food magically became available in the special stores. She made up a shopping list, and the two of them went from store to store searching for the ingredients for *lechón asado, croquetas, yuca con ajo*, and *malanga*. Out of the house they could talk without the other family members listening.

"There are so many things I want you to see in the north. I hope next year you are feeling better and El Comandante will allow you to travel out of the country to see for yourself."

"*Ay, mijito*, I wish that were so. The one thing I have always wanted to see for myself is snow coming down. You have so much of that where you live. What is it like?"

"The first year I lived in Minnesota, I decided to go to a movie. It was late October, and I was with my friend Laquesio. It was a cold night, colder than anything that exists in Cuba, so cold that you can see your breath when you speak."

"*Ay, dios mio, mijito.* That sounds like something from Mount Olympus—clouds coming out of your mouth. How does that feel?"

"Strangely enough, it doesn't feel like anything really. I mean, at first I found it odd, but soon enough I got used to it. It is strange what you can get used to.

"After the movie finished and I came out of the theater, I discovered that the ground was white and wet, and snow was falling lazily from the sky. I was ecstatic. 'Snow!' I cried out. Other people looked at me like I was crazy. Of course it was snow. It may have been the first snowfall of the year, but they had seen tons of it already in their lives. But for me it was like magic. I opened my mouth and tried to capture snowflakes on my tongue, but it was harder than it looked. I twitched this way and that way and slipped on a patch of ice and went sprawling on the sidewalk. Oh, *mamá*, it was wondrous." He choked up knowing she would never have this experience.

"You must have so many friends there. But you have not found someone there to love you. That hurts me so. You must be so lonely. I can read that between the lines of your letters."

Antinio had watched many friends die, often painful deaths accompanied by dementia. What could he say about that to his mother? What could she possibly understand about AIDS? He thought these deaths would have prepared him to be with his mother in the time they had together, without thinking about the absence that would come too soon. That was impossible.

"I do get lonely, *mamá*. There are only three people in my life that I care about, *tu y los jimaguas*. I would sacrifice anything for you."

"My son, I don't need your sacrifice, there has been enough in this family and in this life here. So many things are missing that I used to enjoy when I was a child growing up in Old Havana—department stores full of goods, the Jewish tailor shop where I worked until I got married, the bakeries that sold special cakes for each of the holidays. They are all gone. So are the people that ran them and shopped there. So many have left, and over time the rest have died. I fear I am soon to go."

"You cannot die, *mamá*. I can't let you die. My love for you is a bond created even before my birth. One of the most difficult things for me was to shorten my name when I became an American citizen instead of keeping both your surname and father's. It was more American to have a single last name. I never understood why you married *papá*. When I was young and read the book you gave me... Do you remember which one?"

"You mean *The Golden Ages*? You loved that book. Whatever happened to it?"

"I still have it, *mamá*. When I was young, I convinced myself that you became pregnant from one of the Greek gods rather than from *papá*. I thought that was where your passion for the classics came from and why you instilled that in me. I became convinced that is why you gave me the book, to secretly tell me our family's true origins. Why did you marry him?"

She looked at Antinio. "I am not sure anymore why I did that either. My brother warned me against it, but I wasn't sure if I would ever find someone who would care for and love me. In a way, I never did. That is, except for you."

"Have you read the Georgian poet Tabidze? He wrote, 'Immortality cannot exist without love.' The *jimaguas* came from my sperm, and it is likely that I passed down to them another set of *jimaguas* genes that came from you, since you and *tio* were also *jimaguas*. No matter what happens to me, through them I will live on as you live on through me."

Immortality is a sneaky concept that bedevils all that desire it. I grasp this all too well. Antinio recognized that eternal life was not waiting for him; and certainly if life were to continue to be as difficult as it had been, he had no desire for immortality in the literal sense. He would not be deified like Antinous but hoped that, through the memories of his own children and their children in the next century, those who lived on would be telling his story. And that story, like all stories, would change with accidental "remodeling," by adding to parts that catch the attention and dropping those that make little sense in different times. He wanted to bequeath his sons this future all the more because he could not participate in their present life, being so far away and held apart by hostile governments that had more power than the *tiburones* in the channel separating the two lands.

"I want to bring the *jimaguas* and you to live with me in the United States. What do you think of that idea?"

"*Mi amor*, I am an old lady. I have so many family members here and so many friends. How long would my brittle bones last in your cold, slippery place? My body is not meant to travel so far like you. The *jimaguas* are getting older. Like all young people in Cuba, they would love to go to the U.S., but I don't think their mother will let them go so freely. But she understands what is best for them. I will talk to her about this."

"*Gracias, mamá*. When I get home, I will buy the tickets and make arrangements for them to enroll in school."

* * *

The two days in Havana went by fast. Antinio spent a bit of time with Fineo. "Antinio, my sister in Miami finally sent me a visa. My mother left last month, and I am due to go in a few months, after I close up the house here."

"That's fantastic! What will you do in the U.S.?"

"You know me, I can always divine something up," he joked. "Seriously, though, I have to get a job, and I don't have a clue for once what the future holds."

"Come to Minnesota then. I am sure I can get you a job. I have a lot of friends, and we can find something for you. And I know of many men who would love to meet a Cuban man. With your foresight, I think you will do well."

"I don't know if that will hold true in America, but I will take you up on your offer."

The two old friends kissed good-bye, pleased that they would see each other soon again.

*   *   *

Antinio also arranged to meet Cloto. Twenty-two years had passed. He had long ago married out of necessity and had a child. Antinio was struck by how sad Cloto looked. His features had aged quite a bit, even more so than Antinio's own gaunt, AIDS-afflicted face. He was quieter and more reflective. His eyes showed a slight fear, remaining cautious of the world he lived in. The two men who had not spoken since their last fearful phone call whispered as they talked. Both had learned years before that their talking was in itself a political act—two men honestly in love with each other were dangerous to the maintenance of the regime. So, they continued out of comfort and habit, making the few words they spoke of their ordinary lives seem that much more precious and reconnecting them to the days before Antinio was expelled from the University.

Antinio desperately wanted to talk about his life, his sufferings, and all that he had experienced since they were last together, but it would be all so foreign to Cloto, he could not find the words that his friend might understand. For once he did not want to tell a story but wanted to share what had happened to him and what he had become. Instead a different form of unforgettingness emerged as he simply looked into the eyes of the man who had restarted his life and held his hand, still feeling the electricity that flowed between them. Their connection remained as deep as ever, and the same desire and profundity that they once knew was rekindled. Wordlessly, in their remaining hour together they made up for the long absence.

The next morning, Antinio watched from his window seat as the plane circled up from the airport and flew over Havana. He could identify the hill near the family home with the abandoned mansions now taken over by squatters who had chopped up the rooms so that thirty could fit in makeshift apartments. He saw the Capitolio, where he used to wait for the dancers after their required meetings with government officials; and the Hotel Nacional, where he had sex on the rooftop many a time. The harbor was empty of cruise ships from East Germany, as that country no longer existed; or Poland, as they had no interest in solidarity any longer. It was hard to believe that these tiny ships had once been his sole connection to the outside world. As the plane crossed the open sea, he thought he could see the invisible trail of the *Andrea* carrying a group of seasick people to a new home. From above, the sea appeared calm and was a luminous blue green, as if painted on a vast canvas. He remembered the smells and the crowds and the prayers of the women. So did Yemayá and Elegguá, who were guiding his destiny back to his new home.

XXIII

A strange growth in Antinio's mouth had started as a minor irritant, something he could feel but not see. It could have been anything—accidentally biting his cheek, a scrape from chewing on a fish bone, grinding his teeth at night. He had become hyperalert to these changes in his body, cataloging each one in his diary. Some were fleeting, which could mean they were unimportant; equally as likely, it could mean that the initial outbreak was contained, but soon enough there would be a larger outbreak ten times worse. It was not paranoia; it was the reality that any symptom, any side effect, any attack was more likely to get worse than to improve. His body was losing the ability to heal itself.

One afternoon while he was waiting in his doctor's office, I made my way to the forest where I knew I could find Babalú Ayé. Ten years into the AIDS crisis, I had visited him many times. Each time the *orisha* was as contradictory as ever.

"I myself never know what the effects will be and have to wait like everyone to see what happens," Babalú Ayé defended himself when I had explained Antinio's latest symptom. "I have to admit that the HIV beings are shrewd and mutate often. They take advantage of any minor encroachment—a cold turns into full-blown pneumonia; a scratch on the skin develops into an oozing ulcer. Yemayá is always telling others how lazy I am and how my little beings are worthless. Each person she cares for has millions of my beings in their body. Who is the lazy one?

"There are mechanisms in the body to care for itself and to repel certain types of pathogens. I watch the parries and attacks of my microscopic beings as they are repulsed every millisecond without any human awareness, and certainly not with the intervention of human consciousness. If conscious decision making were required to defend their bodies, humans as a species never would have survived. People come to me when this automatic process falters. And in most cases, with time, some herbs or medicines, prayer, and of course proper devotion to me or other *orishas*, the body can be restored."

"This was true as well in my time," I responded. "First it was Apollo, and later his son Asclepius, who took on that role. I am beginning to understand their powers better by listening to you."

"What I find most amazing is that AIDS is creating a whole new realm of human consciousness," Babalú Ayé said. "Scientists can track how effective my beings are in each human body. This accuracy for a disease is a first. Before, humans only knew they had a virus. Now, with the testing, they know exactly how many of those viruses are in their body at any given time. With this information, humans are more aware of each different attack on their system. That helps them to better imagine their cells coming apart. They can feel the very lack of defenses and how their bodily functions or body parts are being assaulted. Yemayá tells me that this level of consciousness is too terrifying to humans, and by itself helped cause the dementia that so many early patients experienced. 'Human beings are not built to be so self-aware,' she keeps telling me. But that's not my concern."

With that he went back to gathering his herbs.

*   *   *

I knew that Antinio felt the disintegrations in his body. When he talked to his doctor about them, he was often dismissed as a complainer. "No," Antinio would say, "I am not complaining. I am telling you how I feel, what is happening to me. I am being objective about this." Once learned, this ability to feel these micro-changes stuck with him. If Yemayá was correct, and she most always was, this would not be a good thing for him.

His mouth felt worse and worse, and eventually the general soreness turned into lesions. He felt repulsed by his own mouth and hated to look into it. He could not kiss anyone for fear of what it might spread; and, frankly, no one, especially Pothos, was interested in that anymore. He finally received a diagnosis that satisfied Reason: he had human papillomavirus, yet another group of Babalú Ayé's beings that were surging out of control in his body. As a temporary fix, Antinio underwent laser surgery to remove the lesions. But without a functioning immune system, they soon came back, growing bigger and spreading faster. Antinio lost the ability to whistle.

As all this was happening, the *jimaguas* came to Minnesota. I thought this a testament to his desire to live life with acceptance of sickness, whereas the mother of all *orishas*, Yemayá, saw it as Antinio's incredible ego at work.

"He thinks he can bring two fourteen-year-old boys to a cold and freezing place to live with their gay father and his lover, neither of whom they are acquainted with." She shook her head and caused some brief snow flurries. "And do I have to mention that he has AIDS and is struggling to keep himself alive and functioning?"

No matter what she said, I saw this as an act of selfless, pure love, something I was never capable of myself. This made me love Antinio more. I was also beginning to see the flaws of the gods. "Yemayá," I said in a tone more thoughtful than admonishing, "you will never understand the human heart."

The blessing of these *jimaguas* did not appear to extend to Minnesota. They arrived on a blustery November afternoon with wind blowing drifting snow around the city streets. Antinio met them at the airport. They looked mistrustfully at both he and Pothos. From the start, Icario and Polideuces were lonely and nervous and missed their mother. They were glad to be out of Cuba, away from the privations of the Special Period, but they hardly knew Antinio and certainly did not know Pothos. Sustaining this new family would be challenging for the four of them.

Antinio did not tell his boys that he was ill. They saw their father as often clumsy and inept, not that his body was being attacked mercilessly. After they went to bed, Antinio cried himself to sleep from pain and worry. Pothos had entered this relationship purely out of sexual longing and desire; Antinio aroused in him a passion that he had never experienced before. He was not interested in being anyone's father. Life was difficult enough with a partner who was dying, in pain, and depressed. The *jimaguas* were too much. Pothos began to act out in jealousy, becoming like the long-lost third brother who instead of dying at childbirth finally emerged, outraged and bitter toward his brothers for leaving him behind.

A very long year went by. Even with his zest for life, Antinio had his limits. At work, he no longer felt the thrill of programming. The logic that had sustained him was not satisfying. For the first time, he could see the limitations of the perfect machine with its "yes" and "no" answers. He wanted something more complex, something that would answer life's questions. While he knew better than to try to get answers from machines, he wanted some explanation, some guidance, some direction.

He would talk to his coworkers about the *jimaguas* and whether to bring over their mother, as the boys had suggested. Everyone had an opinion. But Antinio did not want their answers. He was impatient and wanted the problem to be solved and removed from his life. He became resentful of the people who tried to help. For the first time, Antinio began to lose friends. Coworkers started complaining to each other about him. He was no longer the hero who battled all problems, met all challenges, and survived to laugh and brag. The fall was as swift as that of Icarus, everyone shaking their heads saying, "I told you so."

The *jimaguas* were not meant to live with Antinio; and Pothos and Antinio (and, sadly, Dionysius) were not meant to stay together either. In swift progression, Circe arrived from

Cuba on a humanitarian visa after Dr. Paean submitted a letter stating that his patient had no more than six months to live. She settled in Miami, and Antinio drove the boys down to live with her. He returned to Minnesota, his heart broken, to find that his lover had moved out and taken the dog with him. Antinio sold the house he could no longer afford and moved into an apartment.

He had an appointment with Dr. Paean and caught him up on recent events. "I am exhausted. I have no energy. I give up. I can't stand this life any longer. You know me well, Doctor. What can you do for me?"

"I suggest two things. The first is that you stop working and go on disability. For longer than any patient I know, you have kept on working."

"Work has always sustained me, especially during the hardest times. But now, just the thought of having to go to the office and face my colleagues seems impossible. If I'm going to die, I can't be around all these people who are so bright and cheerful."

"I'll write the necessary paperwork. Disability payments should be enough to support you and pay your bills. My second suggestion is to prescribe you some antidepressants. We've discussed this before, and you have always refused, but I think now you should try them."

"Another set of medicines and more side effects for me to worry about. Are you sure?"

"Antinio, trust me. I think it's what you need right now."

"I have one request. Remember you were going to prescribe some medications that would help Laquesio end his misery? I think I am at that place finally when I might need them too. Watching Laquesio suffer, I decided then and there that if I ever lost the ability to think logically and have my mind in good order, I would not be myself. If that happens, my life has effectively ended."

"I remember that conversation too well. Laquesio, my first patient to die, and by now I have seen too many others go the same way. I can write you a prescription for two drugs—a strong barbiturate and an antiemetic. They can be used when you cannot stand living any longer. Most of my late-stage AIDS patients have them. You'll decide when you are ready."

Despite the strength of my body and my earthly powers, the pain of my grief from the death of Antinous overwhelmed me completely in my last years. As the pain and sorrow grew ever more profound, I grew weaker and weaker, unable to control my own body, let alone my Empire. I decided to take control of the situation and order my right-hand man, Mastor, to kill me in my sleep. My wife had him arrested before he could complete what I had planned as my last command on earth. I suppose this was payback for my years of ignoring her. She watched my suffering and grinned, not trying to hide her true emotions from me. When I finally died at the age of sixty-two, I saw Antinous, rose out of bed, and with my last breath cried out, "My love, my love, wait for me." But he was gone.

Returning from the pharmacy, Antinio took the pills—one oblong and one round—from their containers and examined them closely. He was an expert in medications, and these looked no different from the thousands of others he had ingested over the past ten years. He took many pills in combination, one to prevent one thing and the next to overcome the side effects of the first. These would do the opposite. The combination would effectively shut his body down and allow him to die without significant pain. He tried to imagine what that might be like. *Will I feel death in the act of swallowing? Would the pain and suffering end before I die or only after it? And then what?* Antinio and his friends often joked that the cure for AIDS was death and that the pills they took were practice for that death. He did not have to practice anymore. He put the pills in a small urn on his dresser, and every few days would peek in to make sure they had not disappeared, their presence a comfort to him.

XXIV

A meeting of the gods was rarely called. They usually worked around each other, each with their own affairs to deal with. The accepted rule was noninterference. This meant that humans got bounced back and forth between the gods, between favor and disfavor. Occasionally, they got caught in the middle of the gods' own family issues.

In extreme cases, when they could not work with or around each other, the gods would gather to discuss a matter. After the Middle Passage debacle, Yemayá had assembled a meeting of all the *orishas*. As their mother, she had the power to do that; but she found it so draining, she vowed that she would never instigate another one.

This time it was Elegguá who summoned the *orishas*. Without their preferred mountaintop to meet on, they gathered on the upper deck of the IDS building in downtown Minneapolis. They were not all willing attendants. Changó, so annoyed at idea of being in the presence of the others, created a huge storm that made it difficult for the gods to get to the assemblage on time.

But it was Babalú Ayé who was the most upset. He knew that Yemayá was angry and was the real reason behind the meeting.

"We all are very aware the situation that brings us here today," Yemayá said.

Babalú Ayé interjected, "I don't have any idea why we have been summoned. Nothing is out of order in the universe as I see it."

"Your retrovirus has caused another epidemic," she bluntly answered. The virus was destroying the gays, the only humans that the gods all loved. "Gay humans were created to stop the fighting between men and women. By embodying qualities of both genders together, we developed a better strain of humans. Although human customs and awareness had not yet caught up, we all agreed long ago that gays would be revered as *jimaguas* as signs of good fortune and prosperity."

"Yemayá, I cannot intervene or stop any being from meeting its fate. Yes, I knew that the self-centeredness of these retroviruses would only call attention to themselves in the same way that Changó always puts himself at the center of attention." Babalú Ayé jumped aside as Changó threw a thunderbolt at him. (It missed and fell nosily down to the street below causing a minor explosion.) "I rest my case based on what you have just seen. If we cannot even control Changó and our gods, how can we control these beings?"

But AIDS was not exclusively a gay problem, Elegguá reminded the *orishas*, which was why both the humans and the gods had reached a crossroads.

The *orishas* worried that if left to their current devices, humans were on a path to destroy the earth and all of its beings, including themselves. Some of the gods argued for letting that course of events unfold. Once the humans reached a tipping point, the reasoning went, they would suffer a massive die-off, and in a few centuries equilibrium would be reestablished. They had seen that happen in Yorubaland over and over in all of the animal kingdoms.

Olokun, in charge of the ocean bottoms, argued, "These human beings are causing changes in my realm that if continued could destroy many more species than themselves." This same complaint was echoed by Ozain, *orisha* of the forests, and Aganju, god of the mountains.

Even Elegguá complained that it was almost impossible to be the trickster anymore because humans did not get his jokes, as greed and dishonesty were rampant everywhere. "While I am tempted to let the human race collapse, I recognize too much good would also be lost."

The door slammed open. As they all turned to look, Yemayá announced, "Due to the importance of the issue at hand, I invited another god to our convocation. You all remember Apollo. I beseeched him to share his wisdom with us."

By this time, Apollo was not his randy old self—with a recorded sixty-eight lovers, fifty-nine female and nine male—but a more thoughtful and caring god. He had agreed to attend the meeting because he wanted to atone for being so rash in throwing the plague and other diseases at the Greek troops when they attacked Troy.

"Thank you, Mother of All Beings, for inviting me here. I appreciate that you remember me. Babalú Ayé, I have been in awe of your work for centuries. I have had the same experience of being in charge of so many beings. In my pantheon, I too am in charge of sickness and healing."

Babalú Ayé nodded, pleased by the attention he was receiving from another notable.

Apollo proposed that the HIV beings be eliminated completely, but Babalú Ayé reminded the guest that the Santeria *orishas* did not have the same powers as Greek gods. "That is impossible," he said. "I have no control over my beings."

"Then, if Babalú Ayé is willing, I can assist him in leading the human scientists to some quicker understanding of these little beings, allowing the former to make more effective antidotes against the latter. We will give human bodies a chance to undo the cell remodeling that the retroviruses have done. Restore the balance. Do you agree that is possible, my friend?"

"This is within the powers of the gods, yes," Babalú Ayé replied. "But, Apollo, I am worried about the wholesale slaughter of my beings. I suggest a compromise for us to consider. You and I can lead the humans to an antidote only if my beings can more easily spread around the world. That way we can shift the epicenter away from their gay hosts towards other, non-gay humans as the main carriers."

The gods readily agreed. This might help both to reduce the world's human population growth and continue their project of creating more gay human beings who would take better care of the earth.

This decision by the gods led to the discovery of the first protease inhibitors to interfere with HIV production. These complex drugs had a relatively simple operation to perform: disrupt the action of the virus's protease enzyme. The first such drugs became available in rapid succession by late 1995. Most patients saw immediate improvements in their CD4+ counts and in the viral load tests showing how much virus was in the body. More to the point, most patients felt better and they stopped dying.

For Antinio, who continued to be plagued by mouth lesions, the drugs were not a panacea. He was put on a protease inhibitor in 1996 and suffered from the side effects asthenia, gastrointestinal and neurological disturbances including nausea, diarrhea, vomiting, anorexia, abdominal pain, taste perversion, and circumoral and peripheral paresthesias. Even in his distress and pain, Antinio found humor in the concept of taste perversion, though the metallic taste in his mouth was awful. His lesions kept growing, and he was severely depressed. For the third time, Antinio's doctor told him that he had less than six months to live.

Later that same year, he stopped taking this drug and was put on a protocol for the next protease inhibitor in the pipeline. In a change from procedures that ordinarily would take drug companies ten years or more to bring a drug to market, AIDS activists had convinced the Federal Drug Administration to allow for expanded access, in essence forcing drug companies to open up protocols to many more people to track their reactions before the drug was completely tested, approved, and put on the market. By participating in this protocol, Antinio gained access to the new drug before it came on the market. It likely saved his life. Within a few months, his CD4+ count shot up from the single digits, where it had stalled for five years, to over 300. His viral load became undetectable, meaning the test could not find traces of the virus in his blood.

It seemed like it happened overnight—gay communities around the country went from being death wards with plague-stricken individuals hobbling down the street to vibrant communities again, filled with people celebrating newfound life. Antinio, who had never fully stopped going to the gym, tested out his new energy. He would add an exercise and wait a week to see if he could sustain it; if so, he would increase the time exercising. After a few months, he could see some muscles gaining shape again.

He traveled to Washington, DC, in October 1996 for a public viewing of the AIDS Memorial Quilt. The project, begun in San Francisco almost ten years earlier, allowed a way for lovers and friends to remember their deceased at a time when public funerals were often rejected by family members because of stigma. Antinio had created a three-by-six-foot panel for Laquesio and had not seen it since submitting it to the Quilt project years before. Arriving on the Mall, the 38,000 panels of the Quilt spread to the horizon. Although it had rained the day before the Quilt was to be laid down, the sun came out and dried the soil so the exhibition could go on. Thousands of people were there on the grounds, but except for the steady drone coming from the podium of the reading of 70,000 names of people who had died thus far, the only sounds were hushed whispers and sobs.

It took him about forty minutes to make his way through the trail of panels, each in a square of eight, to the one he had made. On the left-hand side was his lover's beloved grand piano, his name in white against the black top. The black and white keys flew off the keyboard to become the tail of giant white dove on a red background. Antinio bent over to touch the panel, and tears began to flow. All he could think of was how he had survived and Laquesio had not. He remembered the difficulty of watching Laquesio suffer and his own inability to stop or even help mitigate it in any way. He had always felt remorse at not having been at Laquesio's bedside when he died. Antinio's tears flowed in a long torrent that he thought might never cease, staining the panel. Next to Laquesio's panel was one for Theron. In his bones, Antinio knew that he had survived the plague and that he was not about to die. He would be one of the living.

His visit to the Quilt that afternoon began a rebirth, opening his heart to the possibility of love again. Had he looked up at that moment, Antinio would have noticed another man, hardly two squares over, solemnly remembering the friends he had lost at the panel he had made for them. But they were not fated to meet that day. Neither was prepared for the other yet.

In his last day in Washington, Antinio found the solution to his mouth lesions. Through a contact in Belgium (people were resourceful about finding someone who knew something that might be useful in those days), he was able to secure an experimental medicine. Within six months, the lesions were gone.

With his newfound energy, Antinio decided to go back to the university to get a master's degree in linguistics, his first love. He visited the *jimaguas* in Miami and embarked on a trip to Europe. There he met Philippides in Berlin and thought the transformation of the city mirrored his own, from decrepit to energetic, wistful to forward-looking, from divided to whole. He registered to get his Stasi files, had a number of flings, and visited the Egyptian Museum in Charlottenburg. He had been waiting to go there for years as it was on the prohibited side of the Wall during his earlier visit. He strode through the museum to the third floor, where in the Egyptian section in a glass case sat a 3,300-year-old bust of an Egyptian queen. Despite her age, she was still regal, with brown skin and high cheekbones that appeared much softer than the limestone she was made from. Her eyes were half-shut, and one eye was missing. She had a long, delicate neck, and her head jutted forward, her blue crown with several golden bands rising up twice the height of her face.

Nefertiti beckoned him. In her eyes Antinio saw his mother staring back at him, smiling to see that her son was alive and well, blessing him for a reawakened life, for surviving, and for his continued love and remembrance of her. Yemayá, standing behind the bust, reached out, put her hand through Antinio's scar, and pulled out part of the accumulated grief and trauma that he had stored. He fell to the floor, and she realized she could do no more for him. He would have to carry the rest with him, but even relieving this partial burden would give Antinio strength for his next tests. He awoke with a crowd standing over him, and a guard helped him up. He looked up at Nefertiti and saw the last faint remains of a smile before it disappeared. He could go on.

XXV

Antinio was ready for a new life, and that opportunity came when he was offered a job as a computational linguist in San Diego. With a CD4+ count of 546 and a viral load undetectable, he moved from being afflicted with AIDS back to being simply HIV-positive. He joined the new world of people managing and living with, rather than dying from, this disease. The change felt as meaningful as, or perhaps even more so, his change from Cuban to Cuban-American. He was alive and well and functioning as a human.

Twenty years of Minnesota winters had been hard on his Cuban-born (not to mention HIV-positive) body. When he flew to San Diego for the job interview, the first thing he noticed was how his mind and body relaxed simply from the sound of Spanish being spoken on the streets. It was not the letter-dropping, rapid-fire Spanish of Cubans, but a slower, more sing-song, rural accent of the Mexican hinterlands. This world was more like the one in his head, bilingual and filled with the rhythms of salsa, merenge, and cumbia. Most appealing of all was the weather, neither as lethargic, hot, and humid as Cuba nor as frigid and energy-sapping as Minnesota. The houses with their red-tiled roofs, stucco walls, and terrazzo floors brought back happy memories of his family home and neighborhood filled with children playing and music wafting out the windows. Walking the streets of Hillcrest listening to the birds, feeling the warm air on his arms, and smelling the sweet aromas of grass, jasmine, and whatever else might be blooming at that moment, he felt enveloped and welcomed.

As much as he loved his friends in Minnesota, including Fineo who had settled in an apartment nearby, leaving the state allowed him to let go of a place that had so many memories of death. Antinio had by now been witness to the deaths of hundreds of men. Like their grandparents, gay men picked up the newspaper and turned to the death notices first to see who had died. The gay newspaper in Minneapolis often had pages of obituaries until that magical day in 1998 when, for the first time in fifteen years, there was not a single death reported. Even though the plague hit San Diego as hard as the Twin Cities, he did not know the gay men who had died here. Their deaths would not be in his memory.

He was ready to move back to the work world as well. Reason, which had been nurtured while Antinio was getting his master's degree, looked forward to having new problems to solve. He was entering a field that tied together his love of order with making sense of the innate disorder of words and language. He could easily spend hours reading, learning, and thinking about words and their components, of lexemes and morphemes. He was promised that his job would start with a focus on translation and over time would move into more interesting linguistic challenges.

His workplace was multinational and covered all the European languages including the Slavic, as well as Hebrew and Arabic. Antinio would hold court at lunch and ask people about different words in their native language, make comparisons, and search for joint roots. Often he would lead the group in singing in his throaty but sweet tenor. For birthdays and other special occasions, he would learn a song in the celebrant's home language. Oydis, a Greek woman who worked closely with him on a number of projects, became his best friend and colleague.

Antintio was often horny and was pleased to have his sex drive return as strong as ever. In a new city there were many new men, and while the Internet was beginning to take off as the new means of connecting for sex, Antinio preferred the old-fashioned ways of going out to a sex club or bathhouse.

While many of these had been closed down in the midst of the AIDS crisis, they were regaining popularity, albeit with a new awareness—with buckets of condoms in the hallways, they became places where safe sex could be practiced and monitored.

These bathhouses were a far cry from those in Rome during my days. Ours were monuments, temples devoted to earthly delights, with cool and hot communal tubs. Bathing was a process to be savored, not to be rushed. One started in a cool room and, over the hours, induced sweating by gradually moving from warm to hot ones. In the *caldarium*, which had tubs of hot water and steam heated by boilers, my men would anoint me with oil to clean and refresh my body. I had the walls and floors adorned with mosaics of Hermes, Dionysius, and Apollo. Along the way, one could eat, and there were booths selling perfume and reading rooms. My favorites even offered musical performances.

Originally, bathhouses contained separate rooms for males and females. By the time I took power, the fashion had changed and the baths had become co-ed. I immediately changed them back, as I wanted only the most perfect forms of masculinity around me as I bathed. Naked men cannot hide behind their wardrobes of silk and fine cotton. Only the natural musculature, the strength of the chest, arms, and legs, the thickness of the phallus, and the roundness of the *culus* could accurately show what a man had to offer. As much business as pleasure was conducted in the baths, and I wanted to negotiate with my most powerful attributes readily exposed.

Two months after arriving in San Diego, Antinio had yet to unpack half of his boxes. Rather than deal with it, he went to the Thermae, a single-story building near the rundown Warehouse District. The surrounding buildings with graffiti and peeling paint gave off an ambience of danger, a not undesirable characteristic for a bathhouse as it heightened the sense of furtiveness and anticipation. He was buzzed in to a small lobby where a half-naked man in a booth took his money and gave him a locker key, towel, condoms, and lube. Although it was Antinio's first time in this club, it was similar enough to others. The locker room was stark with dirty red carpet, fluorescent lighting, and metal lockers. He undressed quickly, put his clothes in the locker, and slipped the key's elastic band around his ankle.

In the wrong mood or at the wrong time (too early or too late), these places felt seedy; but with the right music in the background and enough good-looking men wearing their towels at exactly the right angle and tightness to accentuate their *culo* or *pinga*, bathhouses lived up to all expectations. Antinio reigned in places like this.

He stepped out of the locker room into the darkened hallway. Temporarily blinded while adjusting to the lack of light, his senses were on high alert as men closely brushed by him, stroking his body and reaching for his *pinga*. Aroused and adjusted to the dim light, he stalked the perimeter, first locating the steam room and sauna in which he could throw himself into an orgy, an unchanged Greek word for the secret rites of Bacchus remodeled appropriately enough in Latin to mean to press hard. He took in the smell of sweat, sex, and cum and sounds of grunts and moans interspersed with hissing of the jets that produced clouds of hazy steam that multiple bodies drifted in and out of. He continued into the labyrinth designed not to contain the Minotaur but instead to trap men in private corners or narrow passageways where bodies could become entangled in the dark. He stalked a man with a perky *culo*, and after a few turns Antinio caught up with him, encircling his arms about the man's smooth chest, and drew him in. His *pinga*, already at attention, fit neatly in the crack of the man's ass as Antinio nibbled on his ear. After a few minutes of play, the man suddenly became uncomfortable and moved away. Antinio was disappointed for a brief moment before he felt a hand grab him and a disembodied voice say, "Let's get a private room."

They made their way out of the maze and searched for a room. Along a long hallway with small rooms with makeshift beds, they passed by men sitting inside stroking their hard *pinga*s or rubbing their chests suggestively, and others with the doors shut from which emitted loud grunts and sounds of pleasure. Once they found an empty room, they jumped on each other, eager to get started.

This pattern repeated itself several times that evening. Although he was in his early fifties, and even with the ravages of AIDS, he looked many years younger. His defined chest and arms covered with black, curly hair, his intense, dark eyes and alluring smile turned all heads, except one. His name was Atropos. And, of course, that was the man Antinio relished.

Antinio had tried a few times to get this man's attention and then gave up, making do with others who barely rated a comment in the tally that he still kept in a diary. Later, while taking a shower, he noticed Atropos leaving the steam room. The mists swirling around when he opened the door made it appear as if he were elevated off the floor. What caught (more accurately, recaught, since he had stared at this intently much earlier) Antinio's eye was the man's physique—his round and muscular *culo*, strong legs, and long torso.

Atropos had short hair, green eyes, a brown trimmed beard, and a smile that hinted at more to be found out. Visiting from San Francisco, he had come to the Thermae after being stood up by a man he had been seeing in San Diego. Atropos was disappointed, having anticipated an enjoyable weekend before a scheduled work conference that started on Monday. Facing a weekend alone, he had some dinner, cleaned himself up, and made his way to the bathhouse, where it took him a while to let his feelings go and enjoy himself. He walked up to this stranger who eyed him from the shower and gave him a deep kiss that lasted for minutes. Once started, they could not stop. They both felt as if they had been waiting for each other for years. Yemayá, watching with pleasure, knew it was twenty years, seven months, and eight days since Antinio had landed in the U.S. and Changó had sent his thunderbolts across the country to Laquesio and Atropos.

Fate requires the arrangement of a million details and actions minute and grand; it cannot be rushed, nor can it be planned. It was no accident that brought them together that night—the accumulation of life events for them both prepared them for their meeting. It could have been anywhere, but nowhere else. It could have been anytime, but now was the time.

It was late in the evening, and both of them, although excited and titillated, were spent. They talked animatedly as Antinio walked Atropos to his car. In this short time, they had already discovered a friend in common who lived in San Francisco. With plans to meet in the morning, the two men parted at 2 a.m. with another long kiss. This is how Antinio met the last great love of his life.

XXVI

Neither of them noticed how easily they got together the next morning and stayed together for the whole weekend. Antinio came by as arranged to pick up Atropos at his hotel; instead, the two men remained in the hotel room for hours. They finally emerged, satisfied that they had done a thorough exploration of each other's bodies. Atropos loved the feel as his hand ran through the hair on Antinio's firm, muscular chest and noted the distinctive metallic taste of his skin. Antinio discovered the tangy, musty smell of his new lover's armpits. These are the small but key things that men notice when discovering each other.

Eventually, they made it outside the hotel, spending the late afternoon walking around San Diego. They bumped into each other as they walked, just for the joy of once more feeling each other's skin, the hair on the other's arms or legs, the feel of the other's muscles. Antinio grabbed Atropos's butt, excited by its firmness and fullness. Atropos would let his hand fall on Antinio's crotch when they were in a somewhat private place, feeling the elongated, hardening shape of his *pinga*, a word Atropos had learned earlier in the day. They flirted wildly throughout dinner in an open-air Mexican restaurant, causing the waiters to smile whenever they passed by. As gay men can be, the two were invisible to the straight tourists and locals but were magnets for any gay man within sight. Whether it was their pheromones, how they walked separately but somehow joined together, or their smiles and laughter, their travels in the city that day were preceded by reports of their whereabouts in the gay community.

Later that evening, they attended a concert of the local Gay Men's Chorus. They nestled together, Antinio's arm over Atropos's shoulder, heads leaning into each other, dicks alert. As I have watched the progress of men, the shapes and shifting of cultures across decades and locales, the evolution of the Greek choruses has intrigued me. In my day, choruses would arrive on stage to express the moral and spiritual ideas of a play, a dramatic device I often found tedious. Now, two thousand years later, a singing chorus of gay men could display their spirit and determination to be seen and heard—despite the pall of death in the community, they could survive as long as they had voices to sing. Antinio not so quietly sang along to several of the songs, both amusing and pleasing Atropos, and making him desire this man that much more.

After the concert, Antinio became serious. "I need to ask a question. This morning, you said that you don't allow anyone to fuck you on the first date," he said. "Are we still on the first date?"

Atropos laughed because he already knew Antinio well enough to anticipate this question. His answer led them to jump into the car and speed back to the hotel, where Antinio fulfilled his wish to understand the reaches and depths of the *culo* he had been studying all day. They stayed up very late that night, making up for the lost time.

Sunday passed much as the day before, with large doses of sex, some food, and walks about the city. Atropos checked in for his conference, being held at a venerable old hotel on the beach. He and Antinio strolled out onto the sand as the sun dropped into the ocean, splashing the sky with orange rays that slowly faded to blue and then black. They stayed huddled together with the lights of the city at their back. When they got up, they saw a full moon rising from the opposite direction. Yemayá's celestial body was the moon, and so this was no coincidence. If Antinio had checked the lunar calendar, he would have realized that he had initially connected with Cloto and Laquesio on the full moon as well. Atropos and Antinio's adoration of the full moon became their secret.

They started a pattern of visiting each other every two or three weeks, usually Friday night to Monday morning. A few weeks after their initial encounter, Antinio traveled up to San Francisco where Atropos owned a house in Bernal Heights high on a hill overlooking the Mission and downtown. Atropos brought him upstairs, and throughout this first night in this bed in this house, Antinio felt propelled and powered by the energy of the city he could see glowing outside the window.

He came to love this city as his second home, the steep hills with houses stacked against each other, holding themselves in place from the forces of gravity. And there were gay men everywhere, cruising, checking each other out on the streets, in the buses, in parks and coffeehouses. It was like his youth in Havana without the air of furtiveness.

Airports and planes became part of their life. Holidays and vacations gave them some longer time together, and almost every night between visits they would talk. They were independent and enjoyed their freedom to have other sex partners, pursue their careers, and follow their own interests. They enjoyed their time together and their time apart.

Sex was an important component in both of their lives. Antinio and Atropos each had too much sexual energy for any one person to fulfill, and they realized that early on. Antinio continued to record in his diary the men with whom he had sex, many of them regulars, what gay men call "fuck buddies." He did, however, mark those times with Atropos with stars or extra comments. Atropos kept no such diaries.

In this third love, Antinio finally became comfortable about being openly gay. The truth of being out and open as a gay man requires a willingness to be honest and vulnerable with everybody. Inner strength is required to deal with the inevitable negative reactions that will arise. Being out is simultaneously a tremendous liberation and burden.

Despite being the military and political leader of my Empire, I had to hide parts of my very being and to manage my image. After my love for Antinous became public, the word "lascivious," which combines playfulness and jollity with lewd and wanton, became attached to my name. While this was a common word thrown about in the Senate, there was always an edge to it when applied to me that hinted at the secretive and public censure.

As his relationship with Atropos matured, Antinio's strength and comfort in his identity increased. More people knew he was gay than did not. He introduced Atropos as his partner or lover and not as his friend. He told his work colleagues about joining and singing in the Gay Men's Chorus and running with the gay track club. He never had a direct conversation about being gay with his family in Cuba. That said, he assumed they knew, even though he acted as though they did not. Over time, Antinio let down his guard and learned to live with more and more unforgettingness.

XXVII

Words fascinated Antinio. He and his colleague Oydis would often talk about the dilemmas of being a translator. "How can you possibly translate from one language to another when the original meaning has changed so many times?" he asked one day. "The same words in sentences written in 1570 and 1975 could mean completely different things! In my lifetime, I have already witnessed how language in the gay community has changed. The 1970s and '80s were especially fertile times for word remodeling and changes of meaning."

A huge challenge for translators involved words that were once epithets being turned around into positive descriptors, he explained. "How do I convey the sense of 'queer,' for example, in Spanish? If the word is directly translated, it loses all the meaning it had in English if spoken by someone gay. And if spoken by someone who was not gay, I have to figure out if the term is being used positively or negatively or even being used to describe someone who is gay. I have to know the word, its meaning, the context, and the speaker in order to take an educated guess at translating."

"Even when you figure that out," Oydis responded, "the next problem is choosing the right word to use in the translated language. If 'queer' is being reclaimed in English, does it follow that *maricón* is being reclaimed in Spanish? Speaking of changes in meaning," she added, "*maricón* comes from the name Maria, Jesus' mother. I am sure that was a long, complicated trail in the making!"

"It is possible," Antinio reasoned, "but not likely that it would be reclaimed at the same time in both languages. To make things more complicated, *maricón* is probably closer to 'faggot' in its intensity, but it is a word that is used in some but not all Spanish-speaking countries."

Antinio loved these complications because they made language interesting and engaged Reason. "How do you translate a word that can have multiple meanings or multiple possible words used in different countries?" Translation issues aside, even in the same language, like Spanish, these issues came up a lot. "Cuban Spanish uses the word *coger* for many purposes, but generally it means to get, to have, or to carry. In Argentina, it means to fuck and nothing else. I forgot this when I traveled to Buenos Aires last year, and boy did I get in trouble for that."

Oydis laughed. She and Antinio were part of a team working on new ways to build a computer program to accurately translate languages. Machine translation had been the most suspect subject area of linguists. The desire had always been to devise some automatic means to go from one language to another, but the ability to make that happen was considered limited if not impossible.

"So, we know all the difficulties in translating words themselves, but the most challenging part of our task is figure out how to mechanize the seemingly easy way that humans can translate between languages," Oydis said. "Remember the Thanksgiving dinner last year at your house?" Atropos had flown down, and Antinio invited a bunch of other guests who spoke French, Spanish, English, and German. In what felt like a logic puzzle one might find on an exam, the German could also speak English, one of the French guests could speak English and Spanish, the other French man could only speak French, a cousin could speak Spanish and English, Atropos spoke Spanish and understood some French, another American guest only understood English, and Oydis spoke Greek, Spanish, and English. "Antinio, you were the only one who could communicate with everyone. I loved watching you jump back and forth in each of the four languages—you did skip Greek, of course, but I forgive you for that—translating from one to another while managing to keep the story going and the punch lines relatively contiguous so that everyone could share in the conversation. I don't know if you know the Biblical Pentecost story, where all of a sudden everyone simultaneously could understand all the different languages that were being spoken and little flames danced about their heads. That is what this was like," she said, "except that the conversation was much more salacious than spiritual."

Antinio smiled. "That evening was so much fun. I was on all evening. It seemed like I was a human machine translator, it was so automatic. If it was the Pentecost, I was the flame itself, a flame that with a bit of wine burned even brighter. It was a magical evening."

"The question in front of us," Oydis continued, "is, Can a machine even come close to replicating that experience? It would take understanding not only the words and grammar of the languages, but also the inflection of the words and the use of slang and idioms and how they are spoken, loudly or softly, with a smirk or a straight face, by a male or female; add to that gay or straight—all of the information that you, Antinio, needed to process and then mimic in a different language with the particular nuances in the vocal attributes to get the point across."

"Perfecting a spoken machine translator seems impossible—that perhaps will always be left to humans—but there remains the question of what can be done with written translation." Antinio went on, "The most important factors that affect language are words, the structure of the language, or morphology, and context. Breaking it down this way, the goal seems within reach. What we have identified so far in our work to make a multiple-language translator is the need for an intermediary to play the role I took on at that dinner.

"We have tried to develop language pairs," he said, "such as English to Spanish or English to French or French to Spanish, but this is so cumbersome and expensive. The software required to perform each of these separately would overwhelm all but the biggest computers we have available. We need to come up with an intermediary whereby one could choose any number of European languages and have translations done between them all using the same software."

This problem flummoxed the team. Using any of the existing languages as the intermediary caused too many problems, so instead they identified the pieces of language they were trying to parse and came up with a verb translator and a noun translator. None of these attempts got very far. After a few years of testing all sorts of possibilities, they were no closer to their goal than when they started.

The dilemma haunted Antinio. He knew he was close to finding an answer. He would lie in bed analyzing the etymology of words hoping to find a link between a word in Greek and its derivative in another language. One evening, his thoughts shifted from where words originated to how language originated. Later that night he dreamed that he was talking to Hermes who not only invented language, but gave humans speech. Looking directly at him, Hermes said, "I wish that I had made one language instead of many."

The next morning, Antinio realized that the answer might be right in front of him. He rushed in to work and sought out Oydis. "I think I found the solution to our problem. A universal language already exists that could function as the intermediary, and of all the linguists in the group, I am the only one proficient in it—Esperanto. As the perfect language, it contains no irregularities of word form, syntax, or grammar."

"Of course, that could be it!" she agreed. "It would be a simple solution if it works. Let's see how we can get started and then bring in the team."

That day marked the beginning of an exciting period of Antinio's life. For the next few years, his team worked on the Heuristic Esperanto-Regulated Multi-Emissary System (HERMES). Antinio became recognized in his field for their breakthroughs. He traveled to conferences around the U.S. and Europe speaking about the development of HERMES. He authored several papers and was in great demand as a speaker.

The number of Esperanto speakers almost doubled during this period as linguists tried to ride the wave.

Atropos often accompanied Antinio on his travels. They spent time in Spain learning Gallego (Galician), Catalá (Catalan), and Eivissenc (a version of Catalan spoken in Ibiza); and in France studying Alsatian, Oc (Occitan), Gallo, and Savoyard. Although I in my human life had bad-mouthed Latin as inelegant compared to Greek, following Antinio around, I could see how Latin had morphed in so many ways to create all of these related languages. Each of them had their own beauty that reflected the evolution of the language in an isolated setting.

In each case, Antinio needed mere days to pick up the outlines of the language and tie it back to the main branch of the language family. He would then start to understand the consonant changes and other variants that made the language unique. Atropos could follow this progression but did not have the ability to retain in his memory all of the words, the grammar, and the changes. He was engrossed by watching the wheels turn in Antinio's mind as he mastered the next language on their list. Antinio was happy and energized by the process of learning, and this expressed itself in his interest in the subject at hand, in meeting new people, in flirting, and, of course, inviting men back to his room for further discussion and adventures. Wherever they went, Antinio and Atropos left behind a trail of men with fond memories of nights soaked in sexual pleasure and fascinating conversation.

But the good times were not destined to last. When he arrived back in San Diego, a phone call came from his aunt in Cuba. Antinio's mother, Anticlea, was dead.

XXVIII

The loss of his mother reopened the wounds that seemed to have disappeared in the previous period of grace. Coming at another time of freeze in U.S.-Cuba relations, Antinio was not allowed to be with the family to prepare her body and stay up all night remembering, grieving, and celebrating her life as was custom. He felt alone despite the presence of Atropos.

Years before, under the dying elms in Minnesota, Antinio had missed hearing the first reflection of Buddha—*I am of the nature to age; I am not beyond aging.* As much as he wanted to remain young and vital, he had no power to stop the aging process. AIDS had not ravaged his body as badly as it had many other men, and his bimonthly shots of testosterone and daily gym workouts kept him fit. For a few years he had dyed his hair and beard to appear more youthful. The hair on his head, although thinning, remained mostly dark, as did all of his body hair. Still, his mother's death was another reminder of the inevitability of his own aging and death.

HERMES moved along slowly but surely. There were barriers to overcome, many of which were assisted by rapid advancements in the capacity of ordinary computers and the growth of the Internet. The team envisioned a day when their software could be used by individuals in their homes. What they could not see were the corporate changes that would destroy their project. Over a five-year period, the company was bought and sold three times. Antinio and his teammates would come to work to find a new name going up on the building, new letterhead being ordered. They would be ushered

237

into the conference room and informed of what subsidiary or sub-subsidiary of which new company they had become a part. Inevitably, these changes would be accompanied by reductions in staff and the hiring of new team members fresh out of college.

The technology world is one of young people, and Antinio was in his late fifties. In his new company, no one on the board of directors was over forty-two. Younger minds brought new ideas into the company; and they were less expensive and more willing to work ten-to-fifteen-hour days. For a long time, his fame protected Antinio from the culling of the team's older members until he one day found himself the oldest person in the company. He kept up with his energetic new colleagues, and they respected him for his vast breadth of linguistic expertise.

A severe blow came after the fourth corporate takeover. When Atropos called that evening, Antinio was heartbroken. "HERMES is being shut down," he said, "and Oydis was given a month's notice."

"How can that be possible? What is going on?"

"We just got bought up again, and they said that the new owners were interested in more profitable projects. On top of that, a thirty-three-year-old woman came in as manager to lead us into new areas. She has no expertise in linguistics. I just can't manage this..."

"But you are the one that invented HERMES and made your company so valuable that it was bought up over and over. Surely they recognize that."

"They don't seem to recognize anything anymore. Ever since I got my health back, I have thrown everything into my work." Indeed, Reason was satisfied, and Antinio's demons had been kept at bay. "I always wanted to achieve recognition and admiration for my work, work that I loved. That finally happened, and now the meaning of my life is being taken away."

"What does this new manager say about all of this?"

"The new project focuses on statistical analysis of words, the up-and-coming trend in machine translation. I can appreciate the mathematical algorithms, but something of the personal is lost in this approach. HERMES had some limitations, but they could be overcome. To work on this new project, I have to learn new computer languages the younger members of the team already are well versed in. I'll have to work even longer hours.

"They say my new boss is a micromanager. I have always been in charge of my own activities, and already she spoke to me today like I was a child in my first job. What does she understand about what we are doing? What will happen to me, Atropos? I feel like I am being killed off."

"*Bebito*, I think you are overreacting," Atropos said. "Let's see how it goes. And if it does not get better, you can look for another job. You have colleagues all over the world that respect you and would love to work with you. What is Oydis going to do next?"

"She's not sure yet," he sighed. "Let's see what happens tomorrow."

Antinio's work life went downhill. Half of his week was spent in filling out performance reports that served one purpose—to document that he was going nowhere on the project. His wisdom and insight, long traits his colleagues depended on him for, no longer appeared important. The voices returned, starting with the Lamenters. Although he thought they were long gone, they reemerged as strongly as in his younger years. And they had a new line of attack—he was getting old.

Surrounded by young coworkers who had very different lives from his own, he was reminded of the aging process daily. Yemayá, who had been following Antinio's progress in life from a distance as she was not needed much these days, stopped by one day on her way to Tijuana, a few miles away across the border. As we spoke of Antinio, she observed, "One of the biggest problems with gay men is, their fabulousness seems to depend on the illusion of not aging."

"That is an apt choice of works, Yemayá. My times would recognize the word *fabulosus* immediately, meaning rich in myths."

"I cannot think of any other group of beings, human or otherwise, who are so rich in myths that they believe they can resist aging like gay men do. When we invented them, we never thought they would turn out this way. And if this is a cultural norm, sadly Antinio appears to be even further in its grip than most."

"Antinous died at the age of nineteen and never once reflected on aging. What young person does? I helped freeze him in time with the sculpted images I created. I hope these memories, which I have implanted in Antinio as well, have not somehow influenced him in this matter."

"You are learning about what it means to be a demigod and the perils of love." On that enigmatic note, she disappeared.

Antinio's voices harped on his age and his inability to keep up with his younger colleagues. They obsessed over his boss and his difficulties in meeting her expectations. They pounced on the loss of HERMES and pinpointed Antinio as responsible for the failure to bring this valuable tool to mankind. And they pointed out every gray hair on his head and body each time he looked in the mirror and forced him to painfully pluck them out.

*   *   *

Two weeks later, Atropos flew down to San Diego for his regular visit. Antinio picked him up at the airport, but instead of their usual long, deep welcome kiss, he found Antinio worked up into a state that he had never before experienced. In addition to his constant worrying, Antinio had taken on a manic form of constant physical and psychological complaints that no one could possibly help. "I can't stand it any longer. I am too old for this work. Look at me—I am starting to look like an old man. On top of that I'm a failure."

"Antinio, how can you say that? You are as handsome and sexy as the day I met you."

"No, I'm not. I'm old, my body hurts, and no one wants me anymore. I am falling apart. I have aches and pains in my legs, and I think I sprained my shoulder today at the gym. I can't even lift anything. This means I can't do any upper-body strengthening, and soon I will lose all of my definition. You should just leave me now. I know you want someone younger."

"Antinio, I don't want anyone else. Why do you say things like this?"

"Just leave me now, you'll be happier. You're getting tired of me, I can tell. I'm always complaining. I'm getting old. You won't want to take care of me if I am sick. I know that."

"Are you even listening to me? I thought you were seeing your doctor today."

"I did. He could not find anything physically wrong with me. Just like when I knew I was HIV-positive long before my body manifested any symptoms, I sense that something else is coming on and that no one seems to be able to help me."

The weekend was off to a bad start.

"Is that psychotherapist you've started seeing helping you?" Atropos asked.

"It's waste of time, I can tell already. He can't do anything for me. All he did was give me a prescription for antidepressants. They're awful."

"Why do you say that?"

"I'm afraid of what antidepressants will do to me, especially my mind. Do you know that the very first side effect listed is suicidal ideation? I feel depressed enough and don't need the drugs driving me to have any worse thoughts. The next side effect is sexual dysfunction. For the first time, I hardly want to have sex with you and am afraid that I can't actually have an orgasm. It has been ten days since I felt like having sex. Is this being caused by the depression or the antidepressant? It's like when I first had HIV and one never knew if the disease or the drugs to fight it were more horrible."

He paused to gather his thoughts.

"*Bebito*, I am afraid that my mind is going. My fatigue, the loneliness, the focus on my past and present failures make me think that dementia might be encroaching. If it does, I want to be dead before it hits. I can imagine managing all forms of illness. I have done that already and survived everything that HIV could do to me. I'm a survivor when so many died. But I cannot imagine my mind turning any worse than it is right now. Reason and curiosity and discovery give my life meaning.

"I never told you this, but during the darkest days of the AIDS epidemic, my doctor in Minneapolis gave me pills that could kill me. I wish I never threw them away when I felt better."

Even with Atropos by his side, the Siren called strongly. Reason tried to keep her at bay, but Antinio had already lost the ability to distinguish between Reason and the Siren's mimicking of Reason. And so, as she called, he began to follow. Under the Siren's guidance, he had compiled a list of known ways to kill himself—cutting his wrist, drowning, suffocating, hanging, overdosing. He was a gentle man who eschewed all violence, so most of these held no appeal. He did not talk of this to Atropos.

Atropos convinced Antinio to seek help from a well-known acupuncturist. This doctor had significant experience with HIV-positive patients and was considered a skilled healer. He held Antinio's wrist and felt for the twelve pulses of Chinese medicine. He measured Antinio's heart rate and blood pressure, listened to his chest with a stethoscope, and examined his face and skin for signs relating to both Chinese and allopathic medicine.

The acupuncturist asked Antinio, "Is it okay for me to perform a treatment today? I am particularly concerned about an area in the mid-thorax."

"You mean you found something wrong? No other doctors seem to think I have any real problems. They think I am making it all up. Yes, please treat me."

As Antinio lay on the treatment table, the doctor applied needles to Antinio's arms, feet, and chest. After about fifteen minutes, he took them out.

"I detect a significant amount of trauma stored in your body," he told Antinio. "This is not unusual because when a person undergoes painful events, the part of the event that cannot be processed psychologically often remains somewhere in the body. For you, it appears to be around the stomach. I sensed something very deeply rooted was blocking the flow of *chi*, or life energy. I am confident that I can help you release this trauma. This first treatment was a step in that direction."

Antinio told the doctor a bit of his life story—the gunshot in the army, losing his lovers, being discriminated against in Cuba and then by the U.S. government, his struggle with AIDS. He left the office skeptical but relieved. "He's the first person that believes me and that has listened to me. I trust him and for the first time think I might gain some help. Already I feel better. Let's go home now. I want to check out that *culo* that I have been ignoring. I'm sorry I felt so bad and treated you so badly. I want to make up for it now."

Atropos stayed for another two days and, feeling that a crisis had been averted, returned to San Francisco.

Once by himself again, Antinio's voices seized on his spell of optimism to bring him down further, accusing him of being naive and stupid for thinking anyone could fix his problems when the fundamental problem was that he was bad and was being punished. *You caused your mother's death from a broken heart! You got AIDS by being a sick homosexual! You brought pain into the lives of the* jimaguas—*who, by the way, have never loved you and never will—and now you are causing pain to Atropos, the man who loves you more than anyone you have known, who has already stood by you longer than any two of your previous great loves put together.* The trauma that the doctor had opened days before, which Antinio had kept tightly wound, compressed around the bullet, started to circulate through his bloodstream. He could feel again the terror of the sugar mill incident, the shame of entering the university room where he was denounced, the interview in Camp McCoy. *Do you take it up the ass? Do you take it up the ass?* The released trauma fed his voices, which reached a fever pitch. The only consolation was the Siren who soothed him and told him there was a way out of his pain. Yes, he could avoid his fate of suffering, of being of the nature to suffer, if he followed the Siren.

After a sleepless night, he walked around the house preparing himself. He pulled out a large kitchen knife and tried to imagine cutting his wrist. Even with the voices screaming for him to do it, he could not pick the knife up off the table. He went upstairs and put a chair by the closet door and found a belt to put around his head, but he could not figure out how to hang himself. He opened the tap on the bathtub and went back down to the kitchen to find a bottle of rum he had bought for a party months earlier. He thought, *How strange that I could have been happy then, and so quickly all my happiness is gone.* He drank as much rum as he could, about a quarter of the bottle—he did not like alcohol—and went up to the bathroom and got in the tub. He tried to lie as flat as he could to make the water go over his face. When he tried to go underwater and open his mouth, he automatically sputtered and coughed and lifted his head up gasping for air. *This is not going to work.* His brain and voices put in overtime, each failure compounding his shame. *You are so ineffectual, you can't even kill yourself.* He went to his bedside and found the full bottle of sleeping pills the doctor had given him. After downing them, he crawled into bed and pulled a plastic bag tight over his head. He fell unconscious as his breathing slowed, his body overcome by the pills.

I was unable to prevent Antinio from taking the pills, though I was able to push away the Siren's voice in his mind and cried out with remorse rising from my heart, "You can't die." Pulling away the plastic bag, I kissed him over and over and opened his mouth to share my own breath with his. I sang to him of life and love and the Underworld not yet ready to accept him. I got under the covers and wrapped my body around his, hoping to keep him safe, protected, and alive. I caressed Antinio's long, limp *pinga*, stroking it gently, kissing it, and rolling it around my mouth with my tongue, imbuing it with life force until I felt it twinge. It soon became hard. I then maneuvered myself astride Antinio and allowed him to enter me. I felt the great length of his phallus go where no man's, even that of Antinous, had ever been before. I gave up the last inviolable taboo from my life as Emperor, riding it up and down, feeling the physical connection so different from the feelings I had of penetrating a man. Vulnerable, with our two bodies united, I experienced sensations emanating from my *culo*, and my own phallus became erect. I understood for once why my Antinous so craved my phallus. I did not want this experience to ever end. As soon as that thought came to mind, I felt a deep orgasm well up in me unlike any I'd felt before and exploded over Antinio's body. I rubbed the cum into Antinio's skin and on his lips. Antinio smiled, and I knew my lover—yes, I will use this word for the first time—my lover was safe.

I was left gasping for air, unable to control my breathing or beating heart. Yemayá appeared to me in a haze. "By this act of love you have kept Antinio alive, for now. Your sacrifice, like that of Antinous nineteen centuries ago, was pure and noble. You have closed the cycle that Antinous's death caused and released yourself from centuries of roaming the earth seeking atonement. In doing so, you virtually exhausted all of your energies and powers. The next time will be the end."

With those words, she faded away. For once, I was not concerned about my state of being and was grateful that Antinio would live on.

XXIX

That evening, Oydis called Atropos, catching him as he was driving home. "Have you talked to Antinio today? He didn't show up at work, and I have tried calling him several times."

"I tried once and he didn't answer, but I didn't think..."

"I'm pretty worried. He has been so depressed—at work he comes into my office and wants to talk for hours at a time about how bad he feels."

"We talked as usual last night," Atropos said. "He sounded very odd, then said, 'No matter what happens, I want you to know I love you.'"

Atropos was seized by fear. "Do you still have his house key? If not, there is one under the flower pot on the front step. Can you check on him? I shouldn't be, but for some reason I'm scared."

"Of course," Oydis answered. "I'll call you as soon as I get there."

The next half-hour was the longest in Atropos's life. He drove aimlessly trying not to imagine the unimaginable. He felt utterly helpless. Whatever had happened he knew he could not undo. He was too far away to help.

Oydis rushed to the house and let herself in, yelling out Antinio's name. She followed the trail of knives, chair, belt, and rum bottle to his bedroom. She gathered her courage and pushed open the door and found him in his bed, under the covers, breathing fitfully with a bag hanging loosely by his head, an empty medicine bottle on his night table. She shook Antinio. He was groggy but alive.

He began to wail realizing he had failed to die. He had thought that by following the Siren, he would peacefully fall asleep and stop living. He had a thundering headache, and his tongue felt thick. Paramedics carried him on a stretcher, and he felt shame for what he had failed to do. Strapped down in an ambulance zooming through darkened streets, he had no idea where he was being taken. *This must be a dream. I am dead and these are the attendants of the Underworld. Where is the River Styx? I can't believe I am dead but won't be able to see the Styx. And why do these attendants ask me questions that make no sense? Am I being judged already by Rhadamanthys? They are moving me somewhere. I want to scream, but I can't move my mouth. Something is blocking my mouth, and there are tubes coming out of my arms draining my blood. Oh, that bright light burns my eyes. And different attendants peer over me in this bright room dressed in green and speaking in Greek. What is my fate?*

He awoke the next day in a strange parallel world. Everything in his room at the County Hospital Psych Ward was made of stainless steel or tile and bolted down. Even the mirror was steel. He was dressed in blue pajamas made of a strange polyester fabric with a top that was open in the back and always felt cold. His socks were orange. The slippers were made of the same fabric as the pajamas. Even in his dazed state, Antinio thought the colors and sizes were wrong.

He slept for hours, unaware of being poked and prodded by nurses taking his vital signs. Finally he awoke and was surprised to find Atropos there holding his hand. Antinio started crying, and for ten minutes could not stop himself or look Atropos in the eye. "I was so scared that you were dead, and I could not stand the thought that you might have left me," were the first words Antinio understood. "I love you so much. How could you do this?"

Antinio could not respond and fell back to sleep.

On one side of the room, Yemayá and Babalú Ayé watched and consulted with each other.

Babalú Ayé spoke first. "My beings are in no way responsible for what is going on, so this is your responsibility."

Yemayá understood. "It is always my responsibility. Neither humans nor *orishas* seem to be able to take responsibility. It always comes back to me. I did my best to remove some of the trauma and pain in Antinio's body. In any case, it is not his fate to die yet. He has to go on with this messy complication."

Awakening more fully the next day, Antinio was hungry and ready to live again. Atropos was still at his side. Antinio was sorry for what he had done, partially sorry that it had failed, and partly pleased to be still alive. The voices in his mind were quieter, though chiding him for his failure, but the Siren no longer called to him. Reason was waking again. Antinio wolfed down the bland, indescribable meal and tried to get up. He was surprised to discover that he had trouble walking. The drugs were working their way out of his system, and it would take a bit longer for him to have full control over his body. When he looked into the odd metal mirror, he saw a distorted funhouse picture, confirming his mental image of himself. In the opposite corner was another bed, empty but with crumpled sheets. There was no privacy. Even the door to his room had to remain open.

Atropos told him, "The ward is isolated from all of the other floors in the hospital. There is a private elevator and a buzzer system to let visitors in through steel doors like a bank vault. We are completely separated from the rest of the building and the rest of the world. Once they let me in, I had to empty my pockets. I think it would have been easier to sneak by Cerberus guarding the Underworld than to get into this place."

Antinio felt dirty and smelly. The only thing clear to him was the love and concern that he saw in Atropos, in his eyes and his smile. Antinio determined not to do anything to hurt this wonderful man and vowed that he would make things right again.

One more time Yemayá shook her head. "I wish for once that humans would understand what it takes to carry out a vow. Raising their voice to the gods alone is never enough.

What are you willing to sacrifice for this vow to be carried out?"

The denizens of this isolated underworld of mixed sanity were varied. Antinio shared a big room in the ward with a quiet man who left daily for electro-convulsive therapy and came back dazed and unable to walk on his own. The man rarely talked and seemed at peace with having this procedure done, a procedure that to Antinio seemed like ancient barbaric torture. Several homeless men and women roamed the halls with a familiarity bred from so many return visits. They would be launched back onto the streets after ten days here, shouting at the demons who followed them around the city. When things got too rough, they would break a storefront window or harass someone near a cop in order to be transported back to the ward, where they received a bed and three meals a day plus someone who would talk to them daily. There was a young woman, Tityus, barely nineteen, with bandages on her back. She believed that vultures were pecking at her, trying to eat her liver. Even amidst his own hurt and confusion, he felt compassion for such a young person experiencing these horrible delusions, and he tried to befriend her. He differentiated himself by thinking he was not delusional and that the voices he heard were from his own mind and of his own making. Other inmates included Tantalus, a skinny man that was forever hungry but could not eat, and Sisyphus, who appeared in constant frustration at his inability to make any headway on complex tasks that only he could see.

There were countless others who reminded him of the Shades from Odysseus's descent to the Underworld. Disheveled in their ill-fitting, drab blue gowns and slippers, they shuffled around, never approaching Antinio, muttering their secret stories to themselves, pale ghosts of the vital humans they must have been at one time.

Finally there was Diotima, a woman in her fifties, a scientist whose worried husband and children would come for tense visits every day. Antinio and Diotima struck up a friendship and recognized each other as fellow explorers in this strange and isolated island. They talked for hours of life, of pain, and of trying to die. Their bond of understanding around the attempt at death, the difficult realization that it had failed, and the aftermath of life again was something that their families would never share. These intimate discussions more than anything else helped them both in their journeys toward recovery.

Antinio, Atropos, Diotima, and her family quickly learned that a psychiatric ward was no place for healing. It was an emergency stop for those who had tried to kill themselves or were about to. It kept people safe as there was no access to drugs, sharp objects, belts, or anything that could be tied up. The nurses and aides were there to feed the inmates, to make sure they did not do any harm to themselves, and to offer them a bit of human contact and hope. The staff doctor, Dr. Minos, was rarely seen and had no significant connection to any of the patients. His principal responsibilities were to determine the type and level of each person's medication and to sign the papers for commitment or release. While he had supreme powers (the nurses and aides were always telling Antinio they could not make any decisions and he had to wait and see the Doctor), he was the least involved of anyone connected to this disconnected world. He rarely encountered patients like Antinio and Diotima who had jobs, family support, and private insurance and was inclined to let them out as soon as the court-ordered ten days were up.

Antinio resented being in the hospital and argued with Atropos that he did not need to be there. "I made a stupid mistake," he tried to rationalize. "I should have known better, and I felt hopeless. I even felt you would abandon me. Don't judge me, help me. Help me get out of here."

"The law is clear, and you can't get out until the ten days are up," Atropos said. "How can I trust that you won't try to kill yourself again? You have never really said what you did was wrong, merely that it did not work. I love you with everything I have and would do anything for you, and you spurned that love. I frankly am at a loss for words."

"*Bebito*, please don't say that. I did not spurn your love. It was not me doing that, it was the illness. You can't blame me for what my illness makes me do. I do love you and I don't want to hurt you. That is why I want to leave right away."

"You've hurt me and scared me like no one ever has before. You have my heart and soul, and it's hard for me not to feel that my love is not good enough. I want to you to get better."

"But that will never happen here. I can barely see Dr. Minos, and when I do, he gives me no help and only asks about what pills I have tried or would like to try."

Atropos could see that there was no possible help that Antinio could receive here. He believed, as many others in the same situation do, that more attention and love could fix his lover. "I'll help you get out of here and take you to San Francisco as long as you agree to get professional help."

They both met with Dr. Minos, and Antinio turned on all his powers of charm. A few days later, he was released from the hospital, and after collecting some clothes and personal items, the two men boarded a plane for San Francisco, unsure of the future.

For the first time they lived together, day-by-day, side-by-side. Antinio attended a psychiatric day program, and while he belittled the activities, Reason started to be fed again and gained a foothold. Soon Antinio's interest in his own mental healing grew. He found hope in cognitive-based therapy that focused on recognizing his reality of circumstances and accepting them rather than dismissing or wishing them away. This helped to clear a path for Antinio that could be rationally analyzed. He was reminded of his revelation under the elm tree in Minnesota, and with this consciousness, he could crank back the destructive voices.

Once Reason returned, Antinio became restless and bored. His program was finished, and he felt in-between lives and places. He spent his time reading and going to doctor appointments. He would cruise men online and meet up with them while Atropos worked. His libido was intact, and he became quite popular in San Francisco. But even this failed to satisfy him.

Although Atropos and Antinio enjoyed this interlude, they agreed after four months together that Antinio should return home and go back to work. This episode had brought them closer, and they realized that they could count on each other in a way that Antinio had never felt before in a partner. He left with a renewed energy and grasp on life.

Antinio's workplace had undergone more changes while he was gone, making it a less than hospitable place to return to. Although he was protected by disability laws while he was out, once back on the job, he was subject to the renewed strict oversight of his manager. She made it clear that he had to perform to her standards immediately upon returning to work and to clear up the backlog that had accumulated in his absence. When Antinio inquired with HR about this, they rebuffed him, saying that if he wanted to work, he had to do so under his supervisor's conditions.

His team had changed, with even more recently graduated youngsters being paid half his salary. The project had shifted to a completely extraneous place, rendering all the previous work useless. The new boss created new initiatives and threw the old ones out as there was no credit to be gained from finishing an old project. While this was not unusual in the tech field, Antinio failed miserably to adapt to this way of working. His talent for natural languages was not needed, and his slow but methodical work style was antithetical to the new expectations. His weekly metrics dropped, and he never met the norm on the exquisite graphs brandished by his supervisor. His team members could see the writing on the wall and, as much as even the newest ones liked Antinio, they never became close.

As the pressure at work increased, so did the voices. Reason was of little help since the only reasonable solution would have been to leave, but this was not so easy. It was the middle of one of the cyclical crashes in the IT world, and there was nothing out there for him. After one interviewer asked him how someone of his age could be expected to learn the correct protocols (an illegal question, but job applicants had little recourse), he wiped his resume clean of dates except for this last position. Even this did not help. He went back to his therapist, who was alarmed by what he saw in Antinio and prescribed more medications. Every day he would drag himself to work and hide in his office.

Atropos counseled Antinio to go back on disability before he was fired. "I can't do that. You understand why. To be on disability is worse than death to me. What will I do on disability? Are you now against me? Why don't you trust me?" Antinio was defiant. He could hear the Siren once more. During that week he had several despairing phone calls with Atropos, each time scaring his lover as well as himself.

He took several days off from work and finally, after consulting with his therapist, filed for disability. In the game of corporate chess, he had scored a mate. The company had not yet built up its case for termination, and the disability trumped everything. He had the doctors file all the necessary documents. Antinio felt sick, and his body pains returned as before. He spiraled downward fast and left town for an extended visit to San Francisco.

Within a week of being there, the Siren called more soothingly than ever before. Antinio had accumulated several bottles of strong antidepressants and sleeping pills, and the Siren assured him that this would be enough. He filled up the bathtub, downed the bottles of pills, and climbed into the tub hoping to drown himself.

It was an old tub with a leaky drain, so by the time Antinio's head dropped down and he lay in a self-induced coma, the water was almost gone. This did not occur by happenstance. As I could do nothing myself, I summoned Yemayá, the goddess of all waters, and asked her to intercede. Once again, this was not Antinio's time to die.

That evening, Atropos returned home calling out Antinio's name. With no answer, he assumed he was at the gym and went to their room. Only when he opened the bathroom door did Atropos find him in the tub. His first reaction was anger,

anger and betrayal. The ambulance came quickly and hauled Antinio off to the hospital, where he lay in a coma for days in the intensive care unit. One of the medications he had used could have caused severe and lasting damage to Antinio's internal organs, Atropos learned, and most suicide attempts with it are successful. The same body that had fought off the HIV beings for so many years protected him once more. Antinio survived. But for how long? I sensed that I could not intervene any longer. How many times would the *orishas* save his life?

XXX

"Most people who try to kill themselves twice will try it three or four or five times until they actually die," a psychotherapist told Atropos. "Statistically, this is what you have before you." Atropos was shaken to the core by this latest event. When he found Antinio, he was frightened that he had lost the person who complemented his life as no other had ever done. He wanted to believe that Antinio was the ultimate survivor and that they would be telling this story together in twenty years, about how he had almost died multiple times, just like when he had AIDS. Atropos genuinely wanted to believe this story, but knew he could not. He had been watching Antinio go downhill and had no confidence in him anymore. He also recognized that he was angry and deeply wounded. He had done everything for Antinio. His suicide attempts were a slap in the face, telling Atropos his love was worthless.

"Humans have such a hard time not taking things personally," Elegguá said to me when he reached the hilly crossroads where Antinio and Atropos lived. "They always think everything is about them. They think disease is about them, not the beings in their bodies. One person gets ill and another looks at the situation not from the sick person's vantage point, but from their own and gets angry. They each believe that the world is there for their own purposes and that all others, especially their loved ones, are supporting actors. Fate is simple—growing old, sickness, and death are the givens of life. How one lives between these givens is what makes a human life interesting or not. The freedom humans have is this very choice, how they choose to live knowing that death is fated and cannot be changed."

Could Antinio and Atropos live within the shadow of death? Antinio came out of this hospital stay weaker than the last time, and his recovery was slower. Without fulfilling intellectual activity to look forward to, Reason had a harder time tamping down the voices that kept telling Antinio that his end was near. He felt hopeless until he found his own plan. He started to accept that he had a mental illness, a disease that was as potentially debilitating and deadly as AIDS. With this view, he could figure out what to do about it. This was a project that Reason could grab ahold of, and Antinio channeled all of his energy toward trying to figure out what was going on. He tried to answer the question, *Why me? Is the cause genetic? Did I get this from my mother? Is it from AIDS or the drugs I take to fight the disease? Is it from the antidepressant and anti-anxiety medications themselves?*

He read all he could and took some classes. He reinforced himself with what he learned from cognitive behavioral therapy. Each of these steps made him feel better. And like before, he eventually got to the point of wanting to go back to his home. He was afraid to tell Atropos, assuming that he would be upset with the idea of his leaving again.

Atropos had come to the conclusion that he could not live with Antinio at this point. He accepted that his love could not make Antinio well. He did not have to withdraw his love, but he still was hurting himself and felt the need for a break. When they finally talked, each found relief in the other's support of the idea of Antinio moving back to San Diego. Two days later, Antinio flew to San Diego and tried to pick up the pieces of his life.

For the longest time in the ten years they had known each other, Antinio and Atropos did not talk daily. Each needed to readjust to this new world where death was accepted. Atropos went on a business trip to Europe and met a friend in southern France afterwards for a vacation. It pained Antinio deeply that his lover was traveling with another man. He imagined them having sex—no, worse, he imagined them making love on the beach at Cannes or in Provence. He called Atropos, but when he did, he would not find the right words to express his deepest feelings, and Atropos would become uncharacteristically angry and yell at him. Despite this, Antinio's voices remained quiet. His grief precluded them.

About a month after Atropos returned from his travels, he agreed to go to San Diego for a weekend visit. They had not seen each other for three months. Atropos had already decided that if it became too painful to be there, he would take an earlier flight home. Each moment Antinio and Atropos were together, they were tested. Could they get along again? Could they develop a different rhythm in their lives together that accepted the proximity of probable death? Could they love each other with this awareness? And, most importantly, did they want to be together? They were both surprised when they decided the answer to all of these questions was yes.

A few weeks later, Atropos flew back down for a multilingual, multicultural Thanksgiving dinner that had by now become a tradition for the couple. Oydis joined them as did several other friends. This was one the best times in their lives. Soon after, the two men decided they would live together, and Antinio put his house on the market.

They went together to Cuba for two weeks. Being with his remaining aunts and uncles and cousins gave even more life back to Antinio. He played the prodigal son, returning with gifts for everyone and money to buy the ingredients for a big dinner that they only had when he was there. Antinio felt great love and acceptance.

Avis called Atropos into her darkened bedroom, where she took her afternoon nap during the hottest hours of the day. She was strong woman with a quiet personality, always listening to the conversations around her. Despite her introspection, she was very loving and always had a smile for Atropos. She asked, "Do you love Antinio?"

He replied, "Yes, I do, very much."

"Good. I want you to take care of him. You are the only one he has in that world, and he needs you."

Atropos pledged that he would do this, and she leaned forward for him to kiss her cheek and then waved him out of the room.

As always, Antinio's time in Cuba appeared to fill his soul. Each block of the city was infused with memories, many of which he described to Atropos. "The fifth-floor apartment on the corner, the one with the balcony, is where I was called up by an older man who begged me to fuck him, a first for me. I received this scar on my leg when I jumped over that wall after a man's wife came home earlier than expected and caught me with her husband. And in this park, let's see...yes, under this very tree, Clotho and I had many a rendezvous."

The sounds of the street, the sweet smells, the languor of the late afternoons, the interactions with the remaining family members, all rendered in the language he was born with, in the language that was forever the starting point when he dreamed, filled him in a way that his life in the U.S. never could. Whenever he used the word "home," whether in English, Esperanto, or German, this is where his mind took him. Anywhere else was away from home.

The house in San Diego sold quickly, and in a few short months Antinio settled into San Francisco. He kept only his clothes, books, diaries and notes, and music. After eleven years of commuting up and down the state, they were together. They made the most of the time that they had, and for the first several months it looked like everything would be fine.

Antinio started a part-time job as a substitute teacher in a bilingual elementary school. He loved being around children, and even though they tried to ride roughshod over him, he charmed them like he charmed everyone. He pretended that he had a second chance with the *jimaguas* and gave the children every attention he wished he had been able to give his own sons. He sang songs in English and Spanish including his favorite about the mosquito that ate a whale for breakfast. He would dance in front of the classroom to illustrate an idea. He was able to memorize each child's name within the first hour of class, which made each of them feel like he knew them forever. Each day he taught, he would come home with valentines and love notes from the boys and girls testifying how wonderful a teacher he was.

That summer he and Atropos participated in the Gay Games, which were held in Cologne, Germany. Antinio trained with a local track team and won medals in three events: bronze for discus, silver for javelin, and a gold medal for the relay race. In the race, Antinio felt a tearing in his foot—ironically enough, his Achilles tendon—as he passed the baton. With my powers faded, I could only watch.

Achilles died quickly after Paris shot him in the heel; for Antinio, this process took another year. An injury to a tendon normally takes up to a year to heal, and the doctors he consulted saw nothing unusual. Antinio, on the other hand, was anxious that his tendon was healing too slowly. He insisted on exercising his leg instead of resting it. Since beginning his gym routine in the family garage, he had filled dozens of notebooks, which sat on a shelf in chronological order. Each contained the prologue of the gods' names he first wrote fifty years before followed by the date and number of repetitions of each exercise he had ever performed.

To Antinio, the recording of each exercise in his diary was an act of writing in the book of life. Each exercise made the case for life, and each repetition increased it. As long as the numbers stayed even or increased, he would be fine. A decrease for any reason was cause for worry. Skipping a day was like skipping a heartbeat. Skip too many and there would be nothing left.

So, despite his doctor's orders, Antinio continued to use the elliptical machine or stationary bicycle. Unable to balance well with his injury, he had to reduce weight for his chest and arm workout. Each time this happened, he would complain to Atropos that something deeper was wrong, he knew it. New pains started in his lower back, and x-rays showed spinal damage. Now the pain was constant, and no amount of pain reliever fully took it away. He explored a number of alternatives, but was impatient if any one of them did not show immediate relief.

His constant pain was apparent to all, as Antinio complained to everyone he knew. He could not stop talking about it. He grew anxious and depressed. Each doctor he visited prescribed something different—one prescription for the pain, another for the anxiety, and a third for the depression. It was clear to him and to Atropos that these symptoms were all related, but it was difficult to find anyone Antinio trusted that could see the relationship. What no one knew, except Antinio himself, was how deep this pain really was for him.

He was in his final battle for life. He understood that and could not understand why no one else saw it, especially Atropos. Antinio felt more isolated than ever. How could the one person in his life who had been with him longer than anyone but his mother not comprehend the depth of his pain? It had started with his heel, then it went to his spine, and now it was within his very soul. He could feel a gaping chasm within his chest open up, and inside there was nothing else but blackness and horror. He could feel the bullet in him rotting out the membranes of his stomach wall. This was as real as anything he felt in life.

The memories of nearly dying twenty years before, the lesions that grew in his mouth and spread without restraint, the constant fear of dementia, the metallic taste in his mouth from the medicine, the night sweats, the lack of energy, the horror of watching as Laquesio was reduced to nothing in a year's time—these things Antinio relived over and over. His abandonment of his mother, the pain and suffering his leaving caused, her depression and cancer haunted him more and more. His voices reminded him of all this and more—the loss of his first love, Cloto, and the shame he lived through with his university mates, teachers, and then his family about his basic desires, only to end up coming to the U.S. to get AIDS. The secrets he held from his mother and the *jimaguas*, from Laquesio and even Atropos, these secrets that he could never talk about because of the shame and rottenness at his core, rottenness eating away at his very body. He believed that nobody ever understood him after his mother.

The worst was that no one's love—neither his mother's nor that of Cloto, Laquesio, or Atropos—could save his life. Yet, he wanted to believe this was possible. He wanted to believe that his love for them could save his own life. He needed to believe that he had not wasted his time on this earth. He was a survivor, yet he was not sure how to survive any longer. His time was up, and his final fate was posted. He did not deserve to live any longer.

I could do nothing for him. By now I had even lost the ability to enter into his dreams. My own heart ached as badly as his did.

This time he made concrete plans. The Internet, once you dug deep enough, was full of hidden places that contained any information you wanted. There are sites describing all the means to kill oneself, doses of medications, the way to cut an artery that will not clot over, how to load a gun and where to shoot, and how to hang oneself. Antinio felt good about doing this research, engaging what he thought was Reason. He did not realize that the voice accompanying him was once more the Siren in her disguise.

The Siren led him through his last week of life convincing him he was returning home. All of his actions were with a single-mindedness not only to come home, but to make amends, and to assure after his long journey things were right.

He called the *jimaguas* individually. At first they did not believe that this was their father. "I love you and have always loved you, do you know that?" he asked. "I am sorry that I left you when you were young and you had to grow up with a missing father, not sure if I was dead or alive. I wish I never put you through this, but now things have changed. No matter what happens, call my name and I will be beside you."

In response, they both called him *papi* and told him how they loved him and missed him, words they had also never used before.

He also talked with their mother and distant cousins and thanked them for what they had given him in life. To Fineo, Boreas, and Oydis, he joked and made them relish the time together and thoroughly convinced them that he was better than ever.

As for Atropos, there was nothing he really needed to clear up with him. They had shared their lives together despite the distance, and together they were living with the consciousness of death. There was nothing more that needed to be said or that could be said. The only thing remaining was to plan how he would die, and that could not be talked about. He had tried many times, but Atropos would not be lured into helping him die and would not accept any role in his dying.

As Antinio finished the chores of life and the Siren completely took over Reason, he started to regress to his time in Cuba, where his soul had always remained. In his last days, Antinio's command of English started to slip. He could not remember words, and he even made grammatical mistakes. He would speak in Spanish to Atropos when he thought he was speaking in English. His brain was slowing down, and he felt like he was going back home to an earlier time when he was surrounded by his large family and the familiar rhythms of his first language around him.

On his last morning on earth, Antinio got up with Atropos, wanting to be with him but unable to talk, to tell him that he would never see him again, unable to tell him good-bye forever. He ate breakfast and looked at Atropos, trying to burn an impression in his mind of the last person he would see alive, the last person who cared and loved him, the person he was hurting the most by this illness, the last person who could not help him in this life. He could see that Atropos was scared to leave him, that he did not trust Antinio to remain alive. Antinio knew that his death would cause his lover greater pain than he ever had felt before or would feel again, but he could not stop himself.

When Atropos came over to him for the last time and hugged him, kissed him, and told him, "I love you," Antinio wanted to shout out, "Don't leave! Don't leave me!" but he could not. Instead, he said, "I love you more than I ever have and ever will," and started to cry. Quickly he pulled back and wiped away his tears so Atropos would leave. When he shut the door behind Atropos and did not run out after him, Antinio knew that this was the end and he would not fail this time.

He called Diotima—they had stayed in touch since leaving the hospital—and told her everything he could. At first she was quiet. Then she said, "You alone have to make a choice, and that choice is to live or to die. I cannot do that for you. I will not tell you to live or to die. You have the strength and are clear in your soul about what to do."

He hung up the phone. Knowing my time was about to end, I stood by to accompany him in his last moments. He pulled a worn book off the shelf. It naturally opened to the story he had read thousands of times over, his story, the story of Antinous and his sacrifice. He remembered back to the time his mother gave him the book and heard her voice once again. Methodically, led by the Siren, he followed his plans. His head was bursting, but the Siren rose above all sounds and led him to his death.

A few hours later Atropos entered the house and was alarmed by its stillness. He glanced about the main floor and, seeing nothing out of order, walked up the stairs, his heart beating loudly, not wanting to see anything. When he found Antinio collapsed on the floor with a noose around his neck, Atropos screamed and screamed until all of the gods and goddesses of all realms heard his cry of pain. They were all there with him and could not stop his outpouring of grief—they never can stop the outpouring of true grief. With Yemayá in charge of all waters, his tears flowed and flowed and flowed.

EPILOGUE

The priest walked into the ceremonial hall in his long black robes while Atropos and the *jimaguas* stood by the altar, where a picture of Antinio had been placed among the flowers. As the priest sprinkled incense on the hot coals, a trail of smoke lifted and curled in the still air, rising to the ceiling, through the roof, and upward into the sky.

For Antinio, his first voyage was complete, his life fully lived out. There was no more to do. He had fulfilled Calypso's oracle and had met all three Fates that she had ordained, all of the loves on his life's journey. His glasses are sitting on his dresser at the house in San Francisco. The picture of him and his mother still looks out over the room where he last lived.

A few weeks later, Atropos drove down the coast about halfway between San Francisco and San Diego to a special place that he and Antinio had enjoyed together in Big Sur. He removed the urn with Antinio's ashes from the car and walked uphill for twenty minutes into the woods and dug a hole a foot deep. He opened the urn and took out a twisted and melted piece of metal. Here he buried the bullet that had festered in Antinio's body for a half-century.

With the bullet finally separated and forever removed from Antinio's remains, Atropos walked back downhill to a small stream, where he tipped the mouth of the urn toward the water. The ashes fell lazily into the current. He watched mesmerized as they swirled in eddies and started their own journey. He followed them as far as he could as they traveled slowly amongst the rocks and sandbars before picking up speed as the stream ran deeper.

He ran ahead as fast as he could to the waterfall downstream that emptied directly into the Pacific Ocean. As he watched the gushing water tumbling to the ocean far below, Atropos was sure he saw an image in the swirling mists. Yemayá, who was watching this scene, smiled. Honoring a love, the strength of which she and the other gods had rarely seen, she combined my energy and memories to the last of Antinio's dissolving ashes so our stories would be eternally intertwined as one, truly as our Fates were meant to be.

ACKNOWLEDGMENTS

This novel might never have occurred if Michael Flotho had not pushed me on a rainy night in Berlin in 2012 to chronicle the stories of my late partner, René Valdés. He was familiar with René's real-life tales and insisted that I was the only one who knew them all. A short month later, Dave Robb, my dear friend and eventual copyeditor, who manages to introduce me to life-changing events with some magical ease, told me he was doing NaNoWriMo (short for National Novel Writing Month), an online challenge to write a 50,000-word novel in a month. Intrigued, I sat down assuming I would use the time to write a biography instead. Before I even finished enrolling myself in NaNoWriMo, I remembered René telling me once that even he could not write his own memoir, and it would have to be a novel since he could not remember accurately all that had happened in his life. With that benediction, I plunged into writing. Six weeks and 85,000 words later, my first draft was completed.

This early draft was read by my book club in San Francisco, the Gay Boys Book Club, a group of very literate men with wide-ranging tastes and no lack of opinions. A number of members of the club were the very doctors that performed the groundbreaking work on AIDS in the early years of the plague; so, in addition to other important literary feedback, I received some spirited guidance on the timeline and state of medical information available at various points in those years. One member, Stephen Follansbee, provided significant insight and commentary that assisted me in getting to a near-final draft.

Over the next two years, I was thankful to a number of readers, including Sam Chong, Gary Nielsen, Blaine Bonham, Rick Spitzborg, Ariane Rüdiger, and Thomas Sander, for their feedback on a number of drafts. The great storyteller Mark Abramson graciously introduced me to his editor, Toby Johnson. It was through Toby's championing of my work that he introduced me to Jameson Currier, editor and publisher at Chelsea Station Editions. I am forever grateful to Jameson for his belief in this work and the guidance he gave, which taught me so much.

Open in the background on the computer while writing this novel were etymonline.com for research into the etymologies of the amazing language that we use, whose own DNA is filled with strands not only from Latin and Greek, but virtually every language that exists; and rae.es, the website of the Real Academia Española, which offered me the historical insights into the Spanish language.

I relied on a number of online source materials for the background information on Greek, Roman, and Santería practices and tales. Wikipedia.org and es.wikipedia.org were invaluable for information about any range of Roman, Greek, and Cuban subject areas, particularly as starting points for the biographies of Hadrian and Antinous and descriptions of the lives of the gods. Roman-empire.net, *Illustrated History of the Roman Empire*; and commons.wikimedia.org provided additional information and useful maps of the Roman Empire in 117 AD. Information on the Santería *orishas* primarily came from santeriachurch.org and aboutsanteria.com.

Thanks finally to Felice Picano and Jim Provenzano for their help and encouragement, Michael Nava for advice, and John Manzon-Santos for introducing me to Michael. David Powers, Jorge Luis Herrero, Flora Ramirez Bustamonte, Sally Luttrell-Montes, Helga Engelhardt, and Bruce Brockway provided inspiration and voice.

ABOUT THE AUTHOR

Alan Lessik is, in addition to being a writer, a zen practioner, amateur figure skater, and non-profit director. *The Troubleseeker* is his first novel. His non-fiction works include news articles published in the *Advocate, San Francisco Bay Guardian,* and *Frontiers* newsmagazine and several academic papers on international development issues. His contribution to KQED Radio Perspectives, "Judge Not His Death," was one of the most commented on in 2014.

CPSIA information can be obtained
at www.ICGtesting.com
Printed in the USA
LVOW08s0019200317

527767LV00001B/105/P

9 781937 627270